CPD BLUE

TRUE CRIME

THIN BLUE LINE SERIES

THE ROOKIE YEARS

A NOVEL

DENNIS PATRICK MURPHY

CPD BLUE / TRUE CRIME
THIN BLUE LINE SERIES
The Rookie Years

For information contact :
THE THIN BLUE LINE SERIES
http://www.thethinbluelineseries.com

ISBN: 9780578676913

First Edition: March 2020

10 9 8 7 6 5 4 3 2 1

For my parents, siblings, and children;
Nicole, Patrick, Kate and Eva.

ACKNOWLEDGEMENTS

I WOULD LIKE TO THANK THE MEN AND WOMEN

OF THE TOWN OF CAMILLUS (NY) POLICE

DEPARTMENT FOR THEIR ANECDOTAL COP

EXPERIENCES AND FRIENDSHIP.

FORWARD

Mac was fading fast. The last of the will he had during the fight was subsiding faster than he thought possible. The front of his baby blue short-sleeved uniform shirt was covered in blood, and he felt the warm stickiness up both arms past his elbows. He supposed it felt like molasses, although he couldn't be sure, because he hadn't been immersed in any substance like that before. He simultaneously thought to himself as he laid there that it was a strange thing to be thinking about. Mac, however, had been around fresh blood before, and the unmistakable coppery smell was all around him. As he looked up from his supine position on the freshly cut grass in whatever backyard he was lying in, he thought he must have some of it in his eyes as well.

He saw figures standing over him, but it was difficult to focus on them through the emerging light of daybreak on this warm September morning. Mac felt bone-tired and thought to himself—maybe he said it out loud to those above him—"Just give me a minute to rest, and I'll be all right. Just one more minute..."and with that, he closed his eyes as the faceless bodies above murmured to one another in an unintelligible conversation that he apparently wasn't meant to be a part of ..

CHAPTER

ONE

Seeing himself in the reflection of the windshield gave him pause. Officer Patrick MacKenna was hired January 15, 1986, and after being on the job full-time for several months, he was still in wonderment of his position. It was just past three in the morning, and the overhead lamp of the police department parking lot was casting the light into his pale blue marked 1986 Dodge Diplomat Camillus police cruiser. He was working alone on A-Watch, the midnight shift, in a medium-sized Central New York town. It was late winter, with the promise of warmer weather in the air.

Officer MacKenna was a twenty-three-year-old

newly appointed police officer working in full uniform, which included the winter uniform of a heather gray long-sleeved shirt, black knit clip-on tie, dark gray pants with a black stripe down the sides, black Bates boots, a black leather gun belt with the complimentary sidearm of a Smith and Wesson 357 magnum, two ammo pouches of circular speed loaders, a handcuff case, mace holder, portable radio holder, and a light gray Stetson cowboy hat that he wore when he was not in the police vehicle. The summer uniform for the Town of Camillus Police Department swapped out the heather gray long-sleeved shirt for a baby blue short-sleeved shirt with no tie. The winter uniform was worn from November through April. A 'Pumpkin' zip-up jacket of dark blue nylon with the color orange on the inside was added to both uniforms during inclement weather.

Being a white male just under six feet tall, weighing one hundred and eighty-five lbs. with an athletic build and broad shoulders, light brown hair, and slate blue eyes, he can see his shiny silver police badge, collar brass, and tie bar reflecting brightly in his image off the inside of the windshield as he sat in the drivers' seat. Mac, as he was generally known, had just left the station after a phone call with his Chief of Police. Still listening to the slow but still active banter of the police radio in the background, he was trying to rectify the conversation he just had with his boss.

This job meant everything to him. After trying to be a police officer for several years, he was starting to second-guess if he was any good at it. And if he wasn't any good at it, what would he do if they fired him? His father had doubted Mac's decision in becoming a police officer from the start and had tried to dissuade him from the undertaking.

The Town of Camillus Police Department (CPD) was located in a converted three-floor school on the main thoroughfare of West Genesee Street. There was still a playground in front of the building and a baseball field in back, and as a plus to the police officers who worked there, there was also a basketball court within the school.

The town was approximately 34 square miles, being the western suburb of the City of Syracuse, New York and had approximately 25,000 residents. It was mostly a middle-class working town, founded in 1899 and named after Marcus Furius Camillus, a Roman military leader. The topography of the land itself featured rural rolling hills with the infamous Eire Canal running east through west.

Even though Mac was the only police officer working for the Town of Camillus that night, he certainly wasn't the only one working A-Watch. There was always a deputy from the Onondaga County Sheriff's Department (OCSD) assigned to Unit #4505A which covered the western towns in the county, and a two-person unit from the New York State Police working out of the Elbridge Barracks, usually Unit #2D41A.

When Mac was alone in the town on midnights for CPD, his unit number was Unit #3103A. Other times, especially on B-Watch (Day Shift) and C-Watch (Evening Shift), Unit #3101 would cover the eastern side of the town, Unit #3102 would cover the western half, and Unit #3103 would be a rover between the two. The A-B-C designators would be interchangeable with the unit numbers to delineate what shift they were working.

The Onondaga County Mobile Radio District Center (MRD) dispatched calls for service in the county. Mac was woken out of his reverie as they called his unit number.

"Unit #3103A...Unit #4505A...Domestic Dispute in progress...your complainant is Fawn Shroedder...5058 Limeledge Road...Town of Camillus...0317 hours," the male dispatcher called over the two-way police radio.

Mac picked up the two-way radio mic and answered "Received," and his de facto partner for this evening, Deputy Howard "Howie" Marcus (OCSD), replied "Copy." Marcus must have been relatively close by, as they both arrived at the same location approximately ten minutes later. Deputy Marcus had fifteen years on the job and preferred A-Watch so he could spend more time with his wife and children. He was a white male, late-thirties, six feet one inch tall with a slight build, dark, close-cropped hair, and a neatly trimmed mustache.

As Mac exited the patrol vehicle, Howie chided him with a small smile on his face, "Still have a job?" Mac answered, "We'll see." They made their way together to the front door of the single-family residence. The house itself was of a modest blue-gray Cape Cod design constructed in the 1950's.

Fawn Shroedder met them at the door before they had a chance to ring the doorbell.

"I'm really afraid this time," she said. "He's been drinking since dinner, and I think Fred is going to seriously hurt me tonight. He hasn't come to bed yet and he keeps yelling up the stairs to me. He's still in the family room drinking beer and watching television, getting angrier by the minute."

Fawn Shroedder was a white female about fifty years old with graying black hair, five feet four inches tall, approximately one hundred and fifty pounds, wearing an older blue terry-cloth bathrobe with small holes in it, and she spoke nearly at a whisper as she stood in the doorway with the front door partially shut behind her.

Howie took the lead. "Ma'am, did you get into a physical altercation this evening with...uh...Fred...is he your husband?"

"He's my husband, and no, he didn't hit me or anything like that tonight. But he has in the past, and I've never reported it. He hasn't gotten this angry before and kept it going. He keeps on saying that I'm a worthless...bitch...and that he should've killed me years ago. We've been married for twenty-three years, and I have a very bad feeling about this."

"Okay. It'll be all right. Can I talk to you out here on the front steps, and I'll have Officer MacKenna go inside and speak with your husband?" Howie asked. Fawn weakly bobbed her head up and down, and then took a step down onto the concrete landing in her bare feet.

Howie nodded his head towards the front door, and Mac made his way into the house. Inside of the residence was an entryway off the main door with a living room to his left, an upstairs stairway directly in front, and dining room to his right. The interior of the house was tidy, with contemporary furniture and family photographs hanging on the walls. The air smelled of a pleasant crock pot dinner made the day before. A television could be heard from the right side of the house, and a faint light was coming from that direction. The rest of the lights were off in this section of the house. Mac made his way towards where he thought he would find the other half of the dispute.

He walked from the dining room into a large kitchen and proceeded off to the right to a sunken converted family room that had once been a garage. The large stone-faced fireplace was lit with wood-burning logs that were mostly down to coal embers now, and a silent figure sat in a brown leather Lazy-Boy recliner facing the television screen that was next to the fireplace. The furniture in the room was large and comfortable, and again, the room was orderly.

Mac could see that the figure in the chair appeared to be somewhat asleep, with his feet propped up in the recliner and a can of Budweiser in his left hand which rested on the arm of the chair. The middle-aged white male in the recliner was balding, with grayish hair on the sides of his head and eyeglasses resting on the lower bridge of his nose. He was maybe five feet ten inches tall, around 225 lbs., with a very thick neck and the body type of a fireplug.

Mac took a breath. A little voice in his head knew that this might not go so well, as he was about to wake an intoxicated man in his own home who was allegedly already having issues with his wife. He kept his position in the doorway of the kitchen, leaving a reactionary gap of about twenty feet or so, from the slumbering man in the chair.

"Um, Mr. Shroedder. Camillus Police Department. Can I talk with you please?" Mac said in an evenly toned voice, hoping not to startle him too badly.

Unfortunately, this was not the case, and the man did jump back to life, dropping his half-full can of beer onto the carpet as he tried to focus in Mac's direction.

"Who the hell do you think you are?" Fred Shroedder bellowed, struggling to come to his feet and get the recliner in the down position.

"Mr. Shroedder, I'm Officer MacKenna of the Town of Camillus Police Department. Your wife had some concerns tonight and asked us to come over and talk to you."

"I don't give a rat's ass who you are or what that lying bitch said. Get out of my house!" he said, taking off his glasses and throwing them down on a side table.

The man was boisterous, with a heavy slurring to his words. He had gotten the recliner down with much effort and made it to his unsure feet. Swaying back and forth in front of the chair, Fred was apparently gathering himself and forming some kind of plan in his head to back up his intention to make Mac leave his house.

For Mac's part, he was watching the man's hands and assessing what might happen next. They teach cadets in the police academy that you always watch the hands. The hands will hurt you if you don't know where they are or what's in them. Fred was balling his hands into fists, and that was not a good sign either.

A dog then began to whine and bark from beyond a door in the kitchen, which Mac assumed was the basement door. Mac then noticed dog bowls half-full of food and water in the corner of the kitchen. He chided himself for not seeing these earlier through the partial light from the family room as he entered the kitchen on the way to the family room. This was another officer safety issue. In retrospect, he should have used his flashlight to traverse the unlit rooms on the way to find Mr. Shroedder.

"I said, get out!" Mac's attention was once again drawn to the man coming at him. Fred had decided that a direct physical confrontation was in order and was making his way towards Mac.

"Mr. Shroedder, please just calm down. I only want to talk to you about—" Mac started to respond.

At that point, the man had made his way to him, and as Mac took a defensive posture with his strong foot back and his left arm extended, Mr. Shroedder reached up with both hands and ripped Mac's clip-on tie off, along with half of his uniform shirt. Buttons could be heard bouncing off the kitchen's linoleum floor.

"I'll kill Fawn for calling the cops on me!" Mr. Shroedder roared.

Things had gone so wrong so fast that Mac didn't think to reach for his pepper spray before the subject was upon him. Mac was being pushed back into the kitchen as Fred continued his assault. He knew that he had to stay between the married couple, or Fawn Shroedder would indeed be hurt by her husband if he made it to the front door.

Mac then instinctively reached for the handcuff pouch on the back of his duty belt and retrieved his handcuffs. He slapped one end on the man's right wrist as it still grabbed his uniform shirt and ripped some more buttons off, sprinkling them to the floor. Mac put his right hand through the open loop of the other cuff, attempting to pull Fred's hand away and get some leverage to get it behind his back, all the while saying, "You're under arrest! Stop resisting!" The dog continued to bark and snarl, only now at a fevered pace.

Fred was apparently averse to having a handcuff placed on his wrist, and concentrated his efforts at shaking it, and Mac off, by tossing them back and forth with his powerful arm. For his part, Mac had found his way to the floor as he furiously held onto the open handcuff. If he let it go, he knew that the subject would have a swinging chunk of steel as a weapon and this wouldn't end well at all. Fred was swinging his arm for all he was worth, like a bull who had caught something annoying on its nose ring.

Deputy Marcus appeared in the doorway to the kitchen and gave a curious look at Mac, who was now half sitting in the dog bowls and was covered with water and Purina, still hanging off the one open handcuff.

"A little help here...?" Mac managed to say to Howie, as he was most certainly losing the battle through attrition.

Howie tackled Fred to the floor by ramming his shoulder into the man's side, with all three of them slipping and sliding in the dog's nourishment on the linoleum floor. Fawn was now screaming, "Fred stop!" and to the cops, "Don't hurt my husband! He didn't do anything! Don't hurt him!" And the dog, it was later learned, a one-hundred and fifty-pound female sheepdog named Margret, kept up her assault on the basement door in earnest.

While Howie and Mac were desperately trying to get the subject on his stomach and his arms wrenched behind his back, their portable police radios simultaneously crackled, "Unit #3103A...Unit #4505A your status?" Neither one of them had time to advise the MRD Center of the predicament they were in. The status checks were given approximately every ten to fifteen minutes after the arrival of a unit on scene, to make sure the responding officers weren't in distress. Which they very much were.

Howie and Mac both knew that if they didn't answer after the third request by the MRD Center, additional units would be dispatched in their direction to find out what was going on at the scene.

Depending on the call, other units from surrounding villages and towns would start to 'slide' that way as a precaution for one another, nevertheless. Especially on A-Watch, since there weren't as many patrol units working on the street, the brotherhood and sisterhood were keen to look out for one another. Technically, town and village police units were supposed to say within their boundaries (Geographical Area of Employment) but Officer Safety was paramount while working their respective shifts, and everyone took care of one another regardless.

Fred, as it was later learned, was a prolific weightlifter who was an executive for a trash hauling company. He had worked his way up from the bottom of the business. He and his wife hadn't had any children during their marriage, and Fred had slowly slipped into an issue with alcohol in the preceding years.

Thus, Mac and Howie had their hands full, literally. They were entirely hands-on while trying to get Fred in a prone position and keep control of his left hand so that they could get the free cuff on it and secure it behind his back. This might seem easy on television or in the movies, but in practicality, there really isn't an easy way to control another human being bent on non-compliance without seriously hurting them in the process.

Seconds turned into minutes and the struggle ensued. Complicating matters were that Fawn was still screaming at everyone and the dog continued with its distress against the door. Mac and Howie were concerned that either Fawn was going to join in the fray in defense of her husband or, even worse, she would let Margret out of the basement.

A wailing siren and screeching tires then erupted from in front of the house. Troopers Roxy McCall and Gerald "Jerry" Hair appeared in no time. This time it was Howie that panted, "We've got it completely under control," to which Roxy said, "Yeah, I see that," as she dove in and grabbed Fred's left arm.

Jerry separated Fawn from the area, directing her back into the dining room and giving the remaining cops unfettered access to the task at hand. In less than a minute after the cavalry arrived, the three officers were able to safely secure Fred with the handcuffs behind his back.

"You...assholes! I'm going to sue you for everything you've got. Do you know who I am?! I know the County Executive, and you clowns will all be looking for new jobs!" Fred sputtered in a drool with his head sideways on the linoleum.

Roxy and Mac looked at each other and then at Howie, as Roxy said with a grin, "Looks like Mac and I are in the clear, since you're the only one that works for the county."

"Very funny...I'm getting too old for this shit," Howie said in response.

They stood Fred up and walked him out to Mac's police car, placing him in the back seat behind the metal cage. There they seatbelted him in on the passenger side of the vehicle.

Jerry came out of the house and said, "I've got the complainant calmed down, and she says she'll sign a harassment complaint against her husband for threatening her earlier. I advised dispatch that we're Code 2—" this meant an arrest—"and to cancel any other units en route."

"Thanks, Jerry. We really appreciated you guys showing up when you did," Mac said, still breathing hard.

Both troopers had about two years on the job. Roxy was a white female, twenty-five years of age, five feet two inches tall, approximately 120 lbs. with black braided hair. She originally was from the Albany, New York area, went to school at Lemoyne College in Syracuse, New York, stayed here after she graduated, took the New York State Police (NYSP) test and was now working out of the NYSP Elbridge Barracks. Gerald was from Mount Pleasant, New York and transferred to Troop D so that his wife could be closer to her family. He was an African American male, twenty-six years of age, six feet two inches tall, with a slender build and his head shaved bald. Gerald had attended Columbia University where he had met his wife.

Mac was slowly regaining his composure, leaning up against his car, trying to figure out how to get his shirt back together as Jerry said, "The two of you look like shit, but Mac, you take the prize. What happened to you?"

Mac filled in Howie and the troopers as to what transpired after he entered the residence and engaged Mr. Shroedder in his chair. There was some good-natured teasing as Howie described finding Mac in the dog bowls when he entered the house. Camaraderie at its best, and one of the main reasons why people who did this job loved it so much.

Jerry went back into the house, took an affidavit from Mrs. Shroedder, and had her sign a Direct Complaint Information for harassment against her husband. She was also advised about the process of getting an Order of Protection against him, and was told that he would be spending the night in the Onondaga County Public Safety Building Jail (PUB).

Mac went back into the house briefly to retrieve his tie and tie bar off the kitchen floor. He started picking up his loose buttons from between the spilled dog food and water, and then just gave up.

Mrs. Shroedder did meekly apologize for her husband, to which Mac told her that it wasn't her fault and that he sincerely hoped everything would work out for her.

Mac was again resting on the hood of his car, trying to figure out how to reconstitute his shirt into something presentable, when his right hand started to ache. The adrenaline was starting to wear off, and the pain was intensifying. Howie walked over and saw Mac looking at it and said, "You ought to get that looked at. It's starting to swell up."

"It'll be fine. Hey, Howie? Do you think I'll be in more trouble because of what happened tonight?"

"You did good, kid. These things happen, and most of the time you have no control over them. Your car accidents, on the other hand..." he gave Mac a devilish grin.

"Thanks Howie...you're not helping."

"No, seriously... get that hand looked at. I'll do the paperwork and have the troopers do the arraignment and the transport to Booking."

"Okay, thanks. I appreciate it. I'm still kind of worried about how all this will play out for you, also. Do you really think he knows the County Executive?"

"Mac, it doesn't matter who he knows. He was one hundred percent in the wrong and we were doing our jobs. End of story. Now get out of here and have your hand taken care of."

After figuring out the logistics, the troopers transferred the suspect from Mac's car to theirs, and then they both wished Mac well as he advised the MRD Center to put himself out on a detail to Community General Hospital.

As Mac got into his police car to drive to the hospital, it was just starting to get light out. With the sky turning shades of red and pink, he again wondered if he would still have a job in the morning. What Howie said was reassuring, but he was still on probation, and anything could jeopardize that...personnel complaints, car wrecks...ugh...this certainly has been one of those nights.

Order without liberty and liberty without order are equally destructive.

-**Theodore Roosevelt**

CHAPTER

TWO

Mac was getting undressed after spending two and a half hours at the Emergency Room. It was just after 8:00 AM, and he had finally gotten back to the station to drop off the marked car and was gingerly changing out of his uniform. His uniform shirt was done for. He'd have to go to the uniform shop and pick up a new one, as this one was headed for the trash.

The day (B-Watch) sergeant walked into the third-floor locker room. "What in the world happened to you last night? There's a dented quarter panel on your assigned vehicle, and that shirt looks like you were doing a strip tease somewhere.

And what's up with the cast?"

Sgt. Jake Smith had thirty-plus years on the job and resembled a tough-looking Humphrey Bogart in a police uniform.

"Sarge, I called the chief last night and told him about the accident with the car. I was trying to catch up to a speeder on Milton Ave., hit some black ice and clipped a cargo van turning into the gas station at Hinsdale Rd. No one was hurt though, and very minor damage to the van."

"Then what the hell happened to your uniform and your hand?"

Mac explained in detail about the domestic dispute call and the arrest of Mr. Shroedder.

"So, what did they say about your hand?"

"Doc said it's commonly known as a boxer's fracture. In the doc's words, it is the break of the 5th metacarpal bones of the hand near the knuckle. The symptoms include pain and a depressed knuckle. She said that I'd be out of work for four to six weeks. When I had my hand inside of the free end of the cuff, I must've gripped it too hard to retain control and it fractured."

"Ah shit, I'm sorry Mac."

"Thanks. Do you think between this being the second crash in two months and the arrest last night, I might be on thin ice here? I know this looks bad, and I really don't want to lose my job. You know I've been waiting for this opportunity my whole life. I mean, seriously Sarge...am I screwed, or what?"

Jake took his time to answer. "The chief just walked into the building. I think you should catch him up to speed on the domestic and your injury. He's a fair man, and what I can tell from what you told me, you should be all right with him. But don't forget, he still must clear it with the Town Supervisor and the Town Board. Being on probation is tricky. I wouldn't sweat it too hard, but after this...I think you could be out of chances."

Mac lowered his eyes, shook his head up and down and continued to get changed as Jake went back downstairs to the Patrol Room. Once back in civilian clothes, also called "civvies," Mac made his way down the two flights of stairs to the Chief's Office on the second floor.

Betty Masters was the chief's secretary. She was a motherly figure for the Camillus Cops and always had a sweet and calming manner. She was about Mac's mother's age, 5' 2" tall, slender build with medium curly brown hair with glasses. Her eyes widened when she saw Mac walk into the office with the cast on his hand. "Mac! What happened?"

"Hi, Betty. I broke it during a domestic last night. I just got back from the ER. It's fine...really! Is the chief busy? I want to tell him what happened."

"Okay, as long as you're fine. Let me check." She picked up the phone and dialed his office and told him that Mac was waiting to speak with him. "He says he's free right now and you can go on in." Betty gave Mac a sympathetic smile as he walked by her desk and into the chief's office.

Chief Ronan Whitlock was a shorter, distinguished man with graying hair. He was wearing a brown suit, white dress shirt, and a blue tie. He looked exactly how a chief of police for a medium sized town should look. He had worked for the Town of Camillus Police Department for thirty-three years, and had been chief for approximately ten of them. Chief Whitlock was quite comfortable with his position, and everyone liked him.

"Good morning, Patrick! Please, take a seat. So apparently it got busy after I got off the phone with you this morning. Are you okay?"

"Yes sir. Thank you. I'm fine."

"Please tell me how you got that," he said, referencing Mac's right hand with a nod of his head.

"Yes sir. Deputy Marcus and I were dispatched to a domestic dispute call at 5058 Limeledge Road at approximately 0315 hours to speak with Fawn Shroedder regarding her husband Fred, who had been drinking all day and was threatening her. When we arrived, Mrs. Shroedder met us at the front door and told us that she was afraid of her husband who was inside, still drinking and watching TV in the family room. Deputy Marcus continued to speak with her as I went inside to speak with Mr. Shroedder. I found him asleep in a chair in front of the tv in the family room. When I announced my presence, he became hostile and threatened to harm his wife for calling the police. He then physically attacked me with his hands and tried to push past me to get to his wife, who was still standing at the front door with Deputy Marcus. I placed one handcuff on his wrist and prevented him from going any further. I attempted to gain control of him, and we wrestled on the kitchen floor until Deputy Marcus heard the commotion and assisted me by tackling Mr. Shroedder to the ground, where we both struggled to get the other hand handcuffed. We missed our status checks by the MRD Center and New York State Troopers out of the Elbridge Barracks, McCall and Hair were dispatched to assist us. Once the troopers arrived on the scene Mr. Shroedder was taken into custody without further incident. He was not injured during the altercation. During the struggle, I broke my right hand and drove myself to Community General Hospital for treatment. Deputy Marcus completed the paperwork and the troopers arraigned, and then later transported Mr. Shroedder to the Onondaga County Public Safety Building Jail where he was lodged on Harassment, Assault in the Second Degree, Obstructing Governmental Administration, and Resisting Arrest."

Chief Whitlock took this all in, nodding his head occasionally and formulating the events in his head as Mac spoke. When Mac was done speaking, he said, "It sounds like you did what was reasonably necessary to prevent the situation from getting worse. You sacrificed yourself to protect the complainant and that was the right thing to do. I'm just glad you didn't get hurt worse in the process."

"Thank you, chief."

"You must be exhausted. Are you okay to drive yourself

home?"

"Yes, sir. I'll be fine driving home."

"How long did the doctor say you would be out of work?"

"Four to six weeks, but I'm a fast healer. I'll be back faster than that."

"Take your time, Mac. We'll survive without you until you're well. Please drive home safely and let me know if you need anything while you're out."

"Thank you, chief. I will."

Mac walked out of the chief's office and said goodbye to Betty. He walked down the flight of stairs to the back-parking lot and made his way to his newer Chevy Camaro. He threw his ripped uniform shirt in the backseat, started up the car and heard Phil Collins singing 'Take Me Home' on the radio. Somehow it seemed fitting with how the night played out, and as he put the car in gear he still couldn't stop worrying if he was still going to have a job after the news of his escapades made their way to the Supervisor and the Town Board.

The boy who is going to make a great man must not make up his mind merely to overcome a thousand obstacles, but to win in spite of a thousand repulses and defeats.

-Theodore Roosevelt

CHAPTER

THREE

Mac drove home, or the equivalent of it, as he was taking care of his maternal grandmother who had symptoms of Alzheimer's. His maternal grandfather had been a senior accountant for Niagara Mohawk Power Company and had passed away some time ago, and his grandmother had slowly developed the familiar signs of forgetting people, places, and things as she aged. It was very sad for Mac to see her this way. She had always been very loving and kind when he was growing up, and now she didn't even recognize him. It was one of life's cruelest jokes.

His grandmother lived in an upscale suburban neighborhood in the Town of Onondaga on a large hill that overlooked the valley of the City of Syracuse. There were brilliant large radio towers down there that burned bright at night with intermittent glowing red warning lights. The expanse of the view was breathtaking in every direction.

The house itself was a large ranch structure containing three bedrooms and two bathrooms with gray shake siding, a finished basement that included the bedroom where Mac lived, and a couple acres of land. Mac took care of the yard work, took the trash out, and kept an eye on his grandmother to make sure she didn't need anything. She couldn't drive anymore, so he took her to his parents' house in Camillus once a week for dinner. Mac's mother did her grocery shopping and came over as often as she could to keep house and do her laundry.

Even though he loved his grandmother very much, the situation was mutually beneficial as Mac was going through a contentious divorce. Mac graduated from West Genesee High School at seventeen and had started attending Onondaga Community College in the Administration of Criminal Justice program when he found out that his high school sweetheart was pregnant. Being a good Irish Catholic kid, he married her at eighteen and they had their first daughter, Bridget, at nineteen. From there he had to drop out of college and work for his father.

Mac was the oldest of five children born to parents who grew up in Central New York. His father James had gone to an all-male Catholic school—Christian Brothers Academy—and his mother Searlait, an all-female Christian school—Convent. They had met at a school dance but had gone their separate ways, his father joining the United States Marine Corps and his mother attending college in the western part of the state. They reunited when James came back home on leave from the service and attended his mother's company picnic at Bristol Myers Inc. where Searlait was now working with her degree as a medical secretary. His paternal grandmother was the head switchboard operator for the company. His paternal grandfather worked at Wells and Coverley Department store in the men's department. They eventually got married and moved to Naval Air Station (NAS) Cherry Point, North Carolina where his father was an air traffic controller. Mac and his sister Mary were born there, and the family lived in North Carolina for two years until his father's enlistment was up. They moved back to the Syracuse area, finally settling in the Town of Camillus where his three younger siblings (Michael, Ann, and Ruth) were born.

Mac was raised Roman Catholic, and as you would expect, he attended church services every Sunday and went to weekly religion classes regularly. For this reason, and because of the upbringings of his parents, Mac seriously considered becoming a priest when he was younger. The everlasting conflict of good versus evil resonated deeply within him.

Mac was a 'C' student at West Genesee High School and had failed chemistry twice. He also had mistakenly been placed in an elevated geometry course by his counselor without having taken the second half of algebra, which demoralized him further. Mac's favorite subjects were English and Social Studies and he liked to read. Theodore Roosevelt, the 26th President of the United States, was an inspiration to Mac, as he was a former Police Commissioner of New York City.

He had worked for his father as a kid. James owned a large restaurant in Camillus Plaza, and he started washing dishes and bussing tables when he was fourteen, before moving on to pizza cook and then cook. The restaurant business was a hard one, with long hours after school and on the weekends. Mac came in early on Saturday and Sunday mornings and cleaned the three hundred seat restaurant, from the bathrooms to behind the bar, to get it ready to open each afternoon.

Even though that first restaurant had closed, his father had just opened a new Irish pub in the Village of Camillus. Mac helped with the renovation of the place which had white stucco walls and a liberal amount of Kelly-green accents. Mac was the sole bartender and de facto manager.

This position lasted until one night a week before Christmas when his father came down to the pub on a slow night at about 7:00 PM. James was a large man, 6' 2" tall, about 250 lbs., who generally had an agreeable disposition. There were few customers due to the inclement weather and Mac and his father talked pleasantly throughout the evening, engaging the few customers as they came and went. Mac's father was a customary drinker of Dewar's White Label on the rocks, and Mac had to open a new bottle for him when he first walked in that night. By the end of the night at 2:00 AM Mac noticed that he had gone through the entire bottle. No one else drank the Scotch other than his father. Mac mentioned this to his father in passing, not thinking too much about it, as he closed up the place by turning off the neon bar lights around the bar. As he was coming down the stairs from the upstairs portion of the pub where there were an eight-foot pool table and a dart board, he was met by his father on the in-between landing where the front door was located. Mac figured his father was on his way home.

Without provocation or warning, Mac's father took his closed right fist and struck Mac directly in the face. Copious amounts of blood gushed from his nose. Mac looked dumbfoundedly at his father as blood continued to run down his white dress shirt and blue tie.

"Don't you ever call me a drunk!" his father shouted.

"But Dad—I didn't—All I said was that you finished off the bottle..."

"You're done. You're fired. Get the hell out of here."

Mac grabbed his coat and rushed out of the pub, nursing his first broken nose, and went home to tell his wife that he wouldn't have a job for the holidays. Although this was heartbreaking for Mac, it taught him a very valuable life lesson...you can never reason with someone who has been drinking.

Mac was fortunate enough to find work as a kitchen manager for a chain restaurant not too long after, and he took multiple other minimum wage professions (car salesman, vacuum cleaner salesman, residential siding salesman, warehouse worker, UPS trailer unloader, hospital supply tele-lift operator, hospital unarmed guard, etc.) as well, sometimes working three different eight-hour jobs in a twenty-four-hour period. He had to, seeing as his wife had since had another child (Joseph), and had also had a full-term miscarriage, and was pregnant (Elizabeth) yet again. Mac was the only one working most of the time and he just couldn't keep up with the bills. As one could imagine, he was extremely miserable and never got a chance to sleep, let alone spend much quality time with his children or his wife.

He finally decided that he couldn't keep up this pace much longer and that he needed to try to come up with a better plan. Mac had just turned twenty-one years old, and he needed a short-term goal that was achievable. He applied for and received his New York State Pistol Permit, and with his limited funds bought himself a used Smith & Wesson 357 caliber, model 586 blued, 6-inch revolver. This was an investment in achieving a job that paid more than minimum wage.

Since Mac's lifestyle decisions cancelled out his first intention of becoming a priest, his second choice was to do something similar where he could still pursue the same lofty goal of preserving good and triumphing over evil. He played sports (CYO Basketball, Pop Warner Football, Optimist Baseball, and backyard versions of the same) his whole life and thought this would be an added asset to becoming a police officer. He ruined the ligaments in both knees prior to high school by playing sports, which prevented him from playing sports at that level, and hoped this wouldn't become too much of an issue in getting hired down the line.

After searching for positions that required a pistol permit, he was relieved to find one that advertised a job as a housing security patrolman. The money wasn't great, but it was better than working for minimum wage!

Mac called and set up an interview with the gentleman who owned the security company, Walter Meade. On the date and time specified, he pulled up in front of 1813 E. Fayette Street in the City of Syracuse. The complex was notoriously known as Hill Top Apartments. It was a massive complex of fourteen large brick buildings, and stretched out over six blocks, with most of the residents being low-income and of African American descent. It was originally built for service men and their families returning from World War II in what had been a predominately Jewish neighborhood. Today, Mac only knew it from the evening news as a place where there were nightly news reports of drug busts, stabbings, shootings, and homicides.

He was the only white face he saw for the last eight blocks on his drive to the complex. Even though Mac was ten minutes early for the interview, he sat in in his run-down car for twenty minutes, trying to figure out how badly he needed the job. It was springtime, and the sidewalks outside the complex that ran parallel with the street were busy with African American men, woman and children constantly walking by his worn car. Most of them stared at him as if he was an enigma in their world.

Mac finally worked up enough courage, got out of the car, straightened his blue suit, and walked to the security office in the back of building 1813. There he was met by Walter Meade, who was an African American male in his early thirties, 6' 2" tall, about 225 lbs. with black hair and brown eyes. He was quite engaging and dressed impeccably in a dark suit and a fashionable tie. Mac apologized for being late, but Mr. Meade dismissed it. He then asked Mac to take a seat and went on to interview him about the position. Mr. Meade also told Mac about himself and his company. It turned out that Mr. Meade was also a pastor and that he had several other security contracts in the city and employed about twenty people.

At the end of their discussion Mr. Meade said, "Patrick, I'd like to hire you, but I've got to tell you first that you would be my first and only white employee."

"Please call me Mac, everyone else does. If you're willing to take a chance on me, I'd be more than willing to give it a try." Although Mac was more than a little apprehensive about the prospect, he generally liked Mr. Meade and thought maybe it would be a good fit for him.

Now that he had a job making a little more money, he had to implement phase two of his short-term plan. Mac wanted to return to college, but knew that wouldn't solve his more pressing money problems.

After much research and forethought, Mac decided to enroll himself in the Central New York Regional Academy for Police Training Basic Course in Law Enforcement at Syracuse University. This would cost him more of his limited resources, but it was a part-time course that lasted only five months that would make him qualified to work as a part-time peace officer in New York State.

Working for Mead's security company was indeed a good fit for Mac. Because of his management background, Mr. Meade asked him within a month to manage his company. Mac oversaw making the schedules for the various sites, figuring out payroll and dealing with any employee issues. This also gave him the chance to coordinate the classes he was attending at Syracuse University with his work schedule. Mr. Meade expressed his gratitude by giving Mac a raise, a take-home company car and a company pager.

The guys who worked at the security company were great, and ingratiated Mac immediately. They had no reason to do so, as he was an outsider who had gotten promoted within the business extremely early and was the only employee who didn't live in the city and didn't really know or understand the culture of the projects. The other security officers warned very early on for Mac not to let anyone take advantage of him. That it would be seen as a sign of weakness by everyone else at the site, and Mac's work life would become a living hell.

They explained that there were two kinds of people who lived there, predators or prey. You never wanted to be the prey. He took this advice to heart, as he soon found out that some people there didn't like him solely because he was white, and they were quite vocal about it. It was most definitely a shock for him to be the minority for eight hours a day.

One particular day as Mac and three of his coworkers were patrolling the complex during a warm holiday afternoon, an African American man about thirty-five years old, who was obviously quite intoxicated, yelled, "Hey Cracker! Yeah, you, cracker! You ain't shit!" The man was leaning up against the building at 102 Croly St., and there was a large crowd of residents out in front of the building who were grilling, drinking, and having a picnic on an impromptu combinations of card tables and assorted chairs.

Mac stopped and looked over his shoulder at the man as he said again, "You ain't shit white boy! You got nothin'!"

The man was approximately fifteen yards away, and there were about fifty people between him and Mac. One of Mac's coworkers looked over at him and said in a low voice, "It's okay, Mac, he's just drunk. Never mind him. We'll just keep on walking and it will be fine."

But all the other residents had stopped what they were doing, as they were drawn into the scene by the belligerent intoxicated male. They were waiting to see what would happen next, and Mac knew it. He was also acutely aware that they were outnumbered fifty some odd to four, and if there was a problem it could deteriorate very quickly.

Mac responded to his coworker, "You told me not to get punked out here or life would get real. Everybody is waiting to see how this plays out. I can't just walk away."

"Sure you can. We'll deal with it another day. There are too many people out here, and they've all been drinking. Nobody would hold it against you to walk away." And with that, the other two coworkers nodded their heads in agreement.

He saw in their eyes that they were generally worried for him. Mac didn't want to leave, and it felt like an out-of-body experience as he involuntarily turned around and his legs started to walk on their own to the drunk man, who was still yelling insults and slurs in Mac's direction. It was like the parting of the Red Sea as people made a wide path for Mac as he crossed the courtyard towards the man. Once there, Mac placed his hand on the side of the building and said, "Do you have a problem with me?"

The man wouldn't meet Mac's gaze and just stared at the ground. Mac waited another thirty seconds before removing his hand and rejoining his partners on the sidewalk. Mac had been terrified. The only reason he went to confront the man was because he knew his coworkers were right. This was a test, and everyone involved knew it. If he didn't take on that war, he'd be fighting small battles everyday once the word got out. Mac stood his ground with the help of his partners, and eventually the residents accepted him, or more accurately, tolerated his presence in their neighborhood.

The work itself was also preparing him for a profession in law enforcement. Mac dealt regularly with domestic disputes, drug dealers, and armed attackers on the properties. There was a constant interaction with the City of Syracuse Police Department (SPD). The police officers would routinely assist the security officers with their duties in the projects and the detectives from SPD would inquire with the security employees as to where suspects lived or hung out.

Mac was then able to take the Onondaga County Civil Service test for police officer with the City of Syracuse, in addition to town and villages. He took it twice in the upcoming year, achieving eighty-four percent each time. Although this wasn't a bad score, the field of applicants was very competitive, and they rarely got down to the eighties for canvasses.

Even so, during the year that he worked for Mr. Meade, he was able to complete the Syracuse University program and applied for a part-time position with the Town of Camillus Police Department for a peace officer opening. Mac's father made amends by reaching out to the town supervisor and members of the town board, who he knew, to try and get him the job. Mac got an interview with Chief Ronan Whitlock and miraculously beat out the two other candidates who also applied for the posting.

To get his foot in the door with a police department and open an avenue to better provide for his growing family was a small victory for Mac. The enthusiasm was short-lived, however, once Mac learned that one of the other candidates for the position had killed himself since he had not gotten the job. This continuously troubled Mac and it truly never left him.

Nevertheless, Mac got sworn in as a peace officer two weeks later for CPD and started a Field Training Officer (FTO) Program, learning the ins and outs of practical patrol techniques in a suburban setting with experienced patrol officers.

The organizational makeup of the Camillus Police was the Chief, one lieutenant, four sergeants, one detective sergeant, and fifteen police officers, with a couple of part-time peace officers who helped with shift coverage.

The senior officers at CPD were all godlike to Mac and he was eager to learn all he could from them. After two months, Field Training was over, and one of his FTOs had laterally transferred to the Onondaga County Sheriff's Department. This created a full-time opening and Chief Whitlock offered the position to Mac.

Mac just about broke down and cried. He held his composure as the chief went on to explain that there were caveats; he would have to take the civil service test again and pass it, since the list was expiring, and Mac would have to attend the next full-time session of the Basic Course for Police Officers at the Central New York Police Training Academy located at Onondaga Community College and graduate.

Up to this point, Mac had still been working for Meade Security as well as CPD. He gave Mr. Meade his two-week notice and thanked him sincerely for the opportunity he provided for him. Mr. Meade told Mac that he was pleased for him and wished him well in his police career.

Mac worked a full-time schedule, which for CPD was six days on, three days off on a two-week rotating schedule. The senior cops usually worked a steady diet of day (B-Watch) 8:00 AM to 4:00 PM shifts and the younger ones worked evenings

(C-Watch) 4:00 PM to 12:00 AM and the rookies were saddled with the less desirable midnight (A-Watch) with 12:00 AM to 8:00 AM coverage. However, Mac being the newest member of the department, he was filling in on all three shifts as officers were either on sick leave, vacation, or in training.

In the meantime, he took and passed the civil service test again, this time with a score of ninety-eight, which was good enough to get hired by any agency, but his commitment was to CPD. Mac started running the track up at the high school, usually after midnight when he got done working C-Watch, to get ready for the police academy. Although he was very active and played more than his share of sports, he never ran for distance and time. This was new to him, but his knees didn't bother him at all, which was his greatest concern. Mac's next worry was getting his mile and a half time down to under fourteen minutes. This was a standard you had to enter the academy at. The most the recruits would run during training was three miles a day. Mac would increase his distances until he could achieve that without huffing and puffing like a winded couch potato.

Mac's future was starting to take a turn for the better.

With self-discipline most anything is possible.

- Theodore Roosevelt

CHAPTER
FOUR

An academy class was convened the following year. Mac had learned a lot by working as a cop on the streets during that time, and had gotten himself in passable running shape. He hadn't had any work-related issues in the interim, and had mentally prepared himself for the rigors of the police academy.

The academy was five months long and involved a lot of classroom training work involving studying and understanding the New York Penal Law (PL) and Criminal Procedure Law (CPL), New York State Vehicle and Traffic Law (VTL), First

Responder First Aid Training, as well as work outside the classroom, such as Physical Training (PT), Defensive Tactics (DT), Emergency Vehicle Operations Course (EVOC), Crimes in Progress, and Firearms. This was the real deal, and a huge departure from the part-time academy that Mac had attended.

Male recruits had to have military-type haircuts and very limited, neatly-trimmed mustaches. Female recruits with long hair always had to have their hair up and neatly pinned at all times. The Class B uniforms issued to the class were either blue or gray plain uniforms, depending on which agency you were assigned to, and black shoes. The police academy instructors were in excellent shape, and their primary job was to separate the wheat from the chaff. They were overachievers with at least ten years of police experience and had been temporarily assigned to the academy from the larger entities of the City of Syracuse Police Department and the Onondaga County Sheriff's Department. Both agencies jointly ran the academy at the college; however, SPD was twice as large as OCSD, and had the largest make-up of the recruits in the class. Towns and villages in the county as well as other smaller police agencies throughout the seventeen counties in the center of the state would also send newly hired recruits to this academy.

The attrition rate, or failure rate, was about one third, with most unsuccessful recruits becoming Drop on Request (DOR) within the first two weeks. This meant that most recruits quit at the very beginning when they were stressed beyond their tolerance levels. The instructors were gauging who really wanted to go through this hellish process to become a police officer/deputy. Injuries weren't factored into this number. If a recruit got injured during training, they would have to be recycled by their agency to the next academy class, which was usually every six months. No one wanted to get recycled, because you would have to repeat the whole entire process from the beginning. It was based on the military boot camp method, and it had the desired effect. It wasn't for the faint of heart.

The academy was operated Monday through Friday, 7:00 AM to 3:00 PM. There were no barracks for the recruits, so they had to commute every day to and from the college. There were homework assignments almost every night, including weekends.

PT was the worst part of the day, and it was intended that way. PT gear included gray hooded sweatshirts, plain white T-shirts, and sweatpants, with the recruit's name block-stenciled on the back of each article of clothing. Running sneakers were also a prerequisite. Muster was at exactly 7:00 AM, where the recruits would be in the gym in formation waiting for their name to be called by the instructors. God forbid if a recruit was late. This only happened once, and everyone quickly got with the program. There was a demerit system in place, but that's not the reason why a recruit wouldn't want to be late. The verbal assault from instructors would be relentless, and the recruit would constantly be singled out for remediation the rest of the day.

At the beginning of the academy the recruits would start by running around the hilly college campus, which was a mile and half in circumference. Shortly thereafter, the instructors would double the trek around OCC to three miles a day. The run was done in a two-column formation led by two instructors, with a third following up the group. If the recruit in front of a runner fell behind by a space in line, the recruit behind them was required to pass them and fill in that space. If one fell behind the formation or fell out altogether, the verbal abuse from the rear instructor would cascade all over the poor soul for the duration of the run.

The run would end back in the gymnasium, where the recruits would again line up in formation. The instructors would then select a recruit to lead a given exercise at the front of the formation. This would be rotated after each revolution of an exercise. The recruit would have to know the number of the exercise, demonstrate it, and then call cadence for it while doing it as the group performed the routine. There were ten different exercises, and memorization with the assigned number attached to it was at first difficult for the trainees. The exercises included push-ups, sit-ups, jumping jacks, trunk twists, bear-crawls, squat-thrusts, assorted stretches, and the dreaded burpee (a squat-thrust with a push-up in the middle.) Under the watchful eyes of the instructors, they expected maximum effort and flawless execution of each exercise. If not, you guessed it—the trainees heard about it at length.

Recruits would PT for the first hour of the day and then hit the showers and get changed into their Class B uniforms for the classroom portion. Usually everyone was miserable after the physical hardships of PT, and there was little talk in the locker rooms while the recruits were getting ready for the long march across the campus to the Academic One building, where the academy was housed.

After Mac's first week, five recruits from his class all decided at different stages that this was not the life for them. He felt bad, but was secretly relieved that he had survived so far. As Mac sat on the wooden locker room bench next to the gray metal lockers, pulling on his black socks, a fellow recruit walked up to him only wearing his tighty-whitey underwear, holding a small blue and white box, and said, "Do you want a Q-tip?"

"Ah...No, I'm good.... Thank you."

Undaunted he said, "I love these things. I couldn't make it through the day without them."

He turned around and went back through the hot steam from the showers to the mirrors in the bathroom and continued with this routine. It was a surreal moment. Somehow, this guy seemed totally unfazed by what they were experiencing and was holding tight to his ritual as an unrealized coping mechanism. The kindness he offered and the timing of it made Mac grin as he continued getting dressed. It was a welcome distraction to the chaos they found themselves in.

Mac had an advantage at the police academy. He had worked as a cop prior to being there and had been given insider information by fellow cops from CPD who had just completed the same program. Most of his contemporaries didn't have this luxury, and Mac tried to reassure them with what he already knew to help alleviate their fears. Mac did find out that some of the other recruits already have family members on the job, and they too provided further information to their classmates about what was to be expected.

Classroom training could be very tedious at times, with very dry material, unengaging trainers, or sometimes, unmercifully, both. Even though this was a lifetime dream for Mac, he occasionally found his head lolling up and down or his eyes closing against his will. Compassionately, the classroom periods were forty-five-minute segments with ten-minute breaks built in to ease the tedium of the day.

During the breaks, the recruits would stand at the end of the hallway in the common area of the first floor of the Academic One building watching the scholars from the college as they came and went.

The configuration of the academy class was currently thirty-three recruits and was sure to keep on shrinking with continued attrition. There were six females and twenty-seven males, including one African American female and one African American male. There were college grads, veterans, and people with assorted professional backgrounds. It undoubtedly was an assemblage of people from very different walks of life and social classes.

During the breaks, Mac would learn more about his classmates and them about him. There was an instant solidarity among the cadets, as they were all attempting to achieve a unique but common goal.

The vetting process to make it this far had been daunting, including the civil service test specified by New York State, the physical fitness assessment, the background check by the departments, medical clearance, and the polygraph examination. Overall, there were quite a few hurdles to overcome before you had a chance at the police academy. Therefore, everyone knew they were all at the same level and trying to achieve the next—graduating from the academy. If they were fortunate enough to do that, they would still have to survive the FTO program which washed out another crop of hopefuls. And then, finally, there was one year of probation to deal with.

When Mac first attended OCC as an undergraduate, he heard students say that it was easy to become a cop and that they would do it as soon as they graduated. But it wasn't easy at all, and he didn't think the vast expanse of the public knew what rigors were involved in taking this civil servant position.

Mac saw different cliques forming among the academy recruits. At first, classmates were drawn to fellow members of the same department. Then other dynamics emerged as the more cerebral members spent time together in the hallways on break. Then the more athletically gifted grouped together. Even the single and married recruits would congregate into two different bunches. All the members rotated through these groups into comfortable subcategories, and then reconfigured again into a dissimilar makeup in another group. Mac often thought about how the academy itself was a microcosm of a larger society.

In the fall/winter academy, Mac slogged his way through the rain, sleet, and snow he experienced during the runs and the marches to the Academic One building. It was a process to go through, but it got easier as time went by. There were always small setbacks as classmates either quit or failed out, but the stress levels wound down as the academy stretched on towards graduation.

With three weeks left to go in the academy, the recruits were being taught Defensive Tactics (DT). This was conducted in the gym on wrestling mats. In this class, the recruits were instructed in the finer arts of boxing, wrestling, and handcuffing procedures. The recruits wore their PT clothes and were paired up with similar-sized classmates. However, Mac was paired up with a 6' 4", lean 240 lb. recruit for the boxing portion. The classmate had 4" of reach on Mac, as well as 65 lbs. The instructors must have thought that since Mac had some road experience, he could fill the gap in size, since there were no other recruits of that comparable build...or, they wanted to see Mac get his ass kicked.

It turned out to be the latter, or at least Mac thought so. There were only three two-minute rounds, which doesn't seem that bad until you're the one with the head gear and boxing gloves on. Mac held his own the first two rounds, and then with a lucky punch, he caught his adversary with his guard down, squarely striking his jaw. Mac suspected that his opponent was laying off a bit because of the size difference, but once struck, all bets were off. The recruit laid into Mac and hit him so hard he was knocked out of his left sneaker. Mac tried to plant his left foot to counter-attack the barrage of blows, but instead caught the bottom on his running shoe on the wrestling mat, turned his left ankle, and came right out of his shoe.

It was part of the training—and not unexpected, as other recruits received their fair share of injuries—but Mac's ankle immediately swelled up, and he had to go to see the police physician at Community Hospital.

The doctor told Mac he had a severely sprained ankle and to ice it, elevate it, rest it, and keep it tightly wrapped when he was doing PT. It would be discovered years later that the police physician had misread the x-rays at the time, and that Mac had actually broken his ankle during that boxing match. Either way, Mac finished out the last three weeks of the academy by running three miles a day on it. No one, including Mac, wanted to be recycled through the academy, so maybe it was a blessing that the doc didn't see the break and take Mac out of training.

Mac and his remaining classmates ended up graduating January 8th of that year and began their assignments with their respective departments. The rest of his class would begin FTO, but Mac had already done this piece in reverse order and was on his own in the Town of Camillus. Mac hoped that he could prove himself and be given more responsibility and an interesting assignment within the department. His true aspiration was to make detective and conduct investigations, but retaining his job and the income stream it provided was of the greatest importance.

It was an exciting time for Mac, and he couldn't wait to see what lay ahead.

Believe you can and you're halfway there.

- **Theodore Roosevelt**

CHAPTER

FIVE

After the incident with the Shroedder's, Mac nursed his right hand for three and half weeks before receiving permission from his doctor to return to work. There were no repercussions from the second vehicle crash or the domestic dispute with the town board or the supervisor, and Mac was grateful. He couldn't wait to get back on the road. He missed police work, and truth be told he needed the money.

The first thing Mac did when he became a full-time police officer at CPD was buy a new car. He had been driving cars that were at least ten years old his whole life thus far, and he wanted a reliable mode of transportation, if not impractical. He bought a new Chevrolet Camaro, a hold-over from the previous year. It was dark blue with a silver interior. It was not practical for all the snow that Central New York received, nor for having three young children, but it did wonders for his self-worth. Although, it certainly added to his worry over money as well.

The other pitfalls to being injured were that Mac couldn't work overtime details. The Camillus Police worked uniform security in their police uniforms at Fairmount Fair and Camillus Plaza, where they would work a walking beat in and around the malls. They were also employed by the West Genny School District to work football, basketball, and hockey games. Of course, there were also OT for the department working STOP DWI, and traffic details like parades, the fourth of July, and so on.

The extra money came in handy with raising his three children, who, even though they lived with their mother, he saw almost every day, taking them to the zoo, movies, parks and playgrounds, Optimist baseball practice, ballet lessons, First Communion lessons, CYO basketball, Pop Warner football and cheerleading practice. Mac also routinely picked them up after school and spent time with them until he had to work. He missed them dearly, but knew what he was doing was important to provide for the children and make a decent future for them.

Mac had also taken up Washin-Ryu karate, and had been practicing three times a week. After being injured, he obviously couldn't participate in the training. The traditional Japanese sport gave him inordinate inner peace and a new self-reliance that he hadn't had before. It was a great workout, and his gi was drenched with sweat each time he finished his lessons.

His first shift back was a day shift, and he was relieved to be back in a marked police car. Chief Whitlock had welcomed him back and was very cordial upon Mac's return. It was springtime in the town, and the sunny days and fresh country air were a welcome change from the long winters in upstate New York.

B-Watch was usually quiet, with most calls being minor accidents or vehicle lockouts in the mall parking lots, or a petty theft from one of the stores. But not on this day

"Units #3101B, #3102B, #3100B, and #4505B respond to Gemini Estates, building 2, apartment 3, Town of Camillus for a forcible rape just occurred...1217 hours," the MRD Center dispatched over channel 4.

All units acknowledged the call and Sgt. Diane Powell (Unit #3100B) coordinated the response and inquired, "Unit #3100 to dispatch...any additional information on the suspect or direction of travel?"

"Your complainant Adalind Holbrook states that the suspect was a white male in his thirties, last seen wearing a white T-shirt and blue jeans...suspect armed with a knife...no direction or means of travel."

"Received...could you see if AIR-1 is working today, and have them start them this way if they are?"

"Affirmative, they are in service at the heliport and I'll start them."

"Received. Thank you," Sgt. Powell acknowledged.

Mac, who was working Unit #3101B, knew that rapes were quite rare in the town, let alone a forcible rape. He activated his lights and siren and started heading in that direction. His shift partner from CPD was Connor Coke in unit #3102B, and he could see him taking a code (lights and siren) pulling out onto West Genesee Street from a side street about a quarter mile in front of him.

The motorists on the road pulled to the side so that Connor and Mac could pass them on the way to the call. Mac was very cognizant to be careful while driving to the scene; even though this was an important call, he couldn't afford another accident.

Within three minutes they both arrived, letting the MRD Center know by their police radios. Connor and Mac exited their police vehicles and went to building 3, apartment 6 where they knocked on the door. A crying and disheveled Adalind Holbrook came to the door, wearing pink sweatshirt and sweatpants. She was mid-twenties, 5' tall, with a slight build, red hair and blue eyes. On opening the door, Adalind cried, "He raped me! He raped me!"

"Ma'am, I'm sorry. Could you please tell me what happened?" Connor said.

Adalind took a moment, composed herself and said, "My apartment door was opened because I was doing laundry in the basement. When I came back into my apartment a man was standing here in the living room. He had a knife and told me to go out the sliding glass door on the back patio. I didn't want to, and I started to scream. He grabbed my arm and told me if I made any noise, he would kill me. My husband's at work and my two-year old daughter was sleeping in her bedroom, so I did what he said."

"Ma'am, what happened once you were both out on the patio?" Connor asked.

Adalind starting weeping as she started tucking in her shirt.

"He forced me to have intercourse with him. He made me lie down on the cement porch. He took off my pants and then he took off his pants. And then he did it." At this, she started crying again.

Sgt. Powell had arrived during Connor's questioning, and she remained silent as Adalind answered the query. At this, she stepped forward and asked, "Did you see where he went?"

"No, after he was done, I went back into my apartment, closed and locked the sliding glass door and called the police."

"Connor and Mac, start by going out back. See if there is a scene or anything that might give us a direction of travel and then start looking for the suspect. I'll have Unit #4505B start checking the surrounding businesses," Sgt. Powell advised.

"Yes Sarge," they both answered, and then went out the back door into the backyard.

Connor and Mac went out through the common access door out the back of the building and took a left around to where the cement porch was connected to Adalind's apartment. There was nothing visible on the pale gray cement. There was a tall grassy area that ran the length of the property and butted up against an eight-foot wire fence that gave way to a major highway.

"You go right, and I'll go left," Connor said as they came to the fence.

Mac traversed the ground against the fence on the right side of the complex as he thought about this being his first rape investigation. Camillus was such a sleepy town that it was hard to imagine. The rapist must've been watching her for a while to get that type of opportunity with the open door while she was doing laundry.

He could hear the rush of rotor-blades overhead and heard AIR-1 call "Arrived on scene" through his portable radio. He looked up and shielded his eyes against the sun as he saw the black and white sheriff's helicopter circling overhead.

As Mac kept walking the fence line and looking for the suspect or evidence of the crime, he saw the WAVES (Western Area Volunteer Emergency Services) ambulance through the break in the buildings pull up to the front of building 2. He also saw the Village of Solvay and a Town of Geddes police vehicles circling through the area. Even though this was just out of their jurisdiction, a call like this got lots of assistance from surrounding police agencies trying to help.

Mac wasn't finding much of anything, and after checking the fence line, he began checking the back of other apartment buildings and common hallways. He saw several curious residents and asked them if they had seen a white male, in his thirties, wearing a white T-shirt and blue jeans, or anyone else suspicious-looking in the area. They all said they hadn't.

After approximately forty-five minutes, Sgt. Powell used her portable radio to call Connor and Mac back to the original scene. Mac got there first, and Sgt. Powell was just shaking her head back and forth as she was on the radio with the MRD Center. "Cancel the Point of Information (PIO) on the rape. You can clear AIR-1 and Unit #4505B. Unit #3101B and I will be clearing shortly, and you can leave Unit #3102B out on it."

Sgt. Powell was a white female, mid-thirties, with blonde hair and blue eyes, 5' 5" tall, with a medium build. She had been on the job for around twelve years and had made sergeant nearly two years ago.

Connor showed up as she was getting off the phone. "What's up, Sarge?"

"It's a false report."

"You got to be shitting me. Really?" Connor said.

"Yup. The sequences didn't make sense to me. Along with the fact that this guy would've had perfect timing, there was no evidence, and the victim's demeanor wasn't making much sense either," Sgt. Powell expounded.

"But why did she call in the rape?" Mac asked.

"It turns out that she was having an affair and she thought she may be pregnant. She wanted a way out to explain the pregnancy that she knew wasn't her husband's child."

"Holy crap! That's some bizarre shit right there!" Connor exclaimed.

"You know it. Connor, could you write this up and arrest her for Falsely Reporting a Crime? Mac hasn't had one of these yet, and I want it done right."

"Sure, Sarge. No problem."

"She says she'll give you an affidavit of why she did it. I read her Miranda, but you should do it again before you take the statement. You can give her an appearance ticket for next week to report for court, we don't want to take the kid if we don't have to."

"You got it, Sarge."

As the helicopter, the ambulance and other police cars left the area, Mac couldn't help but think of the unprecedented emergency response as he sat in his car filling out his log. It was crazy that someone would go to those lengths to hide an infidelity, and the damage it must do to women who were actually assaulted and the police doubting them because of experiences like this. If Sgt. Powell hadn't been so experienced and known what to look for while questioning the victim, it also would've caused a panic in the community and a sense of violation within the town.

It was another nugget of information that Mac would file

away as a lesson learned for future reference.

Courtesy is as much a mark of a gentleman as courage.

- Theodore Roosevelt

CHAPTER

SIX

Mac worked days for the rest of that week and the following week. He liked working B-Watch, but he didn't get that much of a chance unless the more experienced cops were on vacation or training. The lieutenant at the Town of Camillus Police Department was Max Johnson. He was a white male in his mid-forties, 6' 2" tall, with a medium build, brown crew-cut hair that was going gray, and glasses. He looked sort of like Drew Carey. Lt. Johnson did the scheduling for the police department and took care of most of the administrative duties for CPD. He worked solely Monday through Friday B-Watch, and Mac never saw him unless he was assigned during the day.

The chief and all the sergeants were friendly enough to Mac, but he felt that Lt. Johnson treated him differently than the other cops. When Mac first met him, Lt. Johnson told Mac that he knew his father, which everybody did, since he owned several businesses in the town, but the way he said it gave Mac pause. It wasn't what he said, but how he said it. Still, Mac treated Lt. Johnson with reverence as he did with all his supervisors, although he hoped that he wouldn't have to pay for his father's sins.

Another person Mac only saw on days was Detective Sergeant Billy Cole. He also was a white male in his mid-forties, 6' 1" with brown wavy hair, a thin build and a mustache. He oversaw all investigations and follow-ups that came in from the uniform officers. He was quite pleasant, and seemed to be always engaged with his work. Even though Det. Sgt. Cole was busy he always had time to give Mac pointers on investigations. They were greatly appreciated because this was where Mac eventually wanted to gravitate to.

The town itself was a rural middle-class community that didn't really see a lot of crime. Being in Central New York, it usually started snowing in October on into April, and sometimes even May. The weather kept people inside for most of the year. Sure, there were some property crimes like vehicle larcenies, burglaries of garages in the summertime, stolen bicycles and the like, but all in all, there was a lot of downtime for the cops. This lent itself to never-ending practical jokes amongst the employees to keep themselves entertained.

First and foremost, all the cops called each other "Moe." The connotation was never clear to Mac, but it was endless — "Hey Moe, did you see that?" "Hey Moe, where are you going?" "Hey Moe, they're calling you on the radio," and so on and so forth. It was all good natured and eventually even Mac was called "Moe."

One day, Mac came to work and was up on the third floor in the locker room changing. When he went to put on his boots, which he left underneath his locker, he couldn't budge them from the floor. The guys from the previous shift were changing from their uniforms into their civvies and were pretending they weren't watching any of this. The more Mac pulled on the tops of his boots, the more frustrated he became. Finally, the other cops were crying in hysterics as they watched, and one of them said, "Hey Moe! Are you having problems with your boots?" It turned out that they superglued them to the floor.

In retaliation, several days later when Mac was winding down the end of A-Watch, he took baby powder and put it into open white postal envelopes and then taped them to the visors of the B-Watch police vehicles. When the mischievous cops working days went to put the visors down to shield the sun during their shift, the powder slipped out of the envelopes and ended up in their laps. It was all in good fun, and if nothing else, it kept them on their toes for the next prank.

Coats left in the patrol room while they were doing administrative duties would be constant targets. If an officer got up and went to another room, the instigator would either take off the badge and nameplate and put them back on upside down, or trade nameplates entirely with another abandoned jacket. When the cops got calls for service they would quickly put back on their outerwear and go meet with the complainants. During the conversations, the officers would know that they had been had when the citizens repeatedly started looking down at their jackets or by calling them by their wrong last names.

One day, the pranks got a little out of hand. Sgt. Smith was working B-Watch and one of the newer cops cut out a picture of a naked girl and taped it to Sgt. Smith's gun butt as they passed each other in the patrol office. The young cop thought that someone at the station would see it momentarily and bust the sergeant's chops over it. Well, one thing led to another, and the other cops saw it but kept the joke to themselves to see how long it would last. An hour later, unbeknownst to anyone else, Sgt. Smith had a public speaking engagement at a community group. He left the building and made his appearance at the forum, which included ladies from the Rotarian Club. When he came back, he was so mad he couldn't speak. Although it was still kind of funny, no one wanted to intentionally discredit the senior sergeant like that.

The practical jokes stopped for a while and then came back in earnest. Bananas were shoved into police vehicle tailpipes, causing the motor to sputter when started until a loud backfire eventually came from expelling the exploding banana from the tailpipe. Vaseline was put under police vehicle door handles. Sirens were hooked up so that when you started the cruiser it would wail at full blast until you manually turned it off.

Mac was working C-Watch one day, stopped at a busy four-way intersection at Fairmount Four Corners, when CPD officers Jorge "Twist" Lehman and Carl "Wide-Body" Sorbie pulled up behind him at the traffic light in an unmarked police car and wearing plain clothes. Mac didn't see them right away and they were sandwiched between multiple other civilian cars in rush hour traffic. The two academy mates turned on the unmarked police vehicles' siren and let it shriek on and on. Mac originally thought that he had bumped the switch to the siren in his own car. He kept on turning the switch to the 'Off' position but obviously it didn't stop the siren noise. The civilians in their vehicles all around Mac were just staring at him, expecting for Mac to do something. Mac frantically played with the knob until he looked up into his review mirror and saw the duo behind him laughing hilariously at their hijinks. Mac in the end activated his emergency lights to clear the civilian vehicles out of his way so he could escape the mayhem Lehman and Sorbie had orchestrated.

Lehman was a Hispanic male of swarthy complexion, 5' 7" tall and 145 pounds, with brown eyes, and dark full hair. He was known as "Twist" because of his apropos dance moves. Sorbie was a white male with a tanned complexion, 6' 4" tall, 250 lbs., with a head shaved bald and a body of a tank from excessive weightlifting, thus his moniker of 'Wide-Body.' Twist and Wide-Body had attended the academy class ahead of Mac. Twist was pleasant, funny, and endearing, while his counterpart had a subdued mean streak to him, which was never too far from the surface. Wide-Body could be pleasant most of the time, but there was something dark just behind his brown eyes.

The two were tight, as most academy buddies were, but Wide-Body had just gotten married, and that cut into the social time the two had experienced. They were the masterminds behind most of the practical jokes at CPD.

Since Wide-Body got wedded, he couldn't go out with the crew to get drinks anymore. That didn't stop other younger members of CPD from getting together off-duty. When Mac had the chance, he would hang out outside of the PD with Twist and Connor Coke. Connor had about five years as a cop with CPD. He was 6"1" tall, 180 lbs., with brown curly locks, baby blue eyes, and an athletic build. He was a lady's man with a great gift of gab, which the women loved. The only outsider from CPD to the cavorting was a trooper out of the NYSP Elbridge Barracks named Orsen Alvey. Alvey was a white male, 5' 10" tall, 165 lbs. He was balding, with brown eyes and an average build, and was always smiling. He wasn't from Central New York, and had been recently transferred by the state police to the Elbridge Barracks. Alvey had about three years with the state and enjoyed the single life of a trooper. Everyone was about the same age and single, although Mac was the only divorcee among the friends.

After a Friday night when Mac was assigned to C-Watch

and he was changing in the men's locker room, Twist said from the other side of the lockers, "Hey Mac...are we going out tonight?"

"Sure. I guess I can. I don't have any overtime tonight. Did Alvey get back to you?"

"Yep...He's just leaving work now. He'll meet us at Molly Malone's."

"What about Connor?"

"What did you expect? He was off tonight, so he's out with one of his concubines."

"Okay. I'm in, then. Just give me a second to get my locker straightened out," Mac said.

Molly Malone's was a medium-sized pub located at Charles Plaza in the Village of Solvay. It had a twelve-stool bar area with several four-seat tables on the entry side and was separated by a wall with open doorways on both ends, to a small dance floor area and a DJ booth, surrounded by more table and chairs. There was a kitchen in the back, and the guys could get bar food if they didn't get a chance to get something to eat on shift. There was also an electronic dart board by the front door which the guys liked to play. The manager and the bartenders were cop friendly, and knew that the guys didn't get out of work until late and would let them stay a little later than the rest of the patrons.

Twist drove the pair for the five-minute ride through the

spring night to the pub, arriving at about 12:15 AM. Mac left his Camaro at the PD and would get it later in the night. The DJ music was cacophonous as they walked through the front doors. The bar stools were filled with patrons enjoying the start of the weekend. The busy bartender, Johnny, acknowledged Mac and Twist. He stopped what he was doing and got a single Captain Morgan and Diet Coke with a lime in a pint glass for Mac and a bottle of Budweiser for Twist. Twist paid for the drinks and the cops walked over to the other side of the bar and sat at a table near the dance floor as Run-DMC featuring Aerosmith sang 'Walk This Way' over the speakers.

"So...how about that call tonight? I can't believe that the car didn't catch fire when it rolled over," Twist said after tasting his beer.

"Yeah, what a mess. I can't believe that there weren't more serious injuries involved."

"Every now and then people get lucky, I guess," Twist said as he was checking out the girls dancing on the dance floor.

Alvey walked into their side of the bar holding a Michelob Ultra bottle and sat down at the table. "Gents," he said in greeting, tipping his beer toward them.

The lights in the bar were low, and the colorful lights from the dance floor reflected off the glass mirrored walls, as well as the dancers, who were swaying to the rhythm of the beats. The cops recognized several of the women dancing as waitresses from the TJ's Big Boy restaurant in Fairmount. It was a popular place for the cops to get something quick to eat while they were working during their shift.

"Did you have anything interesting tonight Alvey?" Mac said.

"Nah, just a relay of paperwork down to Broome County, and a vehicle stop on the way back. The driver had the un's."

Mac asked, "What are the un's?"

"Unlicensed, unregistered, and uninspected. She also had a warrant out of the Town of Fabius for not answering a summons," Alvey answered. "What'd you guys have tonight?"

"A vehicle rollover on Route 5 at Bennet Corners Road. It was a Ford Bronco, and the driver tried to avoid a deer, overcorrected, and flipped it in the middle of the highway. He'd just gassed up and fuel was all over the roadway," Twist answered.

"He's lucky it didn't spark," Alvey said.

"Yup, we had to have the vollies hose down the road before the tow company could sweep up the debris," Mac said.

The volunteer fireman in the suburbs were referred to by the cops as 'vollies'—volunteers, or 'blue-lighters'—because of the blue courtesy lights they used on the way to the firehouse, or sometimes 'cellar savers'—due to the fact that by the time they got to the firehouse, got their gear ready to deploy, and made it to the scene, all that was left of the house on fire was the cellar.

Twist then abruptly changed the subject as a Madonna

68

song came on. "Hey, we should go dance with the girls." Alvey moved himself away from the table and stood up, putting his beer bottle down. "Mac, you coming?"

"Nah, you guys go ahead."

Twist and Alvey made their debut on the dance floor with Twist doing his thing.

Mac just sat there at the table, sipping on his drink and reflecting on his own disastrous personal life. He missed not being able to check on his kids at night while they were sleeping and giving them a kiss on their foreheads. It was hard to think about getting involved with someone else. He didn't want to explain to his children who any new girl was, although he knew if he ever got that far, it would be inevitable.

The trio had a good time blowing off steam given the rare socializing they got to do outside of work. Twist dropped Mac back off at the station at about 2:30 AM. Mac got in his car and rolled down the windows as 'Alone' by Heart came on the radio station. He drove home with the windows down, listening to the lyrics as he tried to sort out his life in his head.

When he got home, he checked on his grandmother, who was fast asleep, and then he went downstairs to his space. Mac got himself a pint glass, filled it with ice, and made himself a Captain and Diet. He walked out the bottom patio door to the lower outside porch area, which was off his living space, to see the extensive views of twinkling lights in the valley.

Although Mac didn't openly advertise this, he spoke with God quite often, usually late at night during times like this. He would look up at the evening sky and contemplate his life, re-think situations that involved him during the day, and try to figure out the universe and where he might be going in it. Mac never received any concrete information on any of these things from God, but it didn't stop him from reflecting, hoping that someday the world would make sense and he would receive more information leading him towards his destiny, wherever that may be.

Keep your eyes on the stars, and your feet on the ground.

- Theodore Roosevelt

CHAPTER

SEVEN

Mac woke up the next day around 10:00 AM, checked on his grandmother, who was already watching television, and then got ready to cut the grass. With his grandparents' riding lawn mower, it would take about four hours to mow the lawn. He figured that he should be done around 2:00 PM and that would give him enough time to shower, change, and pick his two children up after school in Solvay. His youngest, Elizabeth, was still a toddler at home with her mother, but the timing should work out to get them all at the same time. Mac had today off from CPD and didn't have any overtime details lined up, so he was looking forward to spending some quality time with his children after he got his chores done.

Mac often wished the time he could spend with his children wasn't so limited. His marriage ended because his wife was habitually "accidently" pregnant for their entire five-year union. She had been his first significant girlfriend from high school, and being a good, Irish Catholic kid, he married her when she became with child. According to her, she was on birth control through all her pregnancies, which left Mac in the dark on the whole family planning thing. It wasn't that he didn't want children; he just knew that it wasn't fiscally responsible to keep on having children that you couldn't afford. With his wife pregnant all the time and not working as a nurse, Mac was left perpetually working, which left him with very limited time with his children, who he loved so much. The resentment for his wife, who was seemingly becoming pregnant on purpose so she wouldn't have to work, drove a wedge in the high school sweethearts' marriage after the birth of their last child, Elizabeth.

After the dissolution of the marriage, Mac made his children his priority, but the bills still had to be paid. Getting divorced just added more weight onto Mac's already burdened life, as he had to pay child support for his three kids. Their mother did not spend much, if any, of that money on them, and Mac still had to buy all their school clothes, coats, sneakers and whatever else they needed. Therefore, the divorce was just more insult added to injury in Mac's life. In spite of all that, however, he was still glad to be able to spend the day with them.

The sun was climbing up into the sky on a nearly perfect spring day. There were only wispy clouds in the heavens and only the trace of a warm breeze. The old tractor started right up, and Mac started carving out rows of even passes through the level front yard. The routine was calming and gave him a good sense of order in the world. The fresh cut spring grass reminded him of being a kid and all was right in the universe.

The backyard was on a thirty percent downward grade, and Mac took turns cutting horizontally across the lot with his body shifting towards the gravitational pull of the slope after every turn. He had to gas up the mower halfway through the yard and was able to get the lawn and the trimming done by 2:10 PM. Mac jumped in the shower and dressed in a blue J Crew T-shirt, yellow surfer shorts and brown flip-flops. He put on a blue and red Boston Red Sox's cap on the way out the door. Once in the car he put on his black Ray Ban sunglasses and played with the radio until he found Bob Segar and the Silver Bullet Band playing 'Shake Down.'

The drive was only about fifteen minutes cutting across town. Mac picked up the kids, who were elated to see their father, and took them on the short drive over to Shove Park in the Town of Camillus. The park had three separate playgrounds on each side of the road that ran through the dead-end thoroughfare. There were several baseball and softball fields in the park, and at the top of the hill there was a covered hockey rink, which more notably converted into a box-lacrosse playing field in the summertime. West Genny was one of the best lacrosse high schools in the country.

The rest of the park was backed up by woods on one side and had babbling creek that ran through it, complete with a bridge which took you from one side to the other. There was a path that went along the water and deep into the woods. There were picnic tables scattered all along the park. Residential housing ran along the other side of the park, along with a nice apartment complex.

The children loved coming to the park and it was a perfect spring day for them to enjoy it. Mac played with them on the swings, slides, and monkey bars and then they went on a long walk down the path into the woods. He carried Elizabeth as Bridget and Joseph ran up ahead, exploring as they went.

Once they were done exploring the park, Mac took them up the two-minute drive to Fairmount Hills to see their Grandmother MacKenna and Mac's youngest sister Ruth, who was fifteen years his junior. Mac's other siblings were off at college: Mary was attending Niagara University, Michael was at Boston University, and Ann was beginning Oswego State University.

Mac carried Elizabeth while Bridget and Joseph scurried around his legs as he opened the door to his parents' house, and his childhood home. The house itself was a large four-bedroom, two-and-a-half-bath, shake-shingle Colonial which sat on a third of an acre, bordered by woods on the back hill behind the house. It was on a dead-end street with similar homes all around the neighborhood.

"Grandma! Grandma!" the older two cried as they raced into the house.

"Hi guys! Hi Patrick! Hi pumpkin!" Grandma MacKenna greeted them as she walked into the hallway from the kitchen. Mac's mother was in her early fifties, but looked much younger than her age belied. She was 5' 8" tall, with a medium build, brown hair going gray, glasses, and a permanent smile. Grandma MacKenna was wearing a yellow paisley-printed blouse and brown slacks.

"Where are you guys coming from?" she asked.

"Shove Park. Where's Dad?"

"Where else would he be on a day like this? He's out golfing," she answered.

Ruth came down the stairs, gave Mac a hug, and then she and all the children ran outside to play.

"Have you heard from the kids?" Mac asked, referring to his brother and sisters.

"Yes. They're all doing just fine. Are you still jealous of them for being off at college?"

"Of course, Mom. I really should've gone away to school like they did, but that ship has sailed. I'll go back to OCC eventually and then work on my bachelor's degree. I really didn't know any better, being the oldest and all. I wish I knew now what I didn't know then. It's going to be so hard to go back and do it."

"I tried to tell you back then. But you had your mind made up about staying home," she said.

"I know, but I didn't really know anybody who went off to college. My friends didn't go away. Heck, I never even went on a college visit. Either way, my SAT scores were dismal because I really didn't have that focus," Mac replied.

"I know, Patrick, but you're making the best of your situation as you've found it. How's work going?"

"It's going pretty good lately. I'm still learning a lot, and I haven't been in any car accidents lately. I really do like what I'm doing, Mom. It's not really exciting like working in the city, but I get a chance to help people, and most of the time they appreciate it.

"The other day, a woman wrote a very nice thank-you note about me to the Chief. Her fourteen-year old daughter had run away to a friend's house. I found her by making some phone calls and went over to pick her up. She was still kinda infuriated when I picked her up and she didn't want to go back home. I took some time and spoke with her about the problems that she was having with some kids at school. I gave her some advice and told her I would talk with her parents to try and alleviate the whole running-away-from-home thing with them. She eventually was appreciative that I listened to her. When I spoke with her parents and explained what she had told me, they were understanding and grateful that I found her."

"Well Patrick, that makes my day! I'm glad you have some satisfaction with your work. It makes the rest of the job a little easier, doesn't it?"

"You're right, Mom. Getting a good letter does go a long way with the Chief. It cancels out some of the other bad things in my learning curve with the job."

Mac and his Mom spoke for about twenty-five minutes about the family, how he was taking care of her mother, and how the divorce was going. Then the conversation turned toward Mac's father.

"He's still drinking too much and he's never home. He says he's working, but you know more than anyone else he's just sitting down there drinking," she said.

"Yeah...well...what can you do? Maybe he'll get sick of it. I mean, it's got to get old after a while, don't you think?"

"I don't know, Patrick. It worries me, but you're right. There's nothing I can do. He knows I don't like it, but he's going to have to figure it out for himself."

"Is he still disappointed I became a cop?" Mac asked.

"Well, even though he helped get you the job, I think he still wanted you take over the business someday."

"Yeah, I know. But after he broke my nose, I would've thought that would have ended that dream for him. He knew that this is what I always wanted to do. Besides being a priest, which of course went by the wayside after finding out about girls, but he knew this is what I really wanted to become."

"Yes, he might be a little jealous about that. When he got

out of the Marine Corps, he got offered a job with the State Police. He turned it down, but some of his friends took the job and he said that they would never make any money at it. Your father said they had to brown bag their dinner every day because they didn't get paid enough to buy their dinner while they were working," she said.

"But it's not about the money, Mom. I mean for me, sure, the money is better than what I was doing before, but I love what I do and I'm proud of what I've accomplished to get here."

"I know honey, but he sees his friends now and they are making better money and they have a pension, which he doesn't have. And maybe he is kind of wishing he took the job. He might even feel bad for telling you that it wasn't a good job when you first asked him about it years ago."

"Well...I guess we're in the same boat. He's going to have to figure that one out for himself. I can't make him change his mind on that. The job is what it is, and I like it. If I didn't need the money to take care of my kids, I would do it for free," Mac said.

"Well, Patrick, he could be hoping that if it doesn't work out that maybe you would be able to take over the family business one day. Whether he's right or wrong, I'm pretty sure he's thinking that might happen."

"Great..." Mac said, thinking to himself that his father had a vested interest in seeing Mac fail so his backup plan could be implemented.

It was just about 5:30 PM, and Mac's mother asked if they

wanted to stay for dinner. Mac felt bad, because he didn't tell her ahead of time that they would be stopping by today, so he told her that they already had plans to have dinner down the street. Everyone kissed and hugged, and Mac piled the kids back into the Camaro, waved to his Mom and Ruth, pulled out of the driveway, and went downhill on Terry Town Heights Drive.

Mac took them to Pensabene's Park West Italian Restaurant at the corner of Warners Rd. and Milton Ave. in Camillus. Everyone had a cheese and sausage pizza and fruit punch. The kids really enjoyed dinner, and after, he took them across the street to Pete's Polar Parlor for ice cream, which they enjoyed even more.

When Mac dropped off his children, they were full and tired. This was the worst part of the day. Mac didn't want to leave them, and they didn't want him to leave. He gave them all big hugs and kisses and turned them over to their mother.

As Mac drove away in the slate gray evening on the way back to Onondaga Hill, he had tears in his eyes. One day, he would find a way to rectify this with his children.

That night, while Mac laid in bed, he again talked to God. He tried to understand how people got divorced, and what that did to their children, and to themselves. He received no answers.

The one thing I want to leave my children is an honorable name.

- Theodore Roosevelt

CHAPTER

EIGHT

The next day, Mac was working A-Watch with Wide-Body. After changing into their uniforms in the Locker Room, the cops got the turnover from C-Watch in the Patrol Room one floor down.

The Patrol Room was on the second floor, across the hall from the secretary's anteroom. On Betty Master's secretaries' side there was the Chief's Office, Detective Sergeant's Office, Lieutenant's Office, and a combined one-desk Patrol Sergeants Room. On the Patrol Room side there was a segmented workspace for the patrol officers which consisted of an "L" shaped white laminated table counter which had six orange plastic chairs. There were computer terminals affixed in front of each chair. Adjacent to the workspace, against the interior wall to the hallway, was a low school counter you would find in any Elementary School, attached over floor-height cupboards. There sat a Base Police Radio, a Teletype Machine, charging stations for the portable radios, and individual officers' mailboxes.

On the other half of the Patrol Room, separated by five-foot moveable beige fabric room dividers, was the Breathalyzer Test Room where people were tested for Driving While Intoxicated (DWI), two holding areas complete with a wooden bench and a metal bar (for handcuffing suspects) a foot above the floor running horizontally the length of the bench, and additional work space for the cops. There was also a small half bathroom as you came in the hallway door. The cops would start and end their shifts in the Patrol Room. Here, messages and work assignments would be passed on between the shifts.

"Anything worth mentioning happened tonight?" Wide-Body asked, while Mac got a new battery for his portable from the charger.

"Nope. Just a couple of minor car crashes and a petit larceny arrest at J.C. Penney's," Sgt. Dianne Powell answered.

The rest of the officers had already gone up to their respective locker rooms to change.

"All right, see you tomorrow," Wide-Body replied.

"Goodnight Sarge," Mac said as he made his way out of the Patrol Room and down the stairs to his patrol car.

It was nice having a partner on the midnight shift, even if it was Wide-Body. Putting things in proper context, he was just moodier than anything else. He really wasn't a bad person or a bad cop. And it truly was better than being alone. Even though the sheriff's department and the state police were working, they could be anywhere outside the Town of Camillus and their response times could be twenty or more minutes away.

"Unit #3101A in service," Wide-Body advised the MRD Dispatch Center.

"Unit #3102A in service," Mac followed up on the police car radio.

"Both units...0003 hours," came the female dispatchers' reply over the radio.

Wide-Body would be working the east side of the town and Mac would be patrolling the mostly rural western part on this Tuesday morning. There was "Dead Air," which meant there was no radio traffic. Mac drove out to the farthest reaches of the town to see if anything was going on.

Wide-Body always started off his shift with a cup of free coffee from the Mobile Station at the Fairmount Four Corners. He would talk with the clerk a while before he started patrolling.

The police radio remained mostly quiet for several hours

84

while Mac was lost in thought cruising the backroads of the town.

"Unit #3101A...copy a suspicious vehicle," Wide-Body's voice echoed from the police radio speaker.

The dispatcher acknowledged, "Unit #3101A...what's your location?"

"Unit #3101A...in the parking lot of 107 Myron Road...on New York registration Young Boy Tom...4279...YBT-4279...it should show on a red Ford four-door sedan...occupied by one," Wide-Body said.

"Received...in the parking lot of 107 Myron Rd. on YBT-4279...Unit #3102A can you start that way to assist?"

"Unit #3102A...affirmative...en route," Mac acknowledged.

"0210 hours."

Mac arrived four minutes later. He pulled up behind Wide-Body's police car, got out and walked around to the driver's window.

"I found him just sitting here in the dark. The vehicle was off and parked, but he stepped on the brakes as I passed by, giving him away. He's got no good reason for being parked in the business," Wide-Body told Mac.

Wide-Body then showed Mac the driver's license of the individual. The license said his name was Alex Guise.

"Hey, I saw a point of information on him. He's a burglar who's been hitting Solvay and Geddes," Mac said.

"Oh yeah! Could you check around while I keep an eye on

him?"

"Sure. Let me get my flashlight and I'll check the area."

Mac went back to his patrol unit to retrieve a flashlight and started to check the exterior door and windows to the beauty salon that they were parked in front of. The business was in a converted white Ranch-style house. The front yard had been converted into a small parking lot that held five cars.

When Mac reached the side of the business, he found a window open. He inspected it more closely and found the inside screen to the window pushed in and lying on the floor. Mac walked back to Wide-Body's vehicle.

"I've got an open window with a screen pushed in. I think you should hook him up and we'll call the owner to come down and look to see if anything is missing," Mac said.

"Good deal. Let's get him out of the car."

Wide-Body and Mac walked up to the vehicle. Wide-Body stated, "Out of the car."

"Why? I didn't do anything wrong," said the man, who they'd determined was Alex Guise.

"Get out of the car before I drag you out," Wide-Body repeated.

Alex was feigning being bothered by the process, and the way Wide-Body was talking to him wasn't exactly helping the progression. He was a white male, mid-twenties, 6' tall and thin, with black hair and a scraggly beard. He was wearing a black leather jacket that was too small for him, blue jeans, and black sneakers.

"Okay? Happy?" Alex said as he stood up from the car and pulled his pants up.

"Turn around and place your hands on the roof of the car," Wide-Body instructed.

Alex started to say something, saw Wide-Body's and Mac's facial expressions, and decided to follow the instructions as given.

Wide-Body started expertly patting down Alex. He found a folding knife in his back-right pocket. Wide-Body didn't say anything. He just took it from Alex and put it in his right-front pants' pocket. Wide-Body then reached behind his duty belt and removed his handcuffs from his pouch and placed one strand on Alex's right wrist, brought Alex's right arm down behind him, then his left and secured the open end of the cuff to the other wrist.

"Am I under arrest?" Alex asked.

"This is just for officer safety at this time. We have an open window on the side of the business here. By any chance, did you break into this fine establishment, shitbag?" Wide-Body said.

"I don't know what you're talking about. I just want to go home."

"Alex, you don't have a rational reason to be here at 2:10 AM. It appears the beauty salon has been burglarized and we're going to have to get the owner here to check her business," Mac advised him.

At that point Alex just sunk his eyes to the ground and physically slumped in Wide-Body's hand as he had Alex's right elbow in his right hand. Alex was placed in the rear of Wide-Body's police car.

Wide-Body went to Channel 2 on the police radio to get contact information on the business while Mac went back to checking the surrounding area. Upon checking Rao Florist across the street Mac found a broken widow in the back of the business. Broken glass was freshly on the ground and inside the shop on the floor. Mac got on his portable radio, advised Wide-Body of the situation and that they needed to get the owner of the florist down here also.

Approximately thirty minutes later, the owner of the hair salon showed up at their location. Wide-Body had his interior light on as he was writing down Alex's information. Mac met the woman, who introduced herself as Maureen, the owner. He showed her the open window on the side and asked if she could check to see if anything was missing.

"You mean anything else?" Maureen said.

"What do you mean anything else? Mac responded.

"Well, he's wearing my black leather jacket..."

Mac couldn't help but smile. He walked back over to Wide-Body's car and stood by the right rear window. Wide-Body saw him and lowered the window. "Alex you're not too bright to be wearing the victim's jacket. NOW...you're under arrest."

"*Shit!*" Alex whispered without looking up. Wide-Body commenced in reading Alex his Miranda Warnings:

"You have the right to remain silent and refuse to answer any questions. Do you understand?

"Anything you do say may be used against you in a court of law. Do you understand? You have the right to consult an attorney before speaking to the police and to have an attorney present during questioning now or in the future. Do you understand? If you cannot afford an attorney, one will be appointed for you before any questioning if you wish. Do you understand? If you decide to answer questions now without an attorney present, you will still have the right to stop answering at any time until you talk to an attorney. Do you understand? Knowing and understanding your rights as I have explained them to you, are you willing to answer my questions without an attorney present?"

Alex confirmed that he understood his rights.

"Listen...yeah, I broke into both of those places but it's not my fault. I've got a drug problem and I can't get into rehab. All the places are full, and they say it'll be at least six weeks before a spot opens up. So, you see it's not my fault," Alex whined in response.

The owner of the florist shop responded twenty minutes later after searching the shop, and said that two boombox radios were taken along with cash out of the register drawer. Maureen from the beauty salon also said she was missing a portable radio and tip money that had been left in a jar on the desk.

Mac called for a tow-truck to impound Alex's vehicle. When they arrived, he did a vehicle inventory search on the vehicle and found the radios from both burglaries in the trunk of the car. Mac then took the requisite photos of the businesses as evidence.

When Wide-Body was processing Alex, he found $277.11 in his right front pocket, which was the currency missing from the two businesses. Wide-Body arraigned Alex in front of the town judge and he was remanded to the Onondaga County Justice Center on the two burglaries with no bail.

Mac patrolled the rest of the town by himself for the rest of the night while Wide-Body did the suitable paperwork. Even though Wide-Body could be a pain in the ass, he still did a good job spotting a burglary in progress on a quiet Tuesday morning.

At 6:36 AM, Mac was fueling his police vehicle at the end of his shift at the Gas Pumps located at the Town of Camillus Highway Department on Milton Avenue. He had jacked the pump handle as he was completing his patrol activity log from the previous night in the driver's seat. Mac was dog tired and could barely keep his eyes open. When the pump handle turned off Mac knew the vehicle was full of fuel. He set his patrol box down, put the police car in drive, took his foot off the brake, and pulled away from the pumps as he heard a loud BANG from behind. Mac cringed as he slammed on the brakes and looked in the sideview mirror.

The gas pump fuel hose was still attached to his vehicle, hanging out of the fuel door lid. He had completely torn it off the gas pump. Although Mac had an all-out adrenaline dump, all he could muster was a sigh, and mutter, "Shit..."

To educate a man in mind and not in morals is to educate a menace to society.

- **Theodore Roosevelt**

CHAPTER

NINE

Later in the same week, Mac was still working midnights by himself on a dark Friday night. He had completed the requisite business checks in the town and was cruising the outskirts on the western edge of Route 321 heading towards Route 5 when he saw a blinding ball of light off to his left on the horizon. The flash itself started off white hot and then turned to a flickering blue orb.

Mac was frozen while driving his patrol vehicle, if that could be possible, which apparently it was. He seriously considered the possibility of an alien invasion. Mac picked up the police radio mic off the dashboard and then reconsidered and put it back in the holding bracket. What was he going to tell the MRD Center...that he was afraid the Town of Camillus was under attack by Martians?

With great trepidation, Mac continued to drive north on Route 321 and then turned left onto Route 5 in the direction of the flash. Just before the town line on his right-hand side he saw that a telephone pole had been sheared in two. The transformer had exploded, causing the cascading blue light in the sky, and live powerlines were still arcing in the farmer's field, where he could make out a green pick-up truck on its side, with the assistance of the side-mounted spotlight on his police vehicle. The truck was approximately thirty yards into the field, and Mac couldn't tell right away if the vehicle itself was smoking from the beginnings of a fire or that the dust was still settling from the crash.

"Unit #3103A to Dispatch," Mac spoke into the police radio mike.

"Unit #3103A go ahead," MRD Dispatch acknowledged.

"Unit #3103A I have a single vehicle rollover crash in a farmer's field on Route 5 near the Town of Elbridge Townline. Unknown how many occupants at this time or injuries. Wires are down and sparking. Could you please start Fire Control, an ambulance, and Niagara Mohawk to my location?"

"Unit #3103A affirmative...0243 hours. Advise on further."

Mac activated his emergency lights, exited his vehicle with his flashlight and proceeded into the field towards the smoking pick-up truck. When he got through furrowed rows and looked into the open window of the truck with his flashlight, he saw three white males in their early twenties, all on top of each other inside the single cab of the truck. The vehicle had come to rest on the driver's side and gravity was apparently keeping the men from crawling up and out the open passenger's window. Mac didn't see any blood, and no one appeared to be injured, although he could smell plenty of raw alcohol emitting from the cab.

Mac climbed up on the side of the truck and stuck his hand into the open window.

"Give me your hand, and I'll pull you free," Mac said.

"Okay," the trio said in unison.

As Mac grabbed the first one, he said, "Are you guys all right?"

The first man said, "Yeah, we're fine."

Mac got the first guy and the second guy out without much problem. They were both about Mac's size. The third guy, who was the driver, was 6' 5" tall, and weighed about 275 pounds. Mac literally had his hands full and the big guy barley fit through the window.

Mac steered all three men through the field and kept them away from the down powerlines. He had them sit on the hood of his police vehicle as he went back to the truck to see the license plate.

"Unit #3103A to Dispatch."

"Go ahead Unit #3103A."

"Unit #3103A...there are three occupants in the vehicle, and all appeared uninjured. The plate on the vehicle is New York Registration Boy Whiskey Tom...9847...BWT-9847...it should show on a Chevrolet pick-up, green in color," Mac advised.

"Unit #3103A received...Fire Control, WAVES Ambulance, and National Grid are all en route."

"Unit #3103A copy...thank you...could you please start me a tow-truck for this vehicle also?"

"Affirmative...0252 hours," the MRD dispatcher acknowledged.

A short time later the fire trucks and the ambulance arrived on scene. The Emergency Medical Technicians (EMTs) evaluated the men and stated that they just appeared to have bumps and bruises. All three refused to be transported for further evaluation. The vollies checked the vehicle and stated that there was no fire in the engine compartment, and then helped with traffic control, setting up flares.

Mac eventually went back and spoke with the driver of the vehicle, who identified himself as Tony Wilder. Tony was a twenty-one-year old college football player. He told Mac that he and his friends had gone out drinking in the City of Syracuse and were on their way back to Auburn, where they lived. Tony further stated that he was talking to his friends in the truck and took his eyes off the road when the accident happened.

Mac had Tony perform several field sobriety tests to ascertain if he may have had too much alcohol to drink tonight. First, Mac had him recite (not sing) the alphabet starting with the letter 'G,' which Tony couldn't do successfully. Next, Max had Tony do a walk and turn on the fog-line (white-line) of the road, instructing him to walk ten steps forward, turn around, and walk eight steps back. Tony couldn't stay on the line and walked six steps up, turned around, and walked nine steps back. Mac then had Tony hold out one of his legs off the ground six inches and count to ten. Tony tried these three times and could get only to four. Mac finally administered an Alco-sensor Test, which is a pre-screening device to determine the Blood Alcohol Content (BAC) in a person's blood, on which Tony blew a .14 BAC. The legal limit in New York State is .10 BAC. Tony was .04 BAC over the what was advisable by the law.

Mac had Tony turn around and place his hands behind himself. It took two sets of handcuffs to hook Tony up. His back was so broad that his wrists could not come close enough to be handcuffed by him using only one set of cuffs.

Mac recited the New York State Driving While Intoxicate Warning to Tony:

"You are under arrest for driving while intoxicated. A refusal to submit to a chemical test, or any portion thereof, will result in the immediate suspension and subsequent revocation of your license or operating privilege, whether or not you are found guilty of the charge for which you are arrested. Your refusal to submit to a chemical test, or any portion thereof, can be introduced into evidence against you at any trial, proceeding, or hearing resulting from this arrest. Will you submit to a chemical test to determine the alcohol or drug content of your blood?

Tony stated, "Yeah, I'm sorry, of course I will."

Mac helped Tony into the back of his patrol vehicle and seat belted him in the back-right seat. He advised the MRD Center, "I have an arrest for VTL (Vehicle and Traffic Law) 1192. I'll be en route to the station with one. Could you please start a Breathalyzer Test Operator (BTO) that way?"

"Affirmative...0303 hours."

Under New York State law, Mac had two hours to have a Breathalyzer Test administered to Tony after he read him the DWI Warning.

The two passengers had been picked up at the scene by one of their parents and taken home. The tow company winched the vehicle from the field in surprisingly short order and towed it to their garage. Fire Control and WAVES cleared the scene as well.

Mac was met at the station by a good friend of his, Deputy Kevin Charm (OCSD). Mac had met Kevin when he was eighteen years old. Mac's maternal grandfather had fallen off the roof while clearing the rain-gutters and broke his ankle. Coincidently, Kevin was in the same hospital room because of a sledding accident. When Mac's mother went to visit her father, she learned that Kevin's father and brother were both Syracuse cops. Kevin had told her that he was a Boy Scout Police

Explorer for the City of Syracuse Police and he wanted to be a police officer as well. Mac's mother told him that her eldest son wanted to work in law enforcement. She got Kevin's phone number and convinced Mac to call him. Mac joined the Police Explorers and the two had remained friends ever since. Kevin had been hired originally as a Jail Deputy at the Onondaga County Public Safety Center Jail, and then transferred to the road a Police Deputy for the sheriff's department.

Deputy Kevin Charm was a year younger than Mac, tall and slender, with black hair, and had a certain resemblance to a young Clint Eastwood. Before joining the sheriff's department, Kevin had forgone college and did a hitch with the Army as a Military Police Officer. He had just gotten married to a girl that he had been dating since high school, so the pair didn't see each other socially like they once did.

"Hey, Mac!" Kevin said, as Mac got out of his car and was retrieving Tony from the backseat.

"Hey Kevin! Thanks for showing up for the BTO. This is Tony Wilder. He was involved in a crash on Route 5. Tony has been a perfect gentleman to me this evening."

"Hi, Tony. My name is Deputy Kevin Charm and I'll be giving you the Breathalyzer Test this morning. There is nothing to worry about."

"I don't want to cause any trouble guys, but I really need to pee," Tony said.

"No worries Tony. I'll have the test set up in a minute and we'll get it right over with. We can't un-handcuff you though until you take the test. You have to be observed not taking anything orally for twenty minutes prior to the exam," Kevin answered.

"Okay, but can we hurry? I really have to go!"

"Let me get us in, Tony, and it'll be done in no time," Mac said as he pulled the keys to the station off one of his belt keepers and unlocked the station door. The station was unmanned on A-Watch unless another cop happened to be working and was inside doing paperwork.

Kevin administered the Breathalyzer Test to Tony five minutes later. Tony blew a .15 BAC on the official test. He was un-handcuffed and taken to the restroom, where he used the toilet. Tony called his father to come get him and he was released on Uniform Traffic Tickets (UTTs) for New York State Vehicle Traffic Laws section 1192-3 (DWI), 1192-2 (DWI-BAC over .10%), and 1131 (Driving on shoulders and slopes).

Mac thanked Kevin for the assist and promised to catch up with him soon.

He finished his shift shortly thereafter and drove back to his grandmother's house. After checking on her, and seeing that she was eating breakfast, he went downstairs and closed the bedroom shutters, got undressed and laid in bed. Mac reflected on the night and chuckled a bit as he thought about advising the MRD Center of the impending alien invasion from Mars. It was fortunate that nobody got hurt. It was said that God takes care of drunks and fools. Tony and his friends had been the beneficiaries of that divine blessing this morning.

Tony wasn't a bad guy, and Mac hoped he would be all right with the legal process that lay before him. If Tony and his friends had been bad guys, or bad drunks, things could've gone much differently. Mac drifted off to sleep thinking it was funny how things worked out for some people and not others, as he continually missed his children.

Absence and death are the same—only that in death there is no suffering.

- **Theodore Roosevelt**

CHAPTER

TEN

The next day, Saturday, Mac had an overtime detail at Fairmount Fair Mall during the evening from 4:00 PM until 10:00 PM. He was in full uniform as he walked the carpeted walkway of the enclosed mall. The atmosphere was controlled by central heating and cooling, with the open clear glassed-in sliding doorways from the assorted shops facing each other with the expanse of walkable thoroughfare between them. Spaced out through the common areas were skylights, water fountains and waterfalls, and lush green gardens that lent themselves to a serene environment for patrons to peruse the wares located within the specialty stores.

Twist and Wide-Body were also working the mall on their night off and had started at noon. Mac had to go back into work at midnight. He left the security office where everyone started their shift by punching their timecard in at the time clock. Mac called on the mall security radio to find out his coworkers' location and made his way there to the Friendly's Restaurant located by the main entrance to the mall.

Twist and Wide-Body were waiting outside the restaurant when Mac arrived.

"Hi guys!" Mac said.

"Hey Moe! Let's go inside and get a cup of coffee," Twist replied.

All three went in and got a booth by the window. The sweet smell of syrup and coffee filled the air. Twist and Wide-Body sat on one side and Mac the other.

"I was at the station before I came in and saw you had a DWI last night," Twist said.

"Yeah...it was a weird scene...right out of Close Encounters of the Third Kind."

Mac told them about the lights in the sky, the damaged utility pole and arresting Tony.

"How drunk was he?" Wide Body asked.

"He blew a .15"

"Holy shit...he was boxed," Twist said.

"I had a guy so drunk last week that he blew Chow," Wide-Body added.

"Did he make a mess out of your patrol car?" Mac asked.

"No...Chow was his dog!" Wide-Body guffawed out loud at his own joke.

Mac and Twist groaned in unison.

A pretty waitress showed up with a coffee pot and poured Twist and Wide-Body their drinks. Mac asked the waitress for a hot chocolate.

Drinking coffee appeared to be a big cop thing. On A-Watch when it was quiet, the men and women from the different departments would gather at the Perkins Restaurant in Camillus Plaza, which was open twenty-four hours a day, and drink coffee. Mac suspected that it was because of the free refills. He tried drinking black coffee to be polite and fit in, but all it did was give him coffee breath and make him piss every thirty-minutes or so. It was not for him. He would rather take the razzing of the guys and get something he liked instead.

As the three cops were talking about the schedule at the PD, the waitress came and gave Mac his hot chocolate. Twist and Wide-Body pretended to smirk. They knew the deal but went along with the teasing, because that's what cops do to one another.

"Do you like working A-Watch Mac?" Twist asked.

"Yeah, it's not so bad. I'm still trying to find my way around, and I get more overtime than I would if I work C-Watch."

"It sucks!" responded Wide-Body.

"Getting sleep is hard," Mac acknowledged, "But I try to sleep in four-hour segments. If I'm lucky to get two of those, I don't feel that bad."

"If you make the best of it, it goes by quicker. I like C-Watch, but I don't need the overtime like you do, with your kids and all. It's nice to go out after work for a pop or two," Twist said.

"I wish I could go out for a pop after work," Wide-Body said.

"You should've not gotten married then Moe, should ya?" Twist replied with a smile.

"Married life isn't bad. It's just not being able to hang out with you guys after work that sucks..." Wide-Body said.

"Sure, it's not bad, until you have to pay child support, not see your kids, pay alimony and give up everything you ever worked for. Yeah, that sounds great. Go ahead and tell him, Mac!" Twist said.

"No, I agree with Wide-Body. I liked being married. Yeah,

the divorce sucks and not seeing your kids, but you can't go into a marriage with that type of attitude. You have to take the approach that it's going to work," Mac answered.

"And how did that work out for you?" Twist said good naturedly.

"Well, at least I don't pay alimony..." Mac said.

"How about that waitress at Big Boy? Twist asked Mac.

"Which one?"

"You know goddammed well which one. The one you always have dinner with by yourself when you're on C-Watch," Wide-Body interjected.

"Oh...you're talking about NMI," Mac said.

"Who the fuck is NMI?" Wide-Body asked.

"The waitress you're apparently referencing. She doesn't have a middle name, therefore No Middle Initial, in cop speak, thus, NMI," Mac responded.

"Very cute, Mac...so what's the story with that?" Twist said.

"She's cute and all, but I'm still screwed up from the divorce, and all my free time is usually spent with my children or working overtime. So, what's the point?" Mac said.

"The point is, it's not healthy to be alone," Twist answered.

"What? That's not a thing," Mac said.

"Sure, it is," said Wide-Body, "You'll end up being 941 crazy!"

"What's 941?" Mac asked.

"New York State Mental Hygiene Law section 9.41. It gives the police the right to commit someone for an evaluation at a hospital who is an imminent danger to himself or a third person." Twist said.

"I know that. But how does being alone qualify me for that? Mac asked.

"You wait and see. We'll be committing you if you stay single too long," Wide-Body said.

"Both you guys are EDP," Mac said in reply.

"Oh, so now we're Emotionally Disturbed Persons, are we?" Twist chimed in.

"I think we're done here. Let's do our rounds of the mall. Shall we?" Mac ended the conversation.

The trio walked around the mall checking on store owners and greeting shoppers as they made their rounds. The mall had a steady stream of people coming and going from the shops and restaurants. Most folks were dressed in late spring ware or early summer clothes, wearing shorts and light clothing. It was a good and promising time of the year, and the cheerfulness was in the air as the cops walked among the throngs of shoppers.

After walking around for a few hours, they decided to stop at Pavone's Pizza and get dinner. All three got cheese slices and soda. They ate in the common area outside the pizzeria, leaning against one of the low walls containing a water fountain.

"What are you guys doing when you get off tonight? Mac asked.

"I've got to go home and see the wife," Wide-Body said around a mouthful of pizza.

"I'm meeting Connor at Molly Malone's. He's bringing a couple of girls. You should bang in and come with us," Twist said.

"That's a nice thought, but I don't have that much time to take off and I'd like to save it to do something fun with my kids," Mac answered.

"Okay, but you don't know what you're missing…"

"I know. Connor always has some amazing talent with him. I'll have to wait until I'm back on C-Watch again to meet you guys out."

They continued working on their meals until they got a call on their mall radios for a fourteen-year-old girl shoplifting at Dey Brother's Department Store.

"I got it," Mac said as he finished up his pizza.

"We're just about done. We'll come with you," Twist said, as he was starting on his second piece of pie.

"I think I'll be good with a fourteen-year-old, but thanks just the same. I'll call you if I need you. Enjoy the rest of your meal."

Mac made the short walk down to the department store. As he walked through the front access to the building he was met by Gladys, the assistant manager.

"Hi, Patrick. We have her in the security office."

"Hey Gladys! What was she stealing?"

"Four pairs of earrings from the Jewelry Department."

"Has she given you any problems?" Mac asked.

"No. Matter of fact she's crying. The earrings only total up to thirty-eight dollars," Gladys said.

"Okay. I'll take care of it. Do you want prosecution?"

"If you could get ahold of her parents and have them come get her, we should be all set."

"Cool. Sounds like a good plan. I'll follow you back."

They walked by the Jewelry Department, Ladies Apparel, the Children's Section and then the Shoe Department on the way to the Security Office, which was located in the rear of the store by the back entrance.

As Mac and Gladys walked into the Security Office, they could see a curly brown-haired girl bent over and weeping in her hands. She was wearing a red T-shirt, brown shorts, and white sneakers. She didn't look up when they came in. The eighteen-year-old female store detective was sitting across from her at a desk, filling out paperwork.

"Hi, I'm Officer MacKenna with the Camillus Police Department. What's your name, dear?

She stopped crying, hesitantly looked up from her hands and with her watery blue eyes and said, "Tina."

"Well, Tina. What happened?" Mac said.

With that, Tina put her head back into her hands and started crying again.

"Tina, it's going to be all right, but it's important that you answer my questions."

She stopped crying again and looked back up at Mac.

"Okay. I'm sorry, my parents are going to kill me. I've never done this before and they're going to freak."

"It's really going to be okay. Just tell me what happened.

"I was at the Jewelry Counter and saw these earrings that I really liked. I don't have enough money to buy them and my mother always tells me I don't need fancy earrings, but my friends all wear them, so I put them in my pocket. I know it was wrong. I really didn't think I'd be caught. Nobody was looking. Then this girl," as she points to the store detective, "Comes out of nowhere and tells me to come with her. My parents are going to ground me forever. Will I have to go to jail?"

"Yes, it is wrong to steal, and you could go to Family Court for it. But the assistant manager says if I can get ahold of one of your parents, she won't prosecute you this time. You'll have to stay out of the store for a year, but you won't have to go to court," Mac said.

"My mom's name is Lisa. Her phone number is 315-474-8481. She's home. I just walked from up on Blueberry Lane not too long ago. Please don't tell my Dad. He'll ground me for a year!"

Mac got ahold of her mom and explained the situation over the phone. She was upset at first, but calmed down after Mac said that the store did not want any legal proceedings to take place. She showed up ten minutes later and chastised her daughter in front of everyone, which made Tina cry harder, and then she took her home.

"Thanks, Patrick. I think that was the right way to go. She looked like she showed remorse, and I don't think we'll have any more issues with her," Gladys said.

"I agree. Sending her to Family Court for that would have caused more problems than the case is worth, and I think her mother will do a better job at metering out the appropriate punishment."

Mac left Dey Brother's and linked back up with Twist and Wide-Body. The rest of their shift at the mall was uneventful. At the end of their tour, Twist went to meet Connor, Wide-Body went back to his wife, and Mac went to work A-Watch.

That was a pretty typical shift at Fairmount Fair. It was more public relations than crime-fighting, but that was okay with Mac. Most suburban policing was the same as walking the mall. People like seeing the police in their community and they were supportive with their encounters with the officers.

Mac was hoping for an interesting midnight shift to make the night go by faster. Working fourteen-hour days could get tiring, and keeping busy was the key to forgetting how weary you were.

Great thoughts speak only to the thoughtful mind,
but great actions speak to all mankind.

- Theodore Roosevelt

CHAPTER

ELEVEN

Unfortunately for Mac, but fortuitously for the Town of Camillus, the rest of the night for him was slow, consisting of business checks, checking the border of the town, and then meeting up with the sheriff's department and the state police for coffee and hot chocolate at Perkins Restaurant late in the morning.

Mac finished off the rest of his rotation on A-Watch without much to speak of; he was coming up on a long stretch of C-Watch shifts for the summer. During the preceding weeks, he drummed up enough support to foster a team for a Sunday morning softball league. Mac treasured sports, and couldn't get enough of the camaraderie they provided.

He organized the team by recruiting other cops to play, raising the registration and umpire fees, coming up with uniform shirts, and by acting as the team's captain. Mac didn't know much about coaching and just wanted to play, but no one else was driven enough to take on the responsibility, and it was left up to him. It wasn't a competitive league, but no one that takes sports seriously ever wants to lose. Especially cops, who are mostly Type-A personalities across the board. They played double headers starting at ten in the morning, and were usually done by around noon. It was a family day, and Mac always brought his kids to the games. They enjoyed being out on the fresh mowed grass or sitting on the bleachers next to their Dad, eating snacks as they watched the cops play. Every now and then, someone would make a bad play and utter a cuss word and Mac would shout out "Family Day!" to remind the cops of their fans.

Back on C-Watch, Mac had to reintegrate being around people and dealing with the traffic he didn't find on midnights. Today he was working with Twist and Connor. They were in the Patrol Room just starting their procedures for the shift when he and Connor received a call from the MRD Center.

"Units #3102C and #3103C...check the status of a resident at 968 Winding Way, Town of Camillus...caller sates that her daughter, Liza Cancel, thirty-eight-year old, white female, is off her meds and not answering her phone. The complainant is her mother and her contact information can be found in the notes...1611 hours."

Mac and Connor acknowledged the call. They filled up the patrol units with their patrol bags and a supply of forms for the night, and responded to the call.

They followed each other up to the front of the residence, which was a green raised ranch-style house on a sloping hill in the middle of a residential neighborhood. Nothing looked amiss from the street as they exited their patrol vehicles. There was a late model sedan in the driveway, and the interior door to the residence was open behind the glass storm door.

"Looks fairly normal," Mac said as he walked back to Connor's car.

"Yeah, it does. That always gives me the creeps on this sort of call. It could be something bizarre or nothing at all. I ran her on Channel 2 (DATA) on the way here. Liza Cancel has a history of EDP. The sheriff's department was here three months ago and transported her to Saint Joseph's Hospital CPEP (Comprehensive Psychiatric Emergency Program) for an evaluation."

"I hope she's not dead," Mac said. "I hate dead bodies."

The sun was out on this warm day, and three little girls were skipping rope in the adjacent driveway next door as the officers walked up to the front door. The girls giggled and laughed as they played, and waved to the officers as they noticed them.

Connor rang the doorbell and knocked on the storm door. After several minutes of repeating this, with no response, Connor opened the storm door and announced, "Camillus Police Department. Is anyone home?"

Connor then stepped into the anteroom and announced their presence again. The worst part about going into someone's home was that they could be very territorial about where they lived, and justifiably so, and wouldn't take to kindly to government intrusion into their space. However, Mac and Connor had a job to do, which was make sure that Liza Cancel was both physically and mentally all right.

Mac stayed in the central hallway as Connor cleared the garage area and downstairs rooms before proceeding up the stairs into the main living area. Connor, not finding anyone downstairs, kept up with announcing themselves as they ascended the stairs.

As they came up the flight of steps, the cops both noticed a very large painting on the wall of the staircase with a leprechaun smoking a pipe lying on a bed of clovers. The style and paint products used looked like that of a third-grade art project, but instead of being on an easel, it was set forth on the grand scale of the wall itself.

Mac and Connor kept going up but took a second to give each other a quizzical look. When they reached the top of the stairs, which came out into a living room, they took in the assorted disarray of the interior of the house. It was the home of a hoarder. Stacks of magazines and newspapers filled the middle of the room, with only paths to cut through the debris. The odor was pungent of spoiled food, urine, and feces.

Both cops covered their mouths with their weak hands, leaving their strong hands on the butts of their handguns as they pushed forward into the untidiness. Connor proceeded left into the kitchen area as Mac held his ground to oversee the hallway, which led to the bedrooms off to his right. Neither officers dared speak conversationally to one another. The thought of someone unexpectantly popping out of one of the numerous hiding spots in the deluge was overwhelming. Connor came back from the kitchen shaking his head to indicate that no one was there, and they again proceeded further into the house through the hallway to the bedrooms. Connor again called out, "Camillus Police," and checked the first bedroom on the right. He returned to the hallway again shaking his head.

They were running out of places to check. Just then they heard what seemed to be mumbling from behind a closed door on the left-hand side of the doorway. Connor knocked on the door and stated, "Camillus Police." They could still hear soft, unintelligible words on the other side of the door. Connor tried the door and it opened into a bright blue full bath. There was a bath/shower combination on the left as you entered the space, and a vanity with a large mirror on the right, and finally a stand-alone toilet further up on the left on the other side of the shower wall. There were dirty towels on the ground and countless bottles of makeup turned over on their sides all over the counter. Kleenex and toilet paper littered the floor.

Sitting on the floor against the commode was an unkempt white female in her thirties, slight in build, with dirty blonde hair plastered to her face. She was wearing a dirty pink sweatshirt and matching sweatpants. Looking up at the officers with searching pale blue eyes, she repeated, "If it is it, then what is it?" It was some kind of riddle with no answer.

"Ma'am...I'm Officer Coke, and this is Officer MacKenna of the Camillus Police Department. Your mother couldn't get ahold of you. She called the police department to have us check on you. Are you all right?" Connor asked.

"If it is it, then what is it?" she kept on repeating over and over. It was if she was a recording for a macabre game show.

Mac looked over Connor's shoulder as her mantra played out.

"Liza, we're going to get you help. Could you stand up please?" Connor asked.

Liza was physically there, but mentally in a different plane of the universe. She acknowledged the cops' presence, but could not bring herself back to this space and time to engage them in conversation.

Connor walked to one side of her and nodded to Mac to get on the other side. Connor gently held her left wrist with his left hand, placing his right hand on her left elbow, and Mac repeated the process on the other side of Liza's body. EDPs could go from serene to exceptionally dangerous in a fraction of a second. They carefully stood her up, and Connor gingerly placed his handcuffs on her behind her back. This was both for her protection and the officers'.

Unlike in the movies, no one ever was cuffed in front. This was a huge officer safety tenet. If they were to be restrained at all, this was the one and only way for it to be done. Other officers across the country had tried to be kind or sympathetic to other detainees in similar or inane circumstances with men, women, and children, and regrettably ended up paying the ultimate price for their benevolence.

"Dear, we're going to find your shoes and take you to the hospital to get you help," Mac said as they led her out of the bathroom.

"I think I saw some sneakers by the front door when we came in," Connor said to Mac as they took her down the hallway.

Mac nodded and proceeded down the stairs with Liza, still holding on to her right arm as he descended.

At the bottom of the stairs Mac saw the white sneakers that Connor had observed earlier. He knelt on the side of Liza, cognizant of not leaning down in front of her legs, and carefully placed the footwear on her feet.

With that done, they led her out of the house, down the driveway, and to the nearest police car, which was Mac's. They gently placed her in the right rear of the vehicle, and seat-belted her in. Liza continued the chant all the while.

The three little girls from next door just stopped in mid motion in the adjacent driveway and watched the cops lead their neighbor to the car. It was if the girls were frozen in time. Their mouths hung open and they just stared unabashedly.

After Mac closed the rear police car door, he asked Connor, "Um...is she a clear and present danger to herself or a third person?"

"I know what the law says Mac," he said softly, "But we can't leave her there like that. Even if we called her mother to come over...what would she do? It doesn't look like she's eaten in a while, and with her repeating that phrase over and over, she's practically in a catatonic state. She definitely can't take care of herself and she needs some medical intervention."

"I agree. I just wasn't sure the docs would feel the same way when we try to 2-PC (Physician Certificate) her."

In New York State, the Mental Hygiene Law states that a person could be detained by peace/police officers, transported, and held up to seventy-two hours in a C.P.E.P (Comprehensive Psychiatric Emergency Program) facility if they were an imminent danger to themselves or a third party. Both Mac and Connor knew that this might not fit the state criteria of Liza, who wasn't actively trying to commit suicide or kill someone else, but they couldn't in good conscience leave her to her own devices; it clearly wasn't working.

"We'll figure it out when we get there," Connor said.

They got in their respective police cars and Mac advised the MRD Center of their intentions.

"Unit #3102C to Dispatch."

"Unit #3102C go ahead," the MRD Center dispatcher answered.

"Unit #3102C...myself and Unit #3103C will be transporting a female to St. Joseph's Hospital CPEP...starting mileage 34,491," Mac said.

"Unit #3102C and #3103C...1657 hours." Dispatch acknowledged.

While Mac drove, Liza's verses became just murmurs in the backseat. Connor, as per regulations, followed Mac's police vehicle to the hospital. All was going as planned for the ten-mile trip until they were on the highway by the Fairgrounds in Geddes, New York. Then Liza started an earsplitting scream that just about had Mac drive off the road as he looked in the rearview mirror to find out what had happened to her.

As Mac looked into the mirror, he could see that Liza had unbuckled her seatbelt and was lying horizontally on the backseat and was kicking her feet against the left rear passenger door with all her might. The steel cage in his patrol car provided a barrier to the front passenger compartment, but did not provide protection for the side doors or windows. Liza was alternating her leg thrusts from the door to the side window. It would just be a matter of time before she broke a window completely out.

Mac had no choice but to immediately pull off the right shoulder of the road and come to a complete stop. He put the police car in park and quickly exited before the dust even had a chance to settle back on the ground from the abrupt maneuver. Connor had pulled over behind him, and before he could withdraw himself from his own vehicle, Mac had opened the left rear passenger door and was trying to corral Liza's legs. She instantly saw a chance to untangle herself from confinement and feverishly kicked Mac's hands with a newfound fervor. Mac's thumbs on both hands paid the price, being bent over until they touched his wrists. Mac grimaced in pain as he tried in vain to get purchase on Liza's elusive appendages.

Connor swung open the other back door and had pulled Liza back up to a sitting position within the car. From there he could control her by hanging on to the chain between the cuffs.

"Liza, you've got to calm down. We're not going to hurt you. It's going to be all right. We're taking you to see the doctor," Connor said in an attempt to calm her down.

"Mac...grab the hobble-restraint from the trunk. We're going to have to place them around her ankles."

Mac ran to the trunk and retrieved the restraint, and met

Connor on his side of the car. Mac made a loop with the black nylon rope, and as Connor held her ankles together, Mac looped it around her legs and pulled the excess underneath the car door. Connor got her buckled again, and as Mac held the rope towards the ground, he quickly closed the rear door. The hobble restraint kept the legs together and in place next to the door, so that even if she got her seatbelt off again, she wouldn't be able to lay on the seat and kick the door or window again.

"Thanks," Mac said as he looked at his swollen thumbs.

Connor grinned good naturedly as he assessed Mac. "Shit happens. It's not the last time you'll get your thumbs hurt with a combative person in the back of a police car. It happens all the time. There's no easy way to prevent them from hurting themselves or damaging the vehicle."

"Yeah, they're not that bad. Just sore, that's all."

Cars continued to rush past the two patrol vehicles on the side of Route 690 East.

"Let's get out of here before the rubberneckers run into one of us or each other," Connor said.

Mac and Connor got back into their cars and finished the rest of the transport without incident. They arrived at CPEP and took the restraint off Liza's legs, and were able to cajole her into the facility without a scene.

They placed her in a holding room while they spoke with one of the doctors and explained the situation at her house. The doctor was understanding and agreed that the cops did the right thing by committing her for evaluation.

Connor had the Data Channel (Channel 2) call Liza's mother before the incident on the highway and advised her that they were taking her daughter to St. Joseph's Hospital for treatment. He further advised that they had locked up the residence before they left.

As Mac and Connor were on their way driving back to the town, Mac reflected on how fragile the human mind was. Liza appeared to have a nice home, in a nice neighborhood, but on the inside of her home and her mind, there appeared to be a struggle for lucidity. No one truly knows the battles of their neighbors, co-workers, or people you pass in the mall or on the street. By the grace of God, we all go on through life.

Nine-tenths of wisdom is being wise in time.

- Theodore Roosevelt

CHAPTER
TWELVE

The summer carried on through August with Mac working C-Watch. He stayed up checking on his grandmother as often as possible, taking care of the chores around the house and spending all his spare time with his children as they went to parks and playgrounds. Overtime was abundant, and trying to squeeze everything in was sometimes chaotic, but Mac made it work.

Mac, Twist, and Connor were working C-Watch with

Sergeant Russ Parker near the end of their shift. Sgt. Parker was in his late thirties and had fifteen years on the job. He was an irreverent soul as a patrolman, but was a good supervisor to the men and women of the Camillus Police Department.

It was late on a warm Thursday night, and there had been the usual calls for service for vehicle lockouts and minor traffic crashes. There was a full moon out on a clear sky and Mac could hear the crickets as he drove around town with his window down on the west side of Camillus.

"Unit #3101C to dispatch...copy a vehicle refusing to yield," Twist said breathlessly into the police radio.

Mac could hear the stress in Twist's voice and instinctively started heading east to get to his territory.

"Unit #3101C...location...direction of travel?" the MRD Dispatcher acknowledged Twist's transmission.

"Unit #3101C...westbound on West Genesee St. coming up on the high school...taking a right onto Hinsdale Road."

In the background of the radio communication Mac could hear the roar of the police engine as he envisioned Twist slowing down to take the turn onto the side-street and then goosing the motor back to full power. Mac engaged his emergency lights and picked up speed himself, trying to get closer to Twist's location.

"Unit #3101C...the vehicle is a dark blue two-door sedan...occupied by one...wanted for speed at this time."

"Unit #3101C received," the dispatcher answered.

"Unit #3100C...I'm monitoring the pursuit," Sgt. Parker advised.

"Unit #3103C show me en route," Connor advised the dispatcher.

"Unit #3102C...me as well," Mac said into his radio mic.

"Both units 2309 hours," the dispatcher acknowledged.

Mac was coming from the Village of Camillus and cranked up his police unit onto Milton Ave., heading eastbound to intercept the suspect vehicle.

The air was quiet as everyone waited for the next update from Twist. It seemed too long without hearing from him.

The dispatcher sensed the same thing, "Unit #3101C...direction of travel?"

Nothing. The eerie silence hung in the summer atmosphere as the Camillus police units were actively converging towards the last known direction of travel.

A mic keyed up with audible hissing in the background, "...Unit #3101C..."

"Unit #3101C...Officer Lehman...your status?" the concerned dispatcher asked.

Silence.

"Unit #3101C...I've wrecked out...Hinsdale Road at...Dunning Drive...I think I'm at Dunning Drive...wires down...vehicle last seen traveling at a high rate of speed towards Milton Ave."

"Unit #3100C...I'm just about there...start a WAVES Ambulance for his location," Sgt. Parker said.

"Unit #3100C...affirmative...2313 hours...please call Dispatch when you have a status on Officer Lehman."

"Unit #3100C...affirm...mark me arrived."

"2313 hours," the dispatcher gave the time in acknowledgement.

The dispatchers at the MRD Center were very close with the patrol officers who worked on the road, tethered together through the police radio. They were their only lifeline at times, and there was certainly a mutual admiration between the two groups.

Mac arrived a minute later and observed a surreal scene. Twist's patrol vehicle had landed in the front yard of a residential house on the corner of Hinsdale Road and the corner of Dunning Drive. The car was parallel and only feet from the front of the residence. A combination of minute road dust hung in the air, along with radiator smoke from the police car. The activated police lights shining through the condensed cloud gave off a prism of red, white, and amber. A telephone pole laid broken in two near the street where the police vehicle had left the roadway, and down, torn power lines sparked and arced on the asphalt and grass, adding to the kaleidoscope of color in the haze.

The front end of Twist's marked car was totaled, but the passenger compartment was intact. He sat behind the steering wheel, dazed and confused as Connor pulled up to the scene and the responding police car headlights lit up his silhouette in the front seat.

"Twist, stay in the vehicle," Sgt. Parker ordered over the police radio.

"Roger that," he groggily answered over his mic.

"Unit #3100C to Dispatch...notify Niagara Mohawk that we have live powerlines down with a trapped officer and need them to respond ASAP. Have Fairmount Fire respond due to a smoking vehicle and possible extraction. Have WAVES stage at Hinsdale Road and Kings Court. Unit #3101C...block-off Hinsdale Road at Kings Court. Unit #3102C block-off Dunning Drive at Dickerson Drive North. I'll be blocking off Hinsdale Road at Edwards Drive with my car and laying a flare-line down on Hinsdale Road at Elm Hill Way."

Mac and Connor repositioned their patrol vehicles and then walked back down to the scene, not getting to close as they knew that the powerlines could conduct electricity through the ground up to twenty yards away. They just watched Twist in his car from their respective viewpoints on opposite sides of the crash, taking it all in.

It still took Niagara Mohawk Power Company forty-five minutes to respond to the scene even though they had a workstation just two blocks away. The workers had to come from home and then retrieve their trucks and equipment before responding. After they arrived, the power to the pole was quickly cut and the wires stopped arcing.

The Fairmount Fire Department responded before Niagara Mohawk and watched helplessly with the cops until the power was cut. The firemen then tried to pry open the driver's door with halogen tools due to the door being jammed into the frame. Twist became impatient and just crawled through the open driver's window. The firemen helped him to the ground.

WAVES Emergency Medical Technician's (EMTs) walked Twist to their ambulance rig where he was evaluated. The EMTs suggested that he go to the Emergency Room (ER) to get evaluated for a concussion. Twist objected, but was overruled by Sgt. Parker.

"Mac, I'm following the rig up to the hospital. Call the MRD Center and advise them on Twist's condition," Sgt. Parker said. "You and Connor stay here. Have the tow-truck haul the police vehicle back to the station and assist Niagara Mohawk with traffic control until they get the pole replaced. A-Watch units are coming on soon, and I'll call the station and have them relieve you as soon as they can."

"Yes Sarge. Have Twist call me when he gets out of the hospital, please."

"I will."

Mac got to a neighbor's house who let him use their phone

and called the MRD Center direct line to the Technical Assistant (TA) Supervisor.

"MRD...TA Flynn," the supervisor answered.

"Hey Felicity, it's Patrick MacKenna."

"Hey Mac! How's Twist?"

"Yeah, the Sarge wanted me to call you guys and let you know he looks fine. He's just going to the ER as a precaution."

"Geez, the radio traffic didn't sound good. We were all worried up here."

The Onondaga County MRD Center was an innovative complex up on Onondaga Hill, next to the Onondaga County's Sheriff's Department South Substation. It was a gated complex with razor wire surrounding the outside perimeter. At any given time, there were twenty to thirty people working. That included call-takers who answered the emergency calls, the dispatchers for both fire and police, and supervisors. During the day there was more administrative staff to keep the center up and running. All phone lines coming into the complex and radio transmissions were taped. Everyone in the process kept that in mind during their conversations.

"I agree. I didn't know what I was going to find when I arrived. Twist got lucky; his unit is trashed."

"I'm glad he didn't get hurt. Just to let you know, I broadcasted the Point of Information for the suspect vehicle in the pursuit over channel three and four and notified the city."

"Did anyone come up with it?"

"Not so far. After Twist 80'd out, we didn't hear anything more about it from anybody."

The City of Syracuse Police Department was on a different radio system than the cops who worked out in the county. A Property Damage Auto Accident (PDAA) was coded on the radio system as a #10-79, while a Personal Injury Auto Accident (PIAA) was coded as a #10-80. The slang in law enforcement was if someone had a bad crash, they 80'd out.

"If no one found it right after, he's good as gone," Mac said.

"Yup. Totally. Too bad Air-1 wasn't up tonight. We might've had a shot at catching him."

'The main thing is that Twist is okay. He's supposed to call me as soon as he gets released."

"Hey, we were going to tell you earlier, but obviously all hell broke loose. We're having a party after shift at Long Branch Park at the Willow Bay Pavilion. We let the other agencies know and people are on their way now. I know it's not optimum for you guys with Twist and all, but if you want to come, we'll be there."

"Are you kidding Felicity? That'll be great! It was a stressful night and I'm sure Twist will want to blow off some steam when he gets out. We've got some confiscated beer in the fridge up in the locker room. Soon as me and Connor get relieved by A-Watch, I'll grab it and we'll meet you there."

"Cool. The girls made some dishes and a lot of dip. The guys brought hamburgers and hotdogs. I'm sure there'll be plenty of booze, but definitely bring the suds."

"Deal. See you soon!"

Mac thanked the residents for their phone and walked over to Connor's position and filled him in. He was just as eager as Mac, and couldn't wait to get relieved. The tow-truck was finishing up pulling the car out of the yard and putting it on a flat-bed. National Grid was going to be a while stringing new powerlines and putting in a new pole.

About fifteen minutes later, Mac and Connor got relieved from their posts and went back to the station to turn in their cars and get changed. He checked the clubhouse refrigerator and found about a case and a half of assorted beer. CPD would get constant calls from citizens about underage drinking in the parks and woods around town. When the cops showed up, the kids would run and leave bottles, cans, and kegs of beer behind.

Technically, the beer was supposed to be turned into the Property Room in case someone claimed it. But that was kind of ridiculous, because the kids would get a summons for Underage Drinking, and if an adult claimed it, they would be arrested for Unlawfully Dealing with a Child. So, the officers put the confiscated brew in their upstairs locker room and would have a couple after shift from time to time.

The Men's Locker Room was separated into two parts. The

locker rooms themselves, the toilets, sinks, and showers were on one half, and the other was furnished with donated used couches and recliners. The CPD Police Benevolent Association (PBA) bought a console television and paid for the cable. It was referred to by the cops as the clubhouse.

As they were changing, Mac took a call on the locker room phone. It was Twist, who was on his way back to the station with Sgt. Parker. He said he was good to go, and Mac told him about the party. Twist thought it was a good idea and told Mac they would be back in less than twenty-minutes.

Mac and Connor waited outside the station with the beer loaded into Mac's hatch. Sgt. Parker and Twist showed up a couple of minutes later.

"Hey, Sarge! You want to come with us?" Mac said as they got out of the patrol vehicle.

"No, I'm good. Twist told me about it, but I've got to get home to the misses. You guys have fun...but not too much fun." He smiled as he went through the doors to the building.

"I'll be out in a second," Twist said and followed the sergeant into the foyer.

Twist was back out in five minutes. They all decided to take their own cars so that they could leave when they wanted to. Sometimes these parties could go until dawn.

When they arrived at a little after 1:00 AM, the party was in full swing. There were approximately fifty people amassed under and around the pavilion. The picnic tables were full of food, and several people were manning the outdoor hibachi grills. There were assorted coolers on the ground and Mac found one with enough room to put the beer in. It was a community type of event, and everyone was welcomed to everything that was brought.

This small section of the park was part of the bigger Onondaga Lake Park. It was on the banks of the north end of the lake. Onondaga Lake was once the most polluted lake in the country, due to a chemical plant dumping toxic waste into it for decades. Now, with the help of the new owner of the chemical plant, Onondaga County, New York State, and the Federal Government, it was being cleaned up.

Technically, no one was supposed to be in the park after hours and the Onondaga County Park Police patrolled the area at night. But the park couldn't have been any safer on this evening. Just about all of the town and village cops who worked C-Watch were there tonight, along with the state police and some sheriff's deputies. There was also one double marked state police car and single unit sheriff's car. The occupants of both units were there for the copious amount of nourishment.

To Mac, this seemed like a scene right out of a Joseph Wambaugh novel depicting choir practice: A subculture that less than one percent of the population would ever be included in. It felt special and right that all these people who protected the sheep from slaughter would come together on this perfect twilight in August.

When people saw Twist arrive, they fawned all over him with concern in their voices as they asked him to recount the pursuit and subsequent crash. Twist, who was still a little sore from being bounced around in the car, appreciated the attention.

Connor found a female dispatcher he was kind of sweet on and moseyed over to have a talk with her. Mac was surprised to find Kevin Charm there, and took up a conversation with him on a picnic bench outside the pavilion. As they were talking, he noticed one of his academy mates from the Town of Dewitt eating potato chips with what appeared to be dip. Just then, one of the troopers put several lit road-flares into a fifty--gallon metal trash can to light up the venue. Mac couldn't believe his eyes as his academy buddy was now illuminated and was in fact not dipping his chips into a can of potato chip dip, but that of a can of cat food.

One of the dispatchers had picked up party supplies after work and some food for her cat that she left in the shopping bag. Before there was light, it looked like a can of dip to Mac's academy-mate.

Mac's body couldn't decide what to do first. Hysterical laughter poured out of him as he fought the urge to ralph right then and there.

Years after the party, dispatchers would quietly 'Meow' into the two-way radio when his academy-mate was working in the Town of Dewitt to remind him of the incident.

It turned out to be a very extraordinary night. There was no better brotherhood or sisterhood than that of the law enforcement community. It was all good clean fun, and everyone in attendance never felt more alive than on this night...especially Twist.

Get action. Seize the moment. Man was never intended to become an oyster.

- Theodore Roosevelt

CHAPTER

THIRTEEN

The next day, Mac was back working C-Watch and was dispatched to a Signal 10-79 (PDAA) at Warners Rd. and Reed Webster Park. It was a cloudy, rain-driven day, and visibility was compromised. There had already been several accident calls the department had responded to. Most had been around the mall areas, but this one was north of the town center and the drivers were waiting in the park.

When Mac arrived, he observed a small gray Honda with a

young girl sitting on the hood and a middle-aged man sitting inside his maroon Silverado pick-up truck. As Mac exited his patrol unit, he walked towards the two vehicles trying to observe the location of the damage. The middle-aged man got out of his truck and had his license, registration, and insurance card in his hand as Mac approached.

"It was my fault, officer. I got distracted by trying to change the radio, and I didn't notice she was turning into the park," he said.

"The main thing is that nobody got hurt. That's why we have insurance. Accidents happen, it's nothing in the grand scheme of things," Mac answered.

"Thanks, officer. It's the girl's first accident, and she's kind of shook up. She says she's not hurt, but you should probably go check on her."

Mac took the documents from the man. "Thank you for having these ready. I'll go see if she's all right."

There was very little damage to either car. The girl had been crying, and standing in the drizzling rain didn't help her appearance.

"I'm sorry officer, I really don't know what to do. I went to a house across the street and called my father and he's on his way."

"There is nothing to worry about. I was just explaining to the other gentleman that these things happen and that's why we have insurance. You're not hurt, are you...um...?"

"Darcy. My name is Darcy. No, I'm not hurt. But it's my parents' car and I feel so bad. I didn't see him coming."

"Darcy, it's not your fault. The other gentleman told me that he was distracted, and he hit you from behind. There's literally nothing you could've done. Your parents' insurance will cover the very minor damage. Seriously, this really isn't a big deal."

"Okay, if you say so, but I feel awful. My Dad just told me the same thing, but I thought he was just trying to make me feel better."

"No, he was telling the truth. You don't even need a tow-truck. The vehicle looks okay to drive. I'm just going to need your driver's license, registration for the car, and the insurance card. The registration and the insurance card are usually in the glove box."

"Oh, that's right. My Mom showed me where they were when I first started driving. I'll get them," she said as she went back into the vehicle.

Mac walked up to her open driver's door as she rummaged through the glove box. She came up with both pieces of paper and opened her purse and pulled out her license.

"Those are it. Thank you, Darcy. You can stay in your car out of the rain while I go back and copy your information down. I'll bring these back to you with the report number for your insurance company. Just sit here and relax. I'll be back shortly and hopefully your father will be here by then. If not, I'll wait with you until he shows up."

While Mac was writing up the Signal 10-79 report, Darcy's father arrived and got into the passenger side of the vehicle after he inspected the car. A check of both registrations and driver licenses were valid and Mac had enough information written down to complete the report later.

Mac exited his patrol vehicle, handed the man his information back, and gave him the Designated Report (DR) number. The man was quite polite, and again apologized for the accident and wished the girl well as he started up his truck and drove out of the parks' parking lot.

Mac then went over to the other vehicle and introduced himself to Darcy's father. He gave him Darcy's information and a copy of the DR number. "Thank you, officer. I appreciate you being so kind and patient with my daughter's first accident."

"These things happen all the time and she shouldn't feel bad about it. Just give that report number to your insurance agent and they'll take care of the rest," Mac said. "Goodbye Darcy. I hope you have a better day!" As Mac walked back to his cruiser, Darcy waved. Mac then watched as her father followed her in his car out of the lot into the gloom of the day.

Mac sat in the park and wrote up the rest of the report. The park had two baseball fields, a tennis court, and a playground area with two sets of swing sets and a pavilion. There was an entrance to the tow path of the Erie Canal across the street, where most people went for walks or runs, or to ride bicycles or walk their pets on better days.

As Mac continued to write, he couldn't help watching a late middle-aged man wearing a tan pork-pie hat hitting golf balls in the field adjacent to the parking lot. The rest of his ensemble consisted of a green zip-up golf jacket, dark blue casual pants, and black and white golf spikes. The older gentleman didn't appear to be affected by the gloom, and went about methodically hitting his pitching wedge about one hundred yards or so with his two sleeves of six golf balls, walking to the landing area and then hitting them back to where he started.

Technically, there was no golfing in the park, and a green medal sign with white writing stated as much as you entered the park. Mac didn't totally understand why the sign was there. If people weren't reckless with the golf balls...how could this be considered wrong? And what would the proper charge be for NO GOLFING in a town park? The man was content to follow his routine. Like most cops, Mac was starting to understand balancing the overreach of the government on people's lives. Yes, there could be a problem if a stray golf ball hit a child or patron of the park, but shouldn't common sense prevail in most situations?

Enough lamenting; it was dinner time, and Mac decided to go to Big Boy's for dinner and see if NMI was working the evening shift. He was delighted to see that she was, and even more pleased when the hostess placed him in a booth in her section. Mac tried not to smile too wide as NMI brought over his silverware and a glass of ice water. She seemed to shyly grin at him, and Mac wondered if there was an unknown conspiracy with the hostess and NMI to be seated in her section.

The ambience of the restaurant was a throw-back to a simpler day, with orange leather-covered booths, Tiffany style lamps, dark colored hardwood tables and chairs, and a hot and cold salad bar in the middle of the restaurant. The kitchen itself could be seen over the half-wood walls behind the waitress station. Chefs in white plume hats stood behind the elevated warming lights of the stainless-steel shelves. They wore white aprons over comfortable black and white striped uniforms. NMI and the rest of the waitresses wore their hair tied up in ponytails or buns and white button-up shirts with a colorful string tied around the collar, black knee-high skirts with a blue colored half apron over the front (with pockets for their guest checks and pens) , black stockings, and black soled shoes. Each waitress had a name tag with white lettering on a blue background with a silver trim pinned to the upper left side of their shirt. "NMI" was not what was printed on her name tag.

"Busy shift?" Mac asked as she came back with the menu.

"Not really. Wednesdays are kind of slow, and the weather didn't help," she said.

"I can see that. Are you and the girls going down to Molly Malone's tonight?"

"I don't think so. I have to work days tomorrow, and a couple of the other girls I think have class."

Mac was kind of disappointed, and it must have shown on his face.

"We're planning on going out on Saturday though. Are you going to be there?"

Mac brightened, "Yeah, I think Twist, Connor and Alvey are going too!"

"Great! I'll let the rest of the girls know!"

Mac was instantly in a better mood as he ordered a chicken sandwich and mashed potatoes. He couldn't help watching her walk away to place his order. He self-consciously looked around after the fact to see if he'd been caught in his dalliance. Mac was getting lonely working all the time and taking care of his grandmother and his children. NMI seemed really nice, and even though she was five years younger than he was, she had the look of an Irish lass and Mac was innately drawn to her.

He finished off the rest of the shift without incident. When he returned the next day for C-Watch, he was going by the secretary's desk when Betty Master's said that the chief needed to see him. Mac's mind instantly turned to dread as he tried in vain to think what he might've done wrong in the last twenty-four hours.

As Mac knocked on the open door to Chief Whitlock's office he was immediately acknowledged by the chief and told to take a seat. Mac was carrying clean uniforms on hangars from the dry cleaners and fumbled with them trying to fold them in half and place them on his lap as he took his chair.

"How's it going Patrick?" Whitlock asked Mac, as he crinkled with the plastic from the dry cleaning, trying to find a happy medium with the unruly garments.

"Good chief," Mac said pensively, not knowing how he should proceed with the conversation.

"Relax Patrick. I just wanted to let you know I received an Atta-Boy letter regarding you today."

"Chief, what's an Atta-Boy Letter?"

"It's a letter that someone writes on your behalf when you do something good at work. It goes in your personnel file and it helps cancel out any 'Ah-Shit' Letters or disciplinary infractions."

"So, it's a good thing then?"

"Yes Patrick. I really like to see these from the public, and it maintains CPD's good image with the community. I made a copy for yourself and I'll place the original in your file. Great job, and keep up the good work!"

"Thank you, chief!"

Mac took the copy of the letter and awkwardly left the chief's office, heading upstairs to the locker room. He was glad he wasn't in trouble, but never quite figured out on how to receive praise from someone. Mac was the only one in the locker room and sat down on one of the recliners to read what the chief had handed him. It read:

Dear Patrick,

I wrote Chief Whitlock a note telling him what a good job you did on Wednesday night at my granddaughter Darcy's accident on Warners Road in Amboy. I wasn't there, but my son and Darcy both said you were wonderful to her. She was pretty shook up to start with, it being her first bout with the police, so I am sure she will always remember your kindness towards her.

It is good to know we have police officers in our town that can be thoughtful and kind and respectful to the public as well as that uniform. A uniform's nothing if there isn't a man big enough to wear it with pride and you sure showed your colors.

I am enclosing $5 for you to have a cup of coffee on me in appreciation.

Thank you again, and God bless you.

Sincerely grateful,

Mrs. Helen Weisbrod

Mac sat there in silence. It was moving to have someone acknowledge his work on such a simple call. CPD was truly a community policing environment, and its residents embraced their officers more than he was first aware. More than that, Mac thought that perhaps he was serving a higher purpose and possibly solidifying his position within the department.

The money was too kind, but police officers could not accept personal gifts from the public. The chief gave it to the

PBA to benefit causes in the community. Giving it back to Mrs. Weisbrod would seem unappreciative, and sometimes these kinds of gifts created more complications in trying to return them.

It was an unaccustomed sentiment from someone he'd never met, and this made Mac feel certain that this was his destiny and calling in life. Police work was certainly not the priesthood, but Mac felt like he was still making a small difference in people's lives. This letter would be forever remembered, not for the act that he was a part of, but for the sentimentality it conveyed on such a personal level to him.

Nobody cares how much you know, until they know how much you care.

- **Theodore Roosevelt**

CHAPTER

FOURTEEN

S aturday finally came. Mac was working C-Watch again and was excited about meeting NMI and the other girls from Big Boy's out after shift. Twist and Connor were working with him, Orsen Alvey was working for the NYSP, and Kevin Charm was working for the OCSD. Kevin was a late addition to the after-shift activities, but assured Mac that he would be there.

The weekends were obviously a bit busier in the town, with residents enjoying the best part of late summer activities in Central New York. The malls and the parks were full of families, and soon the restaurants would be crowded with hungry patrons looking to refuel themselves.

Fender benders in the parking lots of the malls and shoplifters were the norm on this evening shift. Twist and Connor were both out in the malls on separate crashes. Mac was just finishing up on processing a juvenile at the station for petit larceny when a verbal domestic dispute was dispatched a couple of blocks from the station. The kid's parents had just arrived at the front door to the PD, and Mac answered up on his portable radio to take the call. The state was tied up on a transport, and the sheriffs were assisting another one of their units in Tully on a vehicle rollover. Mac knew he was the closest unit and everyone else was busy, so he advised the dispatcher that if he needed another unit to respond with him, he would let them know.

Mac gave the parents a Juvenile Appearance Ticket for their son to appear in Family Court next week and hustled to his cruiser for the short ride to the domestic call. The last of the twilight was hanging in the air trying desperately not to get swallowed up by the impending darkness. Two minutes later, Mac breathed in the early night air through the open driver's window as he advised the MRD Center that he was arrived on scene.

The Aaron Manor Townhome Apartments were located at Milton Avenue and Gordon Parkway. They were nice apartments, and there were usually not that many issues with the residents who lived there.

Mac exited his police car and made his way to the front door of the townhome. He knocked on the door and went to rest his right hand on the butt of his duty weapon when he noticed it wasn't there. Horror went through Mac's mind as he realized too late that he had left his gun locked up in a gun locker at the station while he was processing the juvenile shoplifter.

Before Mac had a chance to think what to do next, the door he had just knocked on began to open.

A youngish female with dark hair opened the door. "Hi, Officer, I'm sorry to bother you. Me and my boyfriend were just arguing about his stupid friends and it got kind of heated. We're fine now, though. I called the emergency number back and they told me you had to come anyhow. I'm so sorry."

Mac was still trying to formulate a plan to address this situation when the dispatcher's voice crackled over the portable police radio, "Unit #3101C...your status?"

It appeared it was a nothing call, but he hadn't talked to the boyfriend yet, and he knew everyone else was still tied up on calls. Not having a firearm on a domestic dispute was beyond frightening.

"Unit #3101C...Officer MacKenna...your status?" the concerned dispatcher asked for the second time.

"Unit #3101C...all set...you can cancel the second unit."

It was an unwise leap of faith and Mac knew it was not bravado that made him cancel his backup, but the embarrassment of his own stupidity being revealed to his coworkers.

Mac kept his hand over the top of his duty holster to camouflage his vulnerability and said, "Miss, could you please have your boyfriend come to the door?"

Mac knew better than to enter a confined space not knowing what lay inside and held the door to the apartment open with his left foot as the girl went a little way into the abode to call her beau.

Mac stood there hiding the right side of his body from view as a disinterested younger redhaired man came to the door. "Is everything okay here?" Mac asked the man.

"Yeah, she kinda freaked when I told her that I was hanging out with my friends again tonight."

"It didn't get physical, did it?" Mac inquired.

"I'm sorry I even called the police. It was stupid, and we never even touched each other," the girl interrupted.

"No, it didn't get that heated officer. Seriously, we're good. We're both kinda embarrassed that you had to come," he said

Mac judged both their demeanors and physical appearances, then decided that they were telling the truth. He copied down their names and biographical data for the report and told them to call back if there were any future issues. Mac wished them a good night and retreated to the sanctuary of his patrol unit.

Once there, and out of sight of prying eyes, he grabbed the steering wheel with both hands and gently pulled his forehead into the upper part of the steering wheel, softly bouncing it up and down and muttering, "Stupid, stupid, stupid..."

It's easy to say that it was another rookie mistake and a lesson learned, but it cut deep to make a mistake like that. Thank God it was a bullshit call and the people were exceptionally nice. All the bad scenarios ran through Mac's head, and none of them ended well. If either one had a weapon and wanted to hurt the other, there was little more he could do than just getting in the way to try and mitigate the damage. Chills ran up and down Mac's spine as he cleared the call and headed directly back to the station to retrieve his handgun.

The malls were closed now, and the parking lots had mostly cleared out. People were still in the restaurants and bars, but the town was winding down. It was quiet enough for Twist to start doing Vehicle and Traffic (V&T) stops. Mac and Connor weren't too keen on running radar and stopping the citizenry for minor traffic violations, but it was Twist's thing when it got slow.

Mac was checking Camillus Park when he saw Connor coming down the drive. The park held the only outside pool in the town; however, WGSH had an Olympic size pool in the basement of the school. The park was wooded with trails, picnic tables, and hibachi grills sprinkled around the grassy areas. At night the kids would have kegs of beer down the trails. Mac knew this because he used to be one of those kids.

Mac angled his patrol vehicle in the parking lot so that Connor could pull up car to car and talk through the driver's windows. It seemed that this was strictly a cop thing, and all of them did it.

"So, are we bringing girls back to the PBA pool tonight?" Connor asked as he pulled up alongside.

The Camillus Pool was referred to as the PBA pool because cops would clandestinely hang out there after the bars had closed. It was no big secret that Mac had started the tradition as a source of bonding and camaraderie amongst the cops. He also didn't mind the female guests swimming in their underwear, or less, under the moonlight.

"Well...I guess we'll see," Mac said with a mischievous grin on his face. The weather would be perfect for a choir practice. Mid-seventies and partly cloudy, with very little breeze.

"You're never going to guess what I did on that verbal domestic dispute," Mac said.

"I thought that was a Code-6 (Settled on Arrival)? I was tied up with a 79 (PDAA) at Fairmount Fair or I'd have been there."

"No biggie. It was bullshit. I just left the station without my gun!

"Holy shit...you stupid motherfucker! Where was it?" Connor said as he laughed, or more like chortled into his hand.

"I left it in the gun locker when I was processing that kid. The call went out and I forgot all about it as I rushed to my car."

"You are so lucky!"

"I know. I feel like a dumbass..."

"Listen Mac, it happens more than you think. Some guys have left their guns, still in their gun belts, hanging in public restrooms. Others have come to work without them and had to run back home as fast as they could."

"You're just trying to make me feel better, Connor."

"I shit you not. It happens a lot. The odds of it happening again to you just decreased because of the ever-lasting trauma it will leave on you."

"I hope so. That was the worst thing ever."

"Seriously, no worries. It happens...just don't make a habit out of it. It's about time we get back to the barn. I'm all gassed up...I'll see you back there!"

"I have to fill up at the pumps yet...I'll see you in a bit," Mac said as he put his police vehicle in gear and started towards the Highway Department.

Mac finished up his log as the jacked pump handle fueled his patrol unit...this time remembering to pull the pump handle out before he took off back to the station.

When he got back to the PD, Twist and Connor were already changed into civvies and were waiting in the parking lot next to their cars.

"C'mon Mac, shake a leg," Twist said as Mac got out of the cruiser with his patrol bag.

"You guys go ahead. I'll be there in ten minutes."

"Are you sure?" Connor asked. "We can wait."

"Nah, you guys go on. I'll be there a little after midnight."

"Okay, we'll see you there," Connor said as he entered his red Honda sports car.

"See you there, Mac," Twist said as he got into his blue Chevy SUV.

Mac passed the midnight crew in the patrol room as he put away his log and pleasantries were exchanged. A favorite saying among the coppers was "Stay safe!" and this was passed on to his relief.

He headed upstairs to the locker room and changed out of his uniform. Mac put on cargo shorts, a loose-fitting T-shirt with a Jimmy Buffet reference on it, a Boston Red Sox's baseball cap, and sandals. He liked the comfortable summer look and checked it once in the mirror before heading down to his car.

Mac started his Camaro and took pleasure in the low rumbling of the exhaust as he let it warm up. Toots and the Maytals were singing 'Sweet and Dandy' on the radio station, and this made Mac smile, as a pleasant summer night out with friends that was just starting to unfold.

Molly Malone's was rocking when Mac pulled into the full

parking lot. The doors to the bar were open and the music spilled into the warm nocturnal air. Mac made his way to the front doors and carefully pushed his way through the gathered patrons clumped in collective groups of guys and gals intermingled with nonsensical chatter.

Mac spotted Twist, Connor, Kevin Charm, and Orsen Alvey standing at the far end of the bar by the door to the kitchen. Mac continued his cha-cha-cha like steps through the crowd until he arrived in the middle of their clique.

Kevin said over the cacophony of noise, "So, Mac...I hear that you're a martial arts master now...no need to carry your duty weapon at work anymore."

Mac shot a look in Connor's direction, and Connor said with an ear to ear grin," What? I thought it was funny!"

Mac smiled in return as Twist handed him a Captain and Diet Coke and said, "You didn't think you were exempt from getting your balls busted, did you?"

"No. I was going to tell you guys when I got here. Connor just beat me to the punch."

Alvey turned around from the bar and passed everyone shot glasses full of Jack Daniels Tennessee Whiskey. "Here's to us, and those like us," he said in manner of a toast, as the assembled cops clinked the shot glasses together in the age-old fashion of friendship and revelry.

As Mac was downing his shot, he spied NMI dancing in the adjacent room with the other girls from TJ Big Boy's. She turned around and shot him a sly 'come hither' glance, then turned back to her girlfriends. Mac knew right there and then it was going to be a memorable night.

Old age is like everything else. To make a success of it, you've got to start young.

- Theodore Roosevelt

CHAPTER

FIFTEEN

The water felt cool and comfortable against his skin as Mac treaded water in the deep end of the PBA pool. The cops had bought a case of Bud Light from Molly Malone's at 2:40 AM and the party had migrated to this oasis with instant relief from the warm humid air. It was a civilized anarchy which started with the storming of the ten-foot chain link fence that kept out the unwanted. It was said among the cops, if a girl wasn't in good enough shape to make it over the fence, then chances were the cops weren't that interested in her unclothed company on the other side of the barrier.

The pool guests, which included NMI and the TJ Big Boy girls, were all stripped down to their skivvies and were parading around the pool deck and/or swimming in the pool itself. The drinking was an afterthought as nubile bodies glistened in the peek-a-boo light of the hovering moon.

The cops were attempting to keep some type of order amongst the guests with constant shushing to keep the noise under control. A neighborhood was less than one hundred yards away, and with the warm summer night there were bound to be open bedroom windows that could hear the muffled fracas going on just beyond the chain linked fence.

The PBA Pool was a modern-day speakeasy of sorts. Yes, it was technically illegal for the cops and their guests to trespass on town property, but as any police officer knows, there was the spirit of the law and the letter of the law. This being said, the off-duty cops oversaw everyone's safety and security while they were currently 'bending' the law in their utopian environment.

Mac and NMI had nestled up against the side of the pool in the deep end away from the other patrons and were getting to know each other outside of their work environment and the loud music of the bar. They talked about their family, high school, their friends, and aspirations for the future.

A marked Town of Camillus Police car rolled through the park around 4:30 AM with its spotlight trained on the pool area.

The spotlight cutout when the A-liner recognized the occupants waiving off her devilish beam of light. The officer just smiled and shook her head through the open driver's window as she continued driving her vehicle, checking out the rest of the park.

The first glint of the sun rising in the east meant that the merriment was coming to an end. Everyone put their clothes back on and the cops policed the area for empty beer bottles or left behind clothing. The process was reversed with one and all climbing back over the pool fence and the empty case of beer bottles being gently passed over the barrier.

Goodbyes were said back and forth as cars started and crept their way out of the park parking lot. Mac had walked NMI to her white Oldsmobile and with the driver's door open, Mac looked into her bright blue eyes and kissed her for the first time. It was a memorable kiss, and Mac said goodbye at her open window as she drove away. He was the last one in the park and took a minute to take it in. It was a perfect night, and for the first time in a long time Mac was optimistic about a personal connection that he had avoided for far too long.

Mac headed home to Onondaga Hill, and after getting some much-needed rest and taking care of his responsibilities with his grandmother, headed back to work C-watch. Upon arrival at the station he was met by Twist in the locker room.

"So...how'd you make out with NMI?" Twist said in greeting.

"Literally or figuratively?" Mac answered in return.

"You know what I mean...spill it!"

"It went swimmingly."

"You're an asshole!"

"I'm kidding...it went great, Twist. I really like her. I just want to take it slow."

"You've been taking it slow for a long time Mac. It's time to get back out there."

"I know, but it's complicated..." Mac said as he pulled his uniform shirt on.

"With you it always seems complicated."

"Yeah, I know...I'm just that kind of guy."

The officers finished getting dressed and walked downstairs to the Patrol Room. They received the turnover from B-Watch, loaded up their respective patrol cars, called into service, and started their eight-hour tour of duty.

A couple hours into the shift, Mac was surprised to be dispatched to the CPD's secretary's house for a missing person complaint. Upon arrival, he met with Betty Masters and her husband at the front door to their home, where he was led down the front hallway to the kitchen table where Mac was offered a seat.

"Mac, I'm so glad it's you. We're so embarrassed to have to call. Our fourteen-year-old daughter, Jennifer, has been missing all day. I called her best friend Kim and she reluctantly told me that Jennifer skipped school with two sixteen-year-old boys. We're so worried and we've looked everywhere for her and we just don't know what else to do," Betty said.

"Jennifer is a straight A student, and this is totally out of character for her. She has been rebelling lately and we've gotten into some arguments with her over it, but her skipping school and not coming home when school got done or calling, is just not Jennifer," Jim Masters added.

"It will be okay. I'll take care of it. As you know Betty, these things happen with teenagers. I'm sure it's just growing pains with Jennifer and she doesn't know the ramifications of her actions at this point. What's Kim's last name?" Mac said.

"McDonald. Kim McDonald. She lives at 215 Germania Ave," Betty replied.

"Okay, give me some time to track her down and I'll get her back home. I'd tell you not to worry, but with me being a dad, I know that's not going to make you feel any better. Just trust me. I'll figure it out and let you know right away," Mac told Betty and Jim.

"Again, Mac I'm so sorry to have to bother you," Betty replied.

As Mac stood up from his wooden kitchen chair, he gave Betty his best smile and said, "Betty, you're like family. It's no bother at all. It's my pleasure. Just give me a little time to work this out."

With that, Mac was escorted to the front door where he crossed the neatly trimmed yard and entered his patrol vehicle that was parked curbside in the street. As Mac put his car into gear, he gave the Masters' a wave, which they both returned with the look of worry still etched upon their faces.

Mac thought about his children who were much younger than Jennifer, but he could certainly sympathize with the Masters' just the same. Being a parent meant that you always had to worry. Worry if you are doing the right thing with the way you raised them. Worry about their safety, their choices, their friends, their schooling, and their social interactions. It never ends. Mac's mother made it look easy, and Mac wasn't an angel either in his teenage years.

"Unit #3101C to Dispatch," Mac said after picking up and activating the police radio mic.

"Unit #3101C...go ahead," the dispatcher acknowledged.

"Unit #3101C show me en route to 215 Germania Ave. in regard to this complaint please."

"Unit #3101C...1823 hours. Do you require another unit?"

"Negative. I'll be all set. Thank you," Mac answered the MRD Center and placed the mic back into the holder clip and continued driving towards Kim McDonald's residence.

As Mac pulled up to 215 Germania Ave., a teenage girl with dark hair was waiting outside the home sitting on the front stoop. She approached the police car as Mac advised the dispatcher that he was arrived.

"Hi! My name's Kim. Mrs. Masters said that you'd be coming," as she came to the open driver's side window.

"Hey Kim! Thanks for helping me with Jennifer," Mac said. "For real. Do you know where Jennifer is?"

"Yeah, I do. But I was afraid to tell them. I didn't know what would happen to Jennifer if I did."

"No worries. I'll cover you with them, so they won't be upset with you. Where is she?"

"She's at Shove Park with Mike and Charlie. Mike is her boyfriend, but her parents don't know. Jennifer is terrified to tell them. She's also scared to go home. She knows that her parents know that she skipped school and she doesn't want to go home."

"Does Jennifer know that you're telling me where she is?"

"Yeah. She's okay with it. She knows you work with her mother. She's not trying to run away from home. She's just kinda freaking out about her parents and being in trouble with them."

"Okay. Cool. I appreciate your help, Kim. You've been great. I'll try and make it all good with everyone."

"You're pretty okay for being a cop," she said.

"People tell me that from time to time. You've been a great help, Kim. Thanks again!" Mac reached for the mic and proceeded to drive away.

"Unit #3101C, please show me en route to Shove Park in regard to this," Mac advised the MRD Center.

"Unit #3101C...1835 hours," they acknowledged.

Twist pulled up before Mac pulled away from the curb and met up with him car-to-car in the street.

"Are you all set?" Twist asked.

"Yea, just trying to help Betty with her daughter."

"What was that all about anyways?"

"Betty's daughter Jennifer skipped school with a couple of older boys and now is afraid to go home. Her friend told me she's at Shove and I'm on my way there to go get her. Easy peasy."

"Okay. Let me know if you need anything, or Betty for that matter. She's the best"

"I know she is. I feel bad we had to get involved. I'll be all set. I just have to figure out on how to make the drama all go away."

"You're good with drama Mac. Let me know if it goes sideways," Twist said.

"Will do," Mac answered as he pulled away, en route to Shove Park.

The park was mostly empty as Mac made his way through the winding curves of the park entrance off of Slawson Drive. Halfway through the park he saw three kids sitting on a picnic table. The two boys were wearing flannel shirts and the brown-haired girl was wearing a faded denim jacket. They all stood up as they saw the marked car coming down the drive.

"Unit #3101C arrived," Mac told the dispatcher.

Mac pulled the car to the side of the road and exited. He walked across the sunlit groomed grass to the picnic table with the teenagers.

"Jennifer, I presume?" Mac said as he approached.

"Yes officer," she said.

"Jennifer, you can call me Mac. I'm sure you know that your mom and I are friends."

"I know. Mom says you're really nice."

"Of course. There is no reason not to be," Mac said.

"I know I did something really bad by skipping school today and I'm sure my parents are royally pissed."

"Yeah, that probably wasn't the brightest thing to do. But it's done, and we just have to work with it," Mac said. "Which one of you is Mike?"

The blonde shaggy haired blue flannel shirt teenager sheepishly raised his hand.

"I'm not here to lecture you guys on whatever relationship you have here, but because you are older, the responsibility rests with you, whether you want it or not. That goes for you too Charlie," Mac said as he looked directly at the brown-haired,

red flannel shirt wearing boy.

Mac directed his gaze back to Jennifer, "I know I can work this out with your parents. More than anything, they're just extremely worried about you. You may have to answer to some sort of penalty for skipping school, but like you said, you knew it was wrong, so you knew that would be coming."

"Yeah. I know I screwed up. I just didn't know what to do next," Jennifer said.

"Okay, how about I get you all back home to your respective residences and get this over with?" Mac said, looking everyone in turn in their eyes.

"Charlie and I live on the backside of the Park on Forsythe St. We can walk from here," Mike said.

"Okay guys. Just remember what I said. I'm really not lecturing. I just want you to know where you stand in the whole picture of events."

"I got it officer. We really didn't mean any harm. It won't happen again," Mike said as he and Charlie turned and started making their way to the back of the park.

"Thanks guys. Jennifer, shall we?" Mac said as he held his arm out in direction of the police car.

"Yeah, I'm ready, but I'm still scared," she said as she slowly made her way to the vehicle.

Mac opened the front passenger door and took his patrol bag off the front seat, putting it in the trunk so Jennifer could sit in the seat. "It will be all right. I'll explain the course of events and say that you learned your lesson, and this was a one-time thing. They'll understand. They both told me you're such a good kid. They want this to be done and over with too."

Jennifer was buckling up her seatbelt as Mac walked around to his side of the car. As he opened the car door and got himself buckled in also, she said, "I sure hope so."

Mac picked up the mic and said, "Unit #3101C to Dispatch, show me back en route back to my original location with one, starting mileage 32,454."

"Unit #3101C received...1901 hours."

Mac transported Jennifer home and sat at the kitchen table with her, Betty, and Jim. They talked through the day's events and Mac was the sounding board as everyone voiced their opinions on what had transpired and the possible consequences. Betty and Jim ended up grounding Jennifer for a week and she promised that it wouldn't happen again. The tension and anxiety were mostly gone from the room as Mac excused himself and started for the door. Betty got up and walked with Mac. At the front door, she gave him a big hug around the neck and with a tear in her eye mouthed, "*Thank you*," as she opened the storm door to let him out.

Mac got into his car and called in service. Feeling that he did some good tonight in his little space in the world, he drove away with the windows down, breathing in the evening air with a smile on his face. Sometimes he felt that he was made for this job. He really liked helping people. Especially really nice people that he had a personal investment in...

If you could kick the person in the pants responsible for most of your trouble, you wouldn't sit for a month.

- **Theodore Roosevelt**

CHAPTER

SIXTEEN

Mac decided that he would return to Onondaga Community College (OCC) to finish his associate degree. He was feeling more comfortable in his professional role as a police officer, although he was still sorting his way through the inherent pitfalls of civil service life in the public eye. He still couldn't completely shake the idea that his dream job was constantly in jeopardy, but needed to press ahead to solidify his future and that of his children.

Mac thought that he should be able to go full-time during the day for regular classes if he switched his shift to A-Watch. He could work from midnight to eight in the morning, and while his kids were in school, he would be able to attend class and pick them up when he got done with school. Mac would be around more during the evening hours to attend to his grandmother's needs around the house and could pick up some more overtime during the evening that he couldn't get while working on C-Watch.

It was ambitious, but he was able to get a full-time timetable at the college scheduling his classes Monday, Wednesday, Friday from 8:00 AM until 2:00 PM. The classes were all back-to-back with no gaps in between, and made the most efficient use of his limited time. Mac checked with Chief Whitlock and received permission to come in a little early so that he could leave before 8:00 AM on class days to make it to the college on time.

He and NMI had started dating, which meant he was starting to spend more time with her and less time hanging out with Twist, Connor, and Kevin at Molly Malone's. He missed hanging out with them, but this gave him structure he needed in returning to college life and balancing the responsibilities of his children and his grandmother.

So, with a plan in hand and a sense of accomplishment in front of him, he enrolled in the fall semester and returned to college at twenty-six years old. It had been eight years since he last attended college classes, but going through the police academy on the same college campus gave him a sense of recent familiarity that settled him on his return.

Mac was taking mostly criminal justice classes in Mawhinney Hall, where the police academy was still located on the first floor in the southwest corner of the building. Even though it had been only a couple of years since the academy he didn't want to be recognized on campus. He just wanted to fit into student life and not appear to be an outsider or a practitioner to the other students. Although with his age being self-apparent, he dressed in baseball caps, t-shirts, jeans or shorts, sneakers or sandals, and carried a backpack, which gave him somewhat of collegiate camouflage. He was careful not to wear anything that would identify him as a police officer for the Town of Camillus. It was comparable to a Twenty-One Jump Street kind of thing, just without the investigatory premise behind it.

Mac also had to make up some of his previous courses. He hadn't been that dedicated at the time of his first semester at OCC. He had been seventeen and not that responsible at the time and wanted to raise his cumulative average to a respectable level.

On his first day of class on a warm Monday in August, he showed up early and sat in the back of the class with his Red Sox's baseball cap pulled down, cargo shorts and sandals. He felt the familiar excitement and apprehension of the first day. Anything was possible, and starting with a clean slate, he vowed to make the most of it this time.

This was a do-over class for Mac of CRJ 101 — Introduction to the Criminal Justice System. He chose a seat in the rear of the dark classroom. Three other students were already there, with two of the three of their heads down on the top of their respective desks. The third was a female, and she was leafing through her book. She barely glanced up from her tome. The other two males were apparently blissfully unaware of Mac's entry into his second act at college.

Shortly the room was filling up with students of every background. Mac was still certain he was still the oldest in the group. Banter gave way as students recognized each other and talked across the spacious classroom. Daylight was still streaming through the outside windows into this learning space, but no one had turned on the classroom lights as of yet. It appeared that would be left to the professor.

Two male students approximately eighteen years of age were having an animated conversation.

"Yeah, that's right, I got pulled over for no fucking reason," student number one said.

"How do you know that?" answered student number two.

"Because I wasn't doing anything wrong, numb nuts!"

"But you didn't have a motorcycle license for your bike."

"Yeah, but he didn't know that!"

"But you said you were racing, Tommy. That sounds like a reason to get pulled over."

"But he didn't see us!"

"How do you know?"

"Because I know!"

"You're not making sense. You say you got pulled over for no reason, but you didn't have a bike license, you were speeding, and your bike wasn't registered or inspected. I'm pretty sure he had a reason."

"Nah, he was just an asshole with nothing better to do. I could've smoked him on my bike, but I didn't."

"I don't know. If you want to be a cop you probably shouldn't be running around racing on a bike without any proper paperwork," student number two counseled.

"Fuck that man! He had no clue what he was doing," student number one finished off the conversation.

Mac was stunned by student number one's attitude. This was a CRJ class, after all. Mac didn't want to be identified so he could just do his work without encumbrance, but he wasn't expecting prospective students aspiring to work within the legal system to have anti-police attitudes.

The professor walked in and switched on the lights, and the students settled down and looked up at him expectantly.

"Good morning fine students! My name is Cash Mahoney. I'm a retired sergeant from the Syracuse Police Department. I had twenty-five years there and received my law degree from Syracuse University while I was still a cop. I currently litigate for National Grid and adjunct for OCC in my spare time. This is an introduction class to The Criminal Justice System. You'll find it quite interesting and informative, as I expect that this is everyone's major."

Heads glanced up and down at the dapper dressed professor. He was wearing an expensive gray pin striped suit, a pink cuff-linked shirt, and a light blue paisley tie with shiny black leather wing-tipped shoes. He was tall with a stocky build, and even being in his fifties looked like he could take anyone in the class in a fight.

Professor Mahoney's classes were Mac's favorites. Mac ended up taking Police Operations, Criminal Investigations, and Special Investigations from him as well. He told war stories of being on the job and firsthand accounts of deaths, crimes, and bad guys as only a practitioner of the criminal justice system could.

Other classes Mac took were just as interesting in the different disciplines which dove-tailed with criminal justice. Over the course of two years in the Criminal Justice Degree Program, he also took Introduction to Speech, Freshman Composition and Literature I & II, General Psychology, Introduction to Sociology, Contemporary Math, Juvenile Delinquency, Anatomy and Physiology, Non-fiction and Popular Writing, Abnormal Psychology, General Ecology,

Ecology Lab, Elementary Spanish I & II, Oceanography, Oceanography Lab, Independent Health Study, Swimming, Judo, and Karate.

Deviance of Sociology was quite thought-provoking. It delved into why groups of people acted against societal norms and peaked into their motivations behind such behavior. Mac learned that the Social Strain Theory by Robert K. Merton tried to explain the goals that a society set for itself and how individuals attempt to fill gaps in those goals by acting aberrant when there is an imbalance in unatonable goals and the means to achieve them through regular avenues. As Mac could see in his work environment, the theory did explain why some people did what they did to end up on the wrong side of the law. Other theories by noted sociologist included different variations to explain the same things, such as Social Strain Theory, Labeling Theory, Social Control Theory, and the Theory of Differential Association.

Abnormal Psychology was another stimulating period with discussions on why certain individuals were hard-wired the way they were and how they thought their actions and responses were quite normal. Different theories included Behaviorist, the Cognitive Approach, the Medical/Biological Approach, the Alternative View, and Sigmund Freud's Psychodynamic approach. In Freud's view, the conflict in which people suffered was organic in the mind and revolved around the Id, Ego, and Superego. This construct led to the belief that unresolved conflict led to abnormality in an individual living in society. All these theories also made sense to Mac as he strived to understand the people he met in his profession.

Other courses that were part of the CJ degree included Introduction to Speech (Public Speaking) which Mac wasn't crazy about. Being a public servant and dealing with the public everyday, he wasn't nervous speaking to people, but standing up in front of his classmates led to nervousness and apprehension. Eventually this would go away, as it did with most of his peers as well, the more they practiced making speeches at the podium.

Mac also had to take physical fitness requirements and chose among them swimming and the art of karate and judo. He had loved to swim as a kid and decided to test out of the New York State requirement. That included retrieving a rubberized ten-pound brick from the deep end of the Olympic sized indoor pool at OCC. That proved to be quite challenging, and Mac nearly drowned in the process. Judo gave Mac a practicality of the self-defense way of using adversaries' weight distribution and strength against themselves. The classes were physically demanding, and the other students being younger gave Mac a worthwhile challenge in executing the techniques. Karate was a different discipline than judo and had beautiful katas and punishing kumite at the end.

One of the last classes Mac took was an internship for Police and Corrections with another retired city cop. Jefferson Adams had just recently retired from the Syracuse Police

Department as a lieutenant in the Special Investigations Division (SID). SID investigated narcotics, organized crime, and prostitution in the city. Adams was put in charge of the internship program as his first assignment as a professor at the college. When he met privately with Mac to outline the assignment, he was pleased to learn that Mac was a police officer with the Town of Camillus. Adams suggested that Mac ride with the city's Neighborhood Anti-Crime Section (NACS) within SID. Adams explained to Mac that he would fix it so Mac could carry his badge and gun and participate in NACS investigations while completing his internship. Mac couldn't believe that he would be able to participate in active narcotic investigations as a student at OCC, but didn't want to look a gift horse in the mouth.

Adams set up the meeting with Lt. Mario Mendoza, who was the commanding officer of the NACS unit. Lt. Mendoza explained to him that since Mac was a certified police officer in New York State, he most certainly could carry his weapon and badge and partake in investigations and arrests in the city. Lt. Mendoza explained that his unit was comprised of six officers who mostly dealt with street corner level drug trafficking; that his officers wore uniforms and rode in marked police cars which were equivalent to a disguise, so that unsuspecting drug dealers and customers would not know the unit's level of skill and surveillance expertise in conducting drug operations.

Lt. Mendoza further advised him that Mac could wear plain clothes and ride in the police cars during the NACS unit regular tour of duty. They routinely worked four o'clock in the afternoon until midnight (which was referred to in the city as Third Platoon) although they did adjust their hours to assist SID on bigger operations as situations dictated.

Coincidentally, Mac had taken a two-week Drug Administration Agency (DEA) course through the Camillus Police Department six months prior, and had a perfunctory aptitude towards this work. Lt. Mendoza was impressed with this and gave Mac a lot of leeway with the unit. Mac took this internship over the summer months, completed eighty hours with the NACS unit, and turned in the requisite ten-page paper outlining his experiences in the internship at the end of the encounter.

Mac was nervous during the early stages of the internship, but gradually felt right at home with the proactive officers in NACS. There was a comradery among the men and women of the unit, and they chased bad guys around the city with their hair on fire all shift, disrupting drug sales of marijuana, crack-cocaine, and heroin in the city neighborhoods.

The internship through OCC and Jefferson Adams was quite fortuitous in introducing Mac to Lt. Mendoza and the City of Syracuse Police Department's NACS unit in ways that were then unmeasurable.

A man who has never gone to school may steal from a freight car; but if he has a university education, he may steal the whole railroad.

- **Theodore Roosevelt**

CHAPTER

SEVENTEEN

While Mac was attending OCC for those two years, he spent his regular work shifts on A-Watch. Even though the Town of Camillus was a sleepy community where severe crime and tragedy was indeed rare, there were certain times during the nightshift when police work became all too real. The community policing aspect which occurred on B-Watch and C-Watch in town slipped away after the witching hour, when the darker side of humanity and life were on display.

The winter months in upstate New York started in late October when snow was first seen in the air, and stretched well on into late April. During these times the nights were long and dark, and people seldom spent long stints outside. At times it was like living on the surface of the moon. Wind chills were often in the negative numbers and residents would barely see their neighbors as they proceeded from their garages to work and back again without any substantial interactions. It was at the end of an uneventful snowy and cold February night that Mac received his first dispatched call of his shift.

"Unit #3103A...check a car off the road on Route 321 between Forward Road and Limeledge Road...a passing motorist called it in...the vehicle is approximately fifteen yards off the road and down an embankment on the westside of the roadway...0631 hours," the MRD dispatcher advised.

"Unit #3103A received," Mac answered.

Mac was the only cop working for the town on this shift. He had heard the troopers out of Elbridge on the air earlier in the night, but apparently, they were still tied up on a call or getting ready to call out of service to end their shift. The dispatched location was on the far west end of the town boundaries and closer to the trooper's barracks in the Village of Elbridge. The weather the previous night had been challenging, with lots of snow accumulation and wind gusts over thirty miles per hour.

Mac had spent most of his night back at the station due to the inclement weather, as it was inadvisable to keep driving over the unplowed roads. He zipped up his Gore-Tex police jacket, pulled on a black knit cap, put on his gloves, and made his way outside to his police vehicle which was covered in snow. Mac cleared off the windows with the snowbrush as the engine warmed up, then got behind the wheel and started making his way on the fifteen-minute journey to the edge of the town.

"Unit #3103A arrived in the area," Mac told the MRD Center as he came down Route 321 off Route 5.

The sun was still trying to rise in the East, and Mac had a hard time discerning what lay off the side of the roadway. When he got to Forward Road, he slowed down to a crawl and crept along looking through the passenger side window, peering over the embankment as he went. Mac didn't see any obvious signs of tire tracks leaving the thoroughfare and thought the caller may have been mistaken in what they saw.

Just before Limeledge Road, Mac saw the glint of sunlight off the top of a full-sized sedan sitting right-side up, parallel to the road, just at the bottom of the embankment. The vehicle was pointing in the direction of the Town of Skaneateles and had come to rest at a slight angle just before the land leveled off.

"Unit #3103A...I'll be out with the vehicle...I'll give you a plate number when I get it."

Mac put on the emergency light-bar flashers to his police car as he exited the vehicle. There was little to no traffic in this area on this cold morning. Mac skidded down the embankment through three feet of snow and made his way to the driver's

190

door. The vehicle had been there awhile, and Mac had to wipe snow off the window with his gloved hand to see inside.

As Mac peered through the frosty window, he could see a dark-haired girl hunched over the passenger seat, as if she were trying to retrieve something from the rear seat. Her hair hung down around her head and obscured any facial features. Mac was caught off-guard. He wasn't expecting to see anyone in the car, and he knew instantly that she was dead.

Mac looked to the greyish-blue sky and inhaled a sharp deep breath of cold air as he said a silent prayer for her soul. He still had the grim task of making sure that she was deceased, and this was not a part of the job that he relished. Mac tried the driver's side door handle and it opened. He gently eased his way into the front bench seat and took off his right glove. Turning around in the car he took his right hand and with the back of it carefully raised the girl's hair away from her face. There he saw the open lifeless eyes of a pretty girl in her late teens or early twenties. Mac fought his first instinct to bolt from the vehicle, egress himself from this tragic sight and leave this horror. But his training prevailed, and he continued on with his mission at hand. He took his right hand and placed it against her carotid artery on the side of the girl's neck and felt for a pulse. She was cold to the touch, and there were no signs of life.

Mac took an extra second to look around the interior of the vehicle. The car was intact with no signs of crush damage or broken glass. A cursory check on the exterior as Mac approached the car down the ravine revealed the same. The girl showed no outward signs of trauma, and there was no blood on her or in the vehicle. Mac checked around the inside of the vehicle and located her purse on the floor and removed her driver's license. He hated the feeling of being inside someone's personal space looking through private items. It was part of the job, but it just seemed wrong.

Her name was Riley Buckler of Skaneateles, New York. The Village of Skaneateles was one of the most affluent communities in Central New York. The village sat on the north end of the Finger Lake of the same name, which the town also shared. Skaneateles was west of Camillus and the village itself was approximately twenty minutes away.

After Mac had a chance to process the scene in his mind, he advised the MRD Center that the call should be reclassified as a one vehicle fatal Personal Injury Automobile Accident (PIAA) and requested that WAVES Ambulance respond to recover Riley's body. WAVES would transport the body to the Onondaga County Medical Examiner's (ME's) Office to confirm what Mac surmised took place. He deduced that Riley had gone off the road sometime between midnight and two in the morning, due to the snowfall on the vehicle and the lack of tire tracks off the road. The position of Riley's body suggested that she wasn't wearing a seatbelt at the time she left the roadway and was thrown from the driver's seat into the passenger's side of the vehicle with great enough force to snap her neck. With her brain stem severed, Riley would lose consciousness, and activity would cease in breathing, heart rate, blood pressure and non-reflective movement. Death would have most certainly been instantaneous, but that didn't make Mac feel any better about the loss of Riley's young life.

Two EMTs arrived on scene approximately twenty minutes later. Mac was back up on the road inside of his vehicle staying warm when the rig pulled up. Like all first responders, everyone sort of knew everyone else after a while in this business.

Donna Johnston jumped down from the driver's seat and started walking back towards Mac's police vehicle as her partner Vaughn McCabe emerged from the other side.

"Hey, Mac. So, you got a DOA?" Donna asked as Mac got out of his car.

The air was still brisk, and vehicular traffic had started to pick up on Route 321 as they gathered between the two emergency vehicles parked on the side of the road. WAVES had activated the emergency lights on the rig and commuting drivers were rubbernecking in great fashion to get a look at the commotion on the side of the roadway.

"Yeah Donna. She's still in the car down there," Mac said as he pointed down the ravine.

"How old was she?" Vaughn asked, as his words were punctuated with steam.

"Nineteen," Mac answered.

"Ah, shit!" Donna and Vaughn said together.

"I know. It sucks. No blood, no mess, she's just gone," Mac said. "You're going to have to use a litter, you're not going to get a stretcher down there."

"All right, I'll get it," Vaughn said as he went back and opened a side door on the rig to retrieve the carrying device.

"Are you sure she's dead, Mac?" Donna asked.

Mac just stood there and looked her in the eyes. He was tired, and this whole macabre process wasn't pleasant. Donna could sense all of this with the look.

"Okay Mac, I know, but I had to ask."

Mac led the way down the embankment as the Pete Kitt's tow truck he requested pulled up behind the emergency vehicles and turned on his yellow overhead lights. Donna and Vaughn were bringing up the rear carrying the litter as Mac reached the passenger side of Riley's car and opened the door. Mac took a few steps back so that Donna could access the open door. She placed the litter close to the door as she also knelt next to the body and checked for signs of life. Donna grimly looked back at Mac and Vaughn without saying a word, then gently reached around Riley's waist and manipulated her body so that she could be turned over and placed in the litter in a supine position. Once in place, Vaughn tightened nylon straps across the body. Vaughn then led the way with the basket up the hill with Donna holding the other end. Donna couldn't get traction with her boots and was stumbling as she tried to carry her half up the hill.

"Here Donna, let me get it. I've got better boots on," Mac said as he took up the other side of the litter.

"Thanks Mac," Donna said as she regained her footing.

The three of them took their time scaling the embankment as to be as reverent as they could possibly be to Riley's remains. They had to place the litter on the ground as Vaughn opened the back doors to the rig and propped them in place. They then put the litter onto the gurney, which was locked in its location in the back of the ambulance. They again strapped Riley onto that and then closed the back doors to the rig.

"All right Mac, we'll be en route to the ME's Office," Donna said.

"Thanks guys," Mac said as he turned around and made his way back to the tow truck.

"How's it going, Jimmy?" Mac said as he reached the tow truck.

"Good Mac. How about you?" Jimmy answered.

"I've had better nights. How difficult is this going to be to get that car back up here?

"Not too bad, Mac. The vehicle looks fine. I just got to get a hook on the front of it and winch it back up the hill and pull it right onto my flatbed."

"Thanks, Jimmy. I was supposed to be done at eight, and I still have to make notification to the family and finish my report. Do you want me to place my police car in a different position so you can get it?

"Naw, it we'll be fine. Just give me fifteen minutes and I'll have it ready to go. The driver's dead?"

"Yeah. A young girl."

"Shoot, I'm sorry Mac. I'll get it done right away."

"Thanks again, Jimmy."

It took Jimmy a little while longer than he thought to get the car settled back on the highway, but twenty-five minutes later Mac was on his way to the station.

"Unit #3103A...show me en route to the PD in regard to this."

"0818 hours," the dispatcher acknowledged.

When Mac got back to the station, Sgt. Jake Smith was waiting for him.

"Hey Mac! I was just going to send you some relief. You doing okay?"

"Yeah Sarge. Just finishing up a one car fatal. I've got to make notifications to the family yet."

"You want to turn it over to B-Watch? I can have one of the day cars take care of that for you."

"I appreciate it, but I don't have school today and I'd like to see it all the way through if you don't mind."

"I don't mind if you don't mind. Let me know if you need any help though."

"I will. Promise," Mac said as he made it upstairs to the Patrol Room and started doing a computer search on Riley, trying to find her parents in the system. He found them entered in the Criminal History Arrest Information Reporting System (CHAIRS) as calling in a loud noise complaint the year before.

Mac put himself out with the MRD Center on a notification detail under the same Designated Report (DR) number and arrived in the Village of Skaneateles. Fortunately, both of Riley's parents were at home and hadn't left for work yet. They were devastated by the news, and Mac felt like the Grim Reaper giving it to them.

Mr. and Mrs. Buckler told Mac that Riley had lived in a nearby apartment with a roommate from high school, and that they were unaware that she hadn't returned from work the night before. They further stated that Riley had been a waitress in Camillus and usually got done with work between eleven and midnight during the week.

Mac again apologized for their loss and left them in their grief. When he first wanted to do this job, events like tonight weren't what Mac expected he would be doing. The television and movie cops aren't often portrayed dealing with the mundane human suffering, nor do they show the process of making death notifications to inconsolable relatives over a routine traffic accident. This was part of the job Mac kept telling himself over and over, but it didn't lighten the burden he felt.

It was almost noon by the time Mac changed in the locker room and started for home. In the ride back to his grandmother's house, he pondered life and death. He had been present on ambulance calls for natural deaths from old age and illness, but this was different altogether. This was the first time that Mac had to reconcile a senseless tragedy to a young person, and the potential long-lasting effects it would have on him after the call had ended. Even more than that, Mac came to the realization that there would be others, and wondered how their deaths might affect him down the road in his career, and beyond.

It is only through labor and painful effort, by grim energy and resolute courage, that we move on to better things.

- **Theodore Roosevelt**

CHAPTER EIGHTEEN

Mac had a rare weekend day off and spent the entire day with his children and NMI. It was a Saturday, and lunch was spent at Chuck E. Cheese in the Town of Dewitt. Usually Mac would be working one of his part-time jobs at the mall or for the school district at a sporting event. He was extremely grateful to spend this quality time instead with the people that he cared so much about. He was starting to find out that life was indeed very short and fragile.

The kids were delighted to spend time with their father and were quite accepting of NMI. Mac was hesitant to introduce her to Bridget, Joseph, and Elizabeth, but after a couple of months he decided that he liked her enough to make this happen. NMI quickly connected with the children as well, and this new strange normal was implemented without a hitch.

The kids were thrilled to spend their Chuck E. Cheese tokens on the rides and games while waiting for the pizza to arrive. Mac and NMI sat across from each other at the orange topped table as a discord of children laughing and shrieking with delight went on all around them. Families were enjoying the atmosphere, and the air was filled with the aroma of Italian comfort food and the sounds of happiness.

NMI had just gotten a full-time job as a teller at a bank in Camillus and was still working at TJ Big Boy's on a part-time basis. With their busy schedules, it was a matter of necessity to incorporate the children into their lives when the opportunity presented itself to them.

"So, are you glad you got the position at the bank?" Mac asked.

"The other ladies and girls are quite nice. It's a very professional setting and it makes me feel like a grownup," NMI answered.

"Well, you're still only nineteen, so this is a pretty big accomplishment for you."

"It feels surreal, but I still enjoy working at Big Boy's for the cash tips. It's just nice to have the extra money. I want to move out of my father's house and get an apartment. Between the two jobs, I should be able to get that done sooner rather than later."

With that, the kids returned to the table. "Daddy, when's the pizza gonna be done?" Bridget asked.

"Soon, sweetie. Do you guys have enough tokens?"

"Yeah, but Joseph is hogging them all. He wants to keep playing Skeet Ball and getting those tickets for a prize."

"Bridget, let's go over to the token machine and get more for you and your sister. The pizza should be ready very soon," Mac said.

With that, Bridget took her father's hand as they walked across the chaotic scene in the dining room to the machine. Mac picked up Elizabeth in his arms as she saw him and toddled over and raised up her arms. He put another five dollars into the machine and gave them the shiny gold tokens. The girls giggled and ran off to try another ride. Mac looked over and saw Joseph intently lining up the skeet ball and rolling it underhand up the elevated ramp to the round holes in the wooden wall. He walked over and ruffled the hair on the top of his head, and Joseph looked up at him with a big grin.

"How you doin' pal?" Mac asked.

"Great, Daddy! Look at all the tickets I've gotten!" Joseph said as he held out both hands, which were filled with red tickets that he took out of the pockets of his jeans.

"That's amazing, Joseph! The pizza should be here shortly,

okay?"

"Okay Dad," he said as he again turned his complete attention to the task at hand, taking another wooden ball from the side rail and lining it up for another shot.

Mac strolled back across the dining room and sat with NMI. He bent over and gently kissed her on her lips before sliding into his side of the booth. She blushed at the public display of affection and looked quickly around to see who might have seen the furtive display of fondness.

"How about we go to the Westhill Movie Theater for a Disney movie tonight?" Mac asked.

"Wow, you're really packing it in today!"

"I know, but free time is such a premium these days. I don't have to work tonight and neither do you. We'll go to a seven o'clock movie with the kids and drop them off at their mother's house after, then we'll have some free time for ourselves. We could go out or go back to my grandmother's and watch television. It's up to you."

"That sounds fine. We can go to the movies and then back to your place and...relax," she said with an impish smile.

Mac gave her a knowing look back and just about blushed himself.

"The pizzas are up," she said, as she glanced over Mac's head and saw the lighted number to their order flashing high up on the bank of numbers on the wall.

"I'll get it while you round up the kids," Mac said.

Mac made two trips with a large brown plastic tray while NMI retrieved the children. Once everyone was settled, Mac started placing food in front of them. He had gotten two All-Meat Combo Pizzas, mozzarella sticks, French fries, and chocolate milks all around. Mac and NMI pulled apart the pie and placed the triangles on each child's plate.

"Daddy, I want the cheese sticks," Elizabeth said as Mac was situating the food.

"I know you do honey," Mac said as he put a couple of them on the plate with her slice of pizza.

Pretty soon everyone was quiet as the feast was underway. The raucous noise around them continued as they munched on the fast food. Mac almost felt guilty as he surmised that the meal had little nutritional value, but then again, he didn't do this with them that often, so he just smiled between bites looking at the kids.

After they were done, the children wanted one more shot at the rides and games, which Mac relented and let them go as he cleaned up the meal and boxed the leftovers as NMI went to the ladies' room to wash up. After thirty more minutes of fun, Mac called it, and he and NMI loaded the kids up into the car.

"How about the zoo before we go to the movies?" Mac asked.

"Yeah, yeah, yeah," the kids all squealed at the same time.

NMI looked over at Mac and playfully rolled her eyes. Mac just grinned as he put her car in drive. The Camaro was not outfitted to accommodate two adults and three children, and NMI's late model white Oldsmobile was the more practical choice.

Fifteen minutes later, they pulled into the Burnet Park Zoo parking lot on the west end of the City of Syracuse. It was located on Tipperary Hill (also locally known as Tipp Hill) which was settled by mostly Irish immigrants around the middle of the nineteenth century. The City of Syracuse was considered the hub for the Erie Canal as it stretched from Albany to Buffalo. Most of the laborers were of Irish descent, and when the canal was finished many of them settled on the western hill overlooking the canal.

One of the claims to fame for the Tipp Hill area is that it has the nation's only upside-down traffic light. In 1925, a traffic light was installed at the intersection of Milton Ave. and Tompkins Street. The red-light portion was on top, the yellow-light in the middle and the green-light on the bottom. This was one of the first traffic lights installed in the country. It is said that Irish youths in the area (a group called the Stone Throwers) resented the British red light being over the Irish green light and threw stones at the red light until it shattered. The City of Syracuse replaced the light several times and finally relented to having the lights reversed (green-light on top, yellow-light in the middle, and the red-light on the bottom) to appease the residents of Tipp Hill.

Another artifact to the area was Coleman's Irish Pub, located at 100 South Lowell Ave. The pub was opened in 1933 after the repeal of prohibition and had been operated continuously by the same family ever since. It started out as a working man's bar and had evolved into a neighborhood gathering place for food, drink, and music.

Mac and his family had a direct relationship to Tipp Hill through his great grandfather, whom he was named after. He emigrated from County Limerick, Ireland on the passenger ship Etruria on May 16, 1903 and lived at 803 Willis Ave. on Tipperary Hill. Mac's great grandfather patronized Coleman's Irish Pub after he worked as a laborer during the day in the city.

Mac's paternal grandparents originally lived on Tip Hill and took him to the zoo when he was a small boy and Mac still had fond memories of their visits. Although he still had nightmares of the wild turkeys attacking him in his dreams. Mac still couldn't figure that one out...

The kids piled out of the car and took hold of Mac's and NMI's hands, as they pulled the adults across the parking lot as fast as they could. Admission was nominal, and once inside, the children decided they wanted to go into the U.S.S. Antiquities cave. Inside the dark cavernous grotto, they found amphibians, invertebrates, fish, and reptiles. The crocodiles were always a big hit with the kids.

"Daddy, would they eat us?" Joseph asked.

"I guess, if they were really hungry and nothing else smaller was around," Mac answered.

"But they ate Captain Hook's hand in Peter Pan...remember?" Bridget said.

Mac laughed and added, "Point taken honey. That's why we don't reach out our hands into the exhibit, right?"

"Right!" all the kids chimed in at the same time.

From the cave, they went to the Diversity of Birds Aviary, which has two dozen types of different birds. They then visited the Nocturnal Animals exhibit and the Social Animals wing before venturing outside.

The sun was on display today, so the wane of winter relinquished its grip on the frozen tundra for the time being. They could still see their breath as they walked along but the kids didn't seem to mind as they made their way around the Wildlife Trail.

Another favorite for the children was the Penguin Coast, where Humboldt penguins were on display. The kids could watch through different windows as the penguins walked on the ice and dove into the frigid water, where they could see them swimming underneath the surface through several of the windows.

Elizabeth was imitating walking like a penguin as they left the exhibit and NMI grabbed Mac's hand and laughed at the sight of it. After checking out the wolves, pandas, lions, and tigers, they ended up at the Asian Elephant Preserve. It was feeding time, and the elephants were being fed by the zoo staff.

"All right guys, we have to hustle to make the movie," Mac told the kids.

They again piled back into NMI's car and headed for the short two-minute drive down the hill to the Westhill Movie Theater. Tickets were purchased, popcorn, candy, and Hawaiian Punch were procured, and the group settled in for the G-rated Disney movie of 101 Dalmatians.

When the movie finished it was dark, and the kids were content and sleepy. Mac drove them to their mother's house and dropped them off, kissing them one by one as they walked up the front porch steps to their mother.

"So, that was a pretty good day, don't you think?" Mac asked as he looked over his right shoulder, backing down the driveway.

"Perfect!" NMI exclaimed.

"How many kids do you want someday?" Mac asked.

Without hesitation, NMI said "Six."

Mac almost braked hard enough that they got whiplash. "Six!" he said. NMI just nodded her head with a mischievous grin on her face. She came from a family of six children, and both sides of her family were just as large.

As Mac put the car back in drive he said, "We'd have

enough kids for a softball team."

"Who said I was going to have them with you?" she said with the same playful grin.

Mac smiled as they drove back to his grandmother's house. It had indeed been a perfect day, and even though dropping the children off subdued Mac's mood, he took conciliation in knowing that he had the company of an exceptional girl. Having been divorced gave Mac the never-ending feeling of failure and that he had let his children down by not staying with their mother, but NMI had given him hope by being a shining light in his otherwise dark world. Life was indeed short, and Mac experienced this fact more than most people. The prospect of having another shot at it with NMI gave him a glimmer of hope in the otherwise murky skies of the new moon they were driving under.

The only time you really live fully is from thirty to sixty. The young are slaves to dreams; the old servants of regrets. Only the middle-aged have all their five senses in the keeping of their wits.

- Theodore Roosevelt

CHAPTER

NINETEEN

Police work on midnights could be agonizingly slow, and attentiveness was the name of the game. Mac knew that most calls-for-service were called in by the public and that they were for sure the eyes and ears of the police department; that's why vigilance was the most important part of A-Watch. Most of the citizens were at home tucked into their nice warm beds, and there weren't a lot of people paying attention to what was going on around town.

Along with this philosophy, Mac more than once on the

midnight shift thought of the George Orwell quote:

"People sleep peaceably in their beds at night only because rough men stand ready to do violence on their behalf."

So even though the silence and the inactivity continued on many of his A-Watch patrols, Officer Patrick MacKenna continued on his way, making numerous paths with his patrol car in and around the Town of Camillus, protecting the good people of the town from things that go bump in the night.

On one of these occasions, Mac was coming northbound down Warners Road (Route 173) just past Oakley Road when on the opposite side of the road he saw a massive orange ball of flame coming from an unattached garage on the side of the road. The fire was being blown by a steady wind into the residential house set farther up the hill from the garage. The house was almost completely obscured by the thick black smoke emitted from the engulfed garage.

"Unit #3103A...put me out with a house fire at 3743 Warners Road. I have an unattached garage fully involved and flames blowing into the main house. Start Fairmount Fire and WAVES ambulance please," Mac said as he pulled his police vehicle to a sudden stop on the narrow shoulder of the road. He undid his safety belt and started running up the long-elevated driveway which led to the main house.

"Unit #3101A...0317 hours...Fairmount Fire and WAVES have been notified and are en route," Mac heard the MRD Center dispatcher say on his portable radio hanging off his gun belt on his left hip.

It was if Mac was in a dream state. There were no other people or cars around, and the carnage that was occurring right in front of him didn't seem real. He was the only witness under the omnipresent shadowy night sky.

The spring air was still quite chilly, and the stillness of the dark night was punctuated with the unmistakable crackle and pop of the fire and the acrid taste of thick smoke. Mac's breathing became labored as he made his way through the dense smoke to the front door. He had left his jacket in the car, and with the exertion of his running he didn't miss it. No lights were on inside of the residence and Mac took the back end of his Maglite flashlight and pounded against the red steel door.

The structure itself was of an odd design. The beige siding had white trim with a second floor that slanted down on the westside of the house. There was a vehicle in the driveway, and Mac was unsure if there was another in the garage due to the lack of visibility of the roaring active volcano getting closer to the house.

Mac continued to pound on the front door, leaving crescent moon dents from his Streamlight on it. He proceeded to beat the portal more intently as he looked over his shoulder and saw the flames now licking the top of the roof above his head. The smoke had enveloped Mac and he was obscured in a dizzying world of only a couple feet of visibility. He found a doorbell and frantically pushed with his other hand yelling, "Camillus Police! Fire!" over and over again.

It had only been a couple of minutes since Mac had been banging on the entrance, but it felt like an eternity as he began to cough from the intolerable mix of smoke and soot. He started looking around the structure to see if there was a less secure point of entry into the dwelling, but was frustrated by the veil of smoke.

Just as Mac decided that he was going to have to take the door, with his right leg raised and coiled, a middle-aged man open the door with a look of horror on his face. He was half-dressed with a button-up shirt hanging unbuttoned from his shoulders and a pair of jeans unbuttoned and unzipped being grasped by his left hand. His eyeglasses were askew on his face and he just stood there looking past Mac at the glow of the fire as it radiated through the gray smoke. In his mind it probably took on alien qualities at this late hour and he was frozen with indecision.

"We've got to go! Is there anyone else in the house?!" Mac yelled over the sound of the roaring fire as it kept up its' progression getting closer now working on the roof of the house as its' second course.

The man just nodded and looked over his shoulder at his wife and two little children huddled behind him in a similar state of disheveled dress. Mac grabbed the man's arm and pulled him into the night and then guided the rest of the family out of the house. He then led them down the driveway out of harm's way and placed them in his patrol vehicle on the street. Everyone was coughing, and Mac had snot unceremoniously coming out of his nose as he stood outside of the car trying to get more unadulterated oxygen into his lungs.

The flames continued to leap from the garage to the roof of the house as everyone helplessly watched. The first sirens could be heard coming from the firehouse, which was less than a couple of miles away. Shortly, the Blue-Lighters made their way down the road, with the fire chief arriving first in his marked take-home GMC Suburban.

Fairmount Fire Chief Mark Bass stepped out of the Suburban with a portable radio in his hand and gave an update to the MRD Center Fire Control and his responding firemen. Once he keyed-off the radio he walked over to Mac and said, "Everybody out Mac?"

"Yeah Bassey, I've got the family in my car. They're half-asleep and in shock, but they appear to be okay. How far out is the ambulance?"

"WAVES is at the Fairmount Four Corners, should be here in a minute. My trucks should be here right after that," Bass said.

The two them stood in the street, just looking up at the unending malevolent destruction.

"You find it, Mac?" Bass asked.

"Yeah, just doing road patrol circles around the town."

"Well, lucky for them that you did. These types of structures go up fast. That garage most likely had stored accelerants like gasoline and oil in it. There's no saving that building at all. It's way too gone."

"Well, you know...that's how come you guys get the nickname of 'Cellar Savers,' isn't it?" Mac said with a flash of a smile as he continued to wipe off the snot.

"Fuck you, Mac!" Bass said playfully.

With that, WAVES Ambulance arrived at the scene of the fire with their emergency lights still flashing. As fate would have it, Donna Johnston and Vaughn McCabe were the responding EMTs.

"Do you have the victims Mac?" Donna asked as she jumped down from the driver's seat.

"Yeah Donna, I have them in my car," Mac answered.

Chief Bass acknowledged the ambulance crew and then made his way to the front of the burning garage and shielded his eyes with the blade of his left hand as he attempted to see past the flames and into the interior of the structure.

"Hey Vaughn!" Mac said as he redirected his attention to the family and opened the rear door to the patrol car.

"I'd like to have everyone checked out by the EMTs," Mac said to the family, who could only silently nod as they kept their eyes on the fire.

Donna peeked her head in the door and asked, "Is everyone all right?"

The mother said, "I think we're fine. We've all been coughing from the smoke, but I don't think we're hurt or anything."

"Okay, that's great. How about I start with the children. I'd like to put them in the rig and listen to their lungs and take their vital signs. Would that be okay?" Donna inquired.

"Sure, I'd like to come with them though," the woman replied.

"Me too," said the father as he opened the front passenger door and started to get out.

"Follow me," Donna said as she guided them to the back of the ambulance.

"Take my hands, kids," Vaughn said as he held each of the children's hands.

Once at the rig, Donna climbed up inside as Vaughn lifted one, and then the other child into the back of the ambulance. The mother followed them up into the treating space and Mac opened the side door so that the father could stand in the opening and look in. The back of the ambulance was not that big of a space, and with both EMTs assessing the two children and the mother inside, it left no room for the father.

Fairmount Fire Department Engines arrived on scene during this process and quickly found a nearby fire hydrant, hooking up their 2.5" hose lines to the pumper. The hoses were quickly charged, and Chief Bass directed the firefighters to start hosing down the main residence with streams of hissing water. It didn't take long for the flames to be put out on the roof of the house. The act of putting the water on the fire spreading on the roof gave off a grey-filled smoke that added to the surrealness of the fiery and foggy environment.

One hose team stayed on the house as the other team was directed by Chief Bass to start directing their hose line on the flames coming from the garage. Mac thought of an old firefighter adage, "Put the wet stuff on the red stuff." With this in mind, the brave firefighters continued their battle with the angry, nebulous dance of flames and the milky-orange smoke lathering into the black night of the dusky sky.

Within thirty minutes, the firefighters had the blaze fully contained. The garage was a total loss, but the house was fully intact with just a little charring to the front of the roof. The firefighters were prodding around the garage with pike poles to make sure there were no hot spots, and other firemen were on a ladder looking at the roofline to the residence.

Mac was sitting on the hood of his patrol vehicle observing the firefighting operation as Chief Bass walked back over to him and said, "I'd say this was a win. Sure, we lost the garage, but the house is almost completely unscathed by the fire."

"I appreciate you guys getting here when you did. Middle of the night fires are a nightmare, and I was having a hell of a time trying to raise the family and get them out," Mac said in response.

"No worries Mac. You made a real difference here by driving by when you did. WAVES is going to take the whole family up to Community General Hospital to get looked at, just to be on the safe side. Smoke inhalation, no matter how slight, is nothing to ignore. Matter of fact, you should get yourself up there too, to get checked out."

"I'm fine, Bassey. But thanks for the thought," Mac said.

"Okay Mac, but if your breathing is still compromised later, I'd get your ass to the ER just the same," Chief Bass said as he walked back to his crew still making their way through the garage.

"Yeah, yeah, yeah," Mac answered good naturedly.

Mac stayed on the scene until the firefighters started putting the lines away and loading up their gear back on the trucks. Chief Bass advised him that the cause of the fire did not appear to be intentional, but he would let Mac know if that changed. It was almost daybreak, and he decided that he would go to Perkins Restaurant at Camillus Plaza and get some orange juice and a Danish. He was writing up the report on the fire in the booth when his waitress said to him, "You reek of a fire."

"You have no idea," he said in response, as she laid down the drink and the small food dish. Mac couldn't smell the smoke on himself, but knew he would need to take a shower when he got home. Having experienced this before, he knew that even when he changed into his civvies that his hair would still retain the scent of smoke until he thoroughly washed it twice.

After writing up the report and taking care of his sustenance needs, he got back into the patrol car and headed to the PD for change of shift. He advised Sgt. Jake Smith of the fire and went upstairs to the locker room to change out of his soot-filled clothes. He bundled up the uniform clothes to take to the dry cleaners and walked back down the two flights of stairs to the parking lot and his Camaro.

Mac thanked God that he didn't have class today, as he was exhausted and just wanted a bed to climb into after the shower. He was finding out that adrenaline dumps were draining and bouncing back from them took a little time for him to recharge after they occurred. Mac just wanted a nice warm bed and NMI to cuddle up with. But the latter wasn't going to happen, as she was working the day shift.

Oh, well—at least he could dream of her as he went off to sleep, he thought, struggling himself to stay awake on the ride home...it was time for other rough men and women to take the watch as he slept peaceably in his own bed.

Great thoughts speak only to the thoughtful mind,
but great actions speak to all mankind.

- Theodore Roosevelt

CHAPTER

TWENTY

Mac's only brother Michael was attending Boston University in Boston, Massachusetts on a full football scholarship after graduating from West Genesee Senior High in Camillus, New York. When Michael came home, it was difficult to make time for him with all that Mac had going on, between taking care of his grandmother, his children, working full-time, overtime and secondary jobs, and college classes, and so he started having Michael ride along with him on the midnight shift.

This was a gray area with CPD. Most civilian riders were Police Explorers, college interns, or regular civilians who wanted to know more about their local police department. They all signed release waivers not holding the Camillus Police Department responsible for serious bodily harm or death. Mac had Michael ride on the down-low, because he didn't want to overextend the number of invitations with Michael and have someone object. Michael never rode the whole shift. Just usually the first three or four hours, and them Mac would drop him off at their parents' house. Mac appreciated his brother's company on A-Watch, and this was the only way for them to bond while he was away at college.

Mac gave Michael a spare police body armor vest in an outside blue quilted carrier that he used to wear before being issued his new one. With Michael being 6'3" and two-hundred and fifty pounds, it provided very little coverage. Mac also gave him an extra Maglite of his so that he could help illuminate the scenes they responded to, but also as a weapon if someone decided to attack him; this didn't seem like a good idea for anybody to do, but you never knew with people you encountered on the midnight shift.

Mac and Michael spent hours riding around the town together talking about family issues, girls, the past, and the prospects of the future for both of them. Michael was an economics major at B.U. and had an innate physical ability for sports. He was an all-state wrestler in high school and loved the game of football. Michael, like every other college football player, dreamed of someday playing in the National Football

League (NFL).

While Michael was finishing up his degree at B.U. he managed a sports bar named *Who's on First.* The bar was just outside of Fenway Park and the home of the Boston Red Sox. The name was a take on an Abbott and Costello baseball comedy skit from the 1940's. Outside of baseball season, it was a townie bar where college students and Boston cops would hang out. Michael started off as a door man/bouncer and then worked his way up to bartender, and now in his senior year, he was the bartending manager of the popular watering hole. It seemed that the family business was hard to get away from for the brothers.

Michael was unsure what he was going to do with his economics degree from BU, but in the near future he was still concentrating on continuing his football career. He had some interest shown him with the Denver Broncos and the New York Jets, but with several knee surgeries under his belt, the franchises were wary of taking a chance with him. The Arena Football League was also calling on him after he finished school. Michael loved to play the game and thought the Arena League would solidify his chances with an NFL team in the future.

While patrolling the streets of the Town of Camillus, the brothers would come across calls for service such as vehicular crashes or conduct vehicular stops where someone was driving under the influence or had an active warrant for their arrest, and inevitably they would be placed in the rear of the police vehicle.

On one of those typical occasions Mac and Michael came across a young man who drove his vehicle into another car at the Fairmount Four Corners. It was just after midnight, and there was a slight mist of rain as they pulled up to the two cars still in the intersection. Mac activated the overhead emergency lights to warn other drivers of the hazard. Michael stayed in the cruiser while Mac exited and spoke with the drivers and sole occupants, who were standing outside their respective modes of transportation.

"Good evening. Is anyone hurt?" Mac asked as he walked up on them.

"No, Officer," a middle-aged woman said as she produced her driver's license, registration, and proof of insurance. She rolled her eyes at a younger white male, the driver of the other car, as she stepped in front of him to hand her information to Mac. Her paperwork revealed her to be Mary Kay Koren of the Town of Geddes.

Mac noticed that the other driver was nervously smoking a cigarette and avoiding eye contact. "Are you okay?" Mac asked while taking a good look at him.

"Yeah, I'm good," he said back, as he slouched against the front quarter panel of his Honda.

"Can I please get your license, vehicle registration and insurance card then?" Mac asked as he moved closer towards him.

Even through the cigarette smoke and being in the open

misty air Mac could smell raw alcohol from his breath. The driver was also disheveled in his appearance, and upon closer inspection his eyes were bloodshot.

Mac looked back at the woman while the young man went back into his vehicle to get the required paperwork. She smiled thinly and gave an abbreviated nod with her head as Mac gave her a knowing look.

Michael watched this scenario play out through the windshield of the police car and was getting pretty good at reading situations before Mac told him what was unfolding during certain calls.

As the male came back out of his car, he gave Mac his New York State driver's license which identified him as Aron Hunter of the Town of Camillus. "I can't find my other stuff. I thought it was in there, but it's not."

"Mr. Hunter, have you been drinking tonight?" Mac asked.

"Only a couple of beers," he answered.

"Can you tell me the last time you consumed alcohol and from where?"

"My buddies' house, about an hour ago."

"Okay. Can you tell me how the crash occurred?

"I was driving home from this way," Hunter said, pointing south towards Onondaga Road. "And when I went to turn onto West Genesee Street this lady was already there. I'm not sure exactly how it happened. It just happened. You know?"

"Not really," Mac said as he listened to Hunter's slurred speech. "Mr. Hunter, I smell alcohol on you so I'm going to have to give you a Field Sobriety Test. Please don't smoke anymore cigarettes until I've given you the test. Give me a minute, because I'm going to have to run your information for your vehicle and insurance since you don't have the paperwork."

Hunter just nodded his head as he looked at the ground.

"Mary Kay, can I speak with you at my vehicle please?" Mac asked, as he started walking the twenty or so feet to the police car.

Mary Kay followed Mac to the rear of his vehicle where the emergency lights cascaded off their faces as they spun around in the light bar. "Can you tell me what happened?" Mac asked Mary Kay.

"Sure, Officer. I was coming home from work at the hospital in Auburn on West Genesee Street and I had the green light at the intersection with Onondaga Road when he—" here she nodded her head towards Mr. Hunter "—came through the intersection and he hit the rear of my Camry. There's not much damage to either car, but I could tell that he was drunk and didn't want him to get back into his car and drive away, so I had the clerk from the Mobil Station call the police."

"You did the right thing. I think he's over the legal limit, so I'm going to give him tests to find out for sure. Why don't you wait in the rear of my patrol vehicle while I copy down your information for the accident report? I don't want you near him, and it will only take a minute."

"Sure Officer," she said as Mac opened the right rear passenger door and she got in.

"I'll be back in a second. I need to get the license plate number off his vehicle," Mac said as he closed the door and left her with Michael.

"Hi!" Mary Kay said to Michael as she looked at the back of his head, trying to see his face.

"Hi!" Michael said back. "Not a good way to start the weekend is it?"

"It's not too bad. There isn't a lot of damage. I can drive it until Monday when I get ahold of my insurance agent," Mary Kay said.

"That's good. It's not fun being without transportation," Michael replied.

"No, it's not. You're right. Soooo...are you a cop?" she inquired.

"Um, no. I'm riding with my brother while I'm home from college."

"Oh..." Then there was an awkward silence until Mac got back into the vehicle.

Mac copied Mary Kay's information on his pad and gave a copy of the Designated Report (D.R.) number on a sheet of paper, she could give her insurance agent with Mr. Hunter's information attached as well. He got back out of his seat and walked around the rear of the car and let Mary Kay out of the back seat and gave back to her the documents and exchange of information sheet.

"I hope you have a good weekend," Mac said as he shook her hand.

"You too, Officer! Thank you," she said as she walked back to her vehicle and drove off towards the Town of Geddes.

Mac walked back to the second vehicle and said, "Mr. Hunter, I'm going to place you in the rear of my police vehicle while I get your vehicle out of the intersection and put it in the parking lot of Ice Cream Shoppe before we start the sobriety tests."

"Does that mean I'm under arrest?" he said forlorn.

"No. I just need to free up the intersection, so we aren't a hazard to other drivers. I do need to pat you down before I place you in the rear of my police car though. Do you have any weapons on you?

"Just a pocketknife."

"That's fine. Don't reach for it, what pocket is it in?

"Back right."

"Okay, I'll get it."

Mac reached into Hunter's pocket and retrieved the knife. He also completed a pat down on the rest of Hunter's person and then placed him into the back of the patrol vehicle where Mary Kay had been sitting moments earlier.

"I've got to move his vehicle out of the intersection and into the parking lot. I'll be right back," Mac told Michael.

Michael nodded his head as Mac jogged over to the car and started it up.

"So, are you a cop too? Hunter asked from the back seat.

"Um...No," Michael answered back.

"Okay then..." Hunter replied.

Insert awkward silence again.

Mac got Hunter's vehicle into the lot and jogged back to the police cruiser and pulled it into the same parking lot. He got Hunter back out of the rear seat and administered a field sobriety test, which he failed miserably. He then administered an Alco-sensor, the Pre-Screening Device, which resulted in a .18 Blood Alcohol Content (BAC).

Mr. Hunter was handcuffed and placed under arrest, read his Driving While Intoxicated Warnings, his Miranda Rights, and then transported back to the Camillus Police Station where a Breathalyzer Test was conducted by Deputy Kevin Charm, who was working A-Watch in southern Onondaga.

Mr. Hunter was issued Uniform Traffic Tickets (UTT's) for passing a red light, Driving While Intoxicated (DWI), Driving While Intoxicated (DWI) with a BAC over .10 %, and then turned over to his father with a return court date in two weeks.

After processing the arrest and completing all the required paperwork, it was 3:30 AM and Mac could tell that Michael was getting tired.

"Let's get in the patrol car and I'll take you back to Mom and Dad's house," Mac said to Michael.

Michael nodded, and they walked down the stairs to the parking lot and their awaiting transportation. As they were both putting on their seat belts Michael said, "Do you know what everyone asks me when I'm alone in the car with them?"

Mac turned to him as he put the vehicle in drive and started out of the parking lot. "No. What?"

"They all ask me if I'm a cop. It happened twice tonight."

"Huh? That's weird. I guess it makes sense. You are in a cop car. You're wearing a vest and carrying a flashlight. Maybe not weird at all."

"I know, but it kills me to say no."

"Well maybe we just found out what you're going to do with the rest of your life after football..."

"Huh..." Michael repeated.

Cue foreshadowing.

No man is worth his salt who is not ready at all times to risk his well-being, to risk his body, to risk his life, in a great cause.

- Theodore Roosevelt

CHAPTER

TWENTY-ONE

When Michael went back to college, Mac was left to his own devices while riding on the midnight shift. Because boredom is the key element in all bad decision-making, Mac would sometimes try and find out how fast the police car could go on the Route 5 Bypass early in the wee hours of the morning.

So not once but twice he blew the square plastic covers off of the overhead light bar during these escapades. The first time it happened, Mac was perplexed by the unfamiliar sound as he careened down the empty highway. He heard was sounded like a THRUMP noise just outside of the vehicle, and in the still and dead summer night he looked frantically around as the cruiser was at one-hundred and twenty miles an hour and climbing down the expanse of the highway.

Mac finally settled in to looking at the rearview mirror as he took his foot off of the accelerator and spied the plastic cover gliding slowly down from overhead and then finally fragmenting into a thousand glittering pieces as it met the asphalt highway.

"Oh shit!" Mac exclaimed as he witnessed the event. He pulled off the shoulder of the roadway and exited the vehicle and looked at the light bar. Sure enough, one half of the cover was missing from the unit. "Ah, man! How am I going to explain this?" He muttered to himself. Mac scratched his head in disbelief.

He climbed back into the police car and headed back to the station to swap it out with another cruiser. There was no need to go back and clean up the mess from his ill-fated adventure since they were practically dust particles.

Since he was the only cop on in the town, he didn't have the luxury of having someone laugh at his misguided exploit and tell him it would be all right. He finished his tour of A-Watch wondering on how to explain the reckless damage to the patrol vehicle.

The next morning, Sgt. Jake Smith was the first to arrive for

B-Watch. Mac was just pulling into the parking lot at the station as Jake was getting out of his pick-up truck and looking at the light bar of vehicle #103.

"Uh...Sarge, I kind of had an incident last night," Mac said as he climbed out of his alternate vehicle.

"I can see that," Jake said as he continued inspecting the light bar.

"Am I in trouble?"

"No worries kid. These things happen. We've got spare light bars in the shed. I'll just swipe it out and no one is the wiser."

"Really?"

"Yeah, it occurs more than you would think. Were you up on the highway when it happened?"

"Yes, I must have been going a bit too fast."

"Yeah, you might want to slow down a bit. We don't have an unlimited supply," Jake said with a wink and a smile.

"Thanks, Sarge. I will. I promise," Mac said feeling quite relieved and twenty pounds lighter.

The next night, Mac was on the graveyard shift again by himself. He didn't have one call all night. He was just driving around in circles doing business checks and putting miles on the car so he could have something on his police log.

Mac was a voracious reader and couldn't be without a book. Currently he was reading the *Hunt for Red October* by Tom Clancy, along with a myriad of other school texts. But trying to read on A-Watch just about put him in a catatonic state.

At approximately 4:00 AM, Mac was going down the Route 5 Bypass for the umpteenth time when he drifted off to sleep as the police car was traveling down the desolate roadway. He woke up about a half of a mile down the road. When he did, Mac's heart almost stopped beating as it jumped out of his chest. Mac had never been so scared. He knew he was tired, but didn't understand how his body and mind had utterly failed him.

Mac was so frightened that he pulled off the Warners Road exit and drove right back to the police station. He backed into a parking space right outside the back door to the building and just sat there replaying the scene over and over in his head. Mac tried to nail down the exact moment he fell asleep and replay it in his mind and how his police car was able to navigate a twenty-five-degree right-hand curve and still stay on the roadway without hitting the guardrails on either side of the highway. When he was jarred awake, his speed was also constant at sixty-five miles an hour, which he assumed would've slowed down when he nodded off but didn't. Mac kept on reliving the event over and over, trying to figure out A) how he didn't crash, and B) if he did crash, how catastrophic would it have been?

Thankfully, Mac didn't have a dispatched call while he sat there for the next several hours running the scenario over and over in his head. The adrenaline dump still caused his hands to shake well after the event, and Mac was unsure how he would be able to regroup and safely drive anywhere at the moment. It made no sense to him, and being a very pragmatic person, he continued to run the equation through his mind as the golden red morning presented itself and the B-Watch cops started to arrive for their day shift.

Some of the guys and girls had already changed as Mac was getting his patrol bag and police utensils from the cruiser. He made his way upstairs into the Men's Locker Room as Twist was finishing up his look in the bathroom mirror. Twist's uniform was always impeccably done before he left the station, and he was checking to make sure everything was just so, as Mac walked to his locker and set the police bag down.

"How'd it go last night, Moe? Twist asked, as he saw Mac through the mirror behind him.

"Holy shit! I almost killed myself...literally!" Mac answered, still dealing with the aftereffects of the unwanted adrenaline in his veins.

"No shit? Really?"

"Yeah, no shit. I fell asleep on the Bypass and woke up a half of a mile down the road. I nearly pissed myself and had a heart attack at the same time when I came to. I was so completely fucked-up I had to sit in the station parking lot for the rest of the night."

"Man, I've almost done that myself. I never could get enough sleep on A-Watch when I was assigned to it. I give you a lot of credit doing it permanently while going to school. You didn't hit anything?" Twist asked as he turned away from the mirror and walked up to Mac's locker.

"No, and I can't figure out how I didn't."

"It's better to be lucky than good, Mac. Just take it for what it's worth. You can't afford to have any other crashes."

"Yea, I know Twist, but it kind of defies logic," Mac said as he pulled off his belt keepers and took off his gun-belt and hung it inside his locker.

"Well, just be thankful, Mac. I've got to get in service. Get some sleep. I'm doing a double, so I'll see you when you come back in."

"Thanks, Twist. Stay safe," Mac said, as he continued to disrobe and shake his head in disbelief as he told the story for the first time to someone else. He knew that sleep was not going to come as easy as Twist wishing it for him. Mac changed into his civilian clothes and headed off to Onondaga Community College for a full day of classes. It seemed like the cycle was endless, but he had to keep his head down and knock it out. A-Watch would be here before he knew it.

Mac made it through the school day unscathed and got segmented sleep in three two-hour shifts, all the while checking on his grandmother, taking care of the house, and bringing Joseph to First Holy Communion Classes. Before he knew it, or was ready for it, he was freshly showered and once again driving the Camaro down Skyline Drive onto Cleveland Road on his trek back to work A-Watch at CPD. He still felt uneasy about falling asleep while driving the previous shift, and put self-imposed contingencies in place: To get out of the police car at the Mobil Station or by going to Perkins Restaurant for a glass of orange juice. Anything to help wake his brain back up if the shift was again mind-numbing in its routine.

As he pulled into the station AC/DC was playing 'Back in Black" and Mac felt a little more amped up as he left his vehicle in the lot and climbed the stairs to the locker room.

"Get any sleep?" Twist asked as Mac walked into the changing area.

"Yeah, but getting six hours in three different sessions just doesn't completely do it. I constantly feel like I'm walking around underwater in a dream sequence," Mac answered.

"Well, you got too much going on obviously. Something has to give, and there's a reason why human beings can't burn the candle at both ends," Twist retorted.

"I know. I really do get it, but I have to take care of my grandmother and my kids. It's not like I have a choice on not working the overtime. Again, I need to provide for my kids. Their mother doesn't afford them with anything. Nor does she take them to religion class or any of their practices. I need to get my associate degree sooner than later, thus the reason I'm on midnights to begin with. As it is, I don't see NMI enough and I can't give up karate, it's the only thing that keeps me in shape and deals with all the rest of the stress I'm under."

"Well, then you're fucked," Twist said in exasperation.

Mac gave him a wry smile as he pulled his vest over his head and said, "I'll sleep when I'm dead."

"It's your funeral, Moe! Be safe...I'm out of here. I'm

exhausted myself. Nothing really to pass on. Just the run of the mill shoplifters and 79's."

"I'll see you, Twist. Maybe we can get together on our rest days and do something normal."

"Sounds like a plan to me. Let me know. See you, Mac!"

Mac walked back down the stairs to the Patrol Room and read the teletypes from the previous shifts to see if there was anything of interest. Not finding anything he got his patrol bag and put it in the front passenger seat and called in service.

"Unit #3103A...0003 hours," the MRD Channel 4 dispatcher acknowledged.

And so, it began again on the boring overwatch shift...until halfway through...

"Unit 3611A...copy a motorcycle refusing to yield!" Officer Kevin "Scooby" Geertzen from the Town of Geddes Police Department advised the MRD Center. You could hear his police engine screaming up to speed in the background.

The Town of Geddes bordered the Town of Camillus on the east side of the town. Its claim to fame was that it was the home to The Great New York State Fair, and unobtrusively, the Village of Solvay Police Department was nestled in the center of it.

The Town of Geddes PD and the Town of Camillus PD were like sister agencies. They would hold joint picnics in the summertime, and members would usually get together off shift as well to socialize. Officer Geertzen received his moniker because he was the dog warden for the Town of Geddes prior to joining the police department. So naturally, everybody affectionately called him 'Scooby,' so much so that no one actually could remember his real first name. Scooby was six feet tall, average build, in his mid-thirties with very curly brown hair worn on the longish side. So actually, he sort of resembled a lovable K-9.

The motorcycle pursuit was called out by Scooby a little after 3:00 AM.

"Unit #3611A, your location and description?" the dispatcher asked.

"Westbound on West Genesee Street crossing Parsons Drive. Black Suzuki crotch rocket...no plate visible," Scooby advised.

"Same bike as previous?" the dispatcher inquired.

"Same guy," Scooby responded deadpan.

Periodically, all summer long, a black Suzuki sport bike GSX-R1000X without a license plate had intentionally gotten into vehicle police pursuits with different police agencies on the western side of the county and would outrun the police cars when they started to engage. The driver was always wearing a full-faced helmet with a tinted face shield, gloves, and a black motorcycle jacket. His race and sex were still unknown. This time of night, the Onondaga County Sheriff's Department AIR-1 was usually in the hangar located in the Town of Camillus, and by the time they got up in the air, the pursuit was already over, with the motorcycle long gone.

It appeared that the operator of the Suzuki was doing this for sport, and had become emboldened with it the more the summer went on. He intentionally swerved into the oncoming lanes of the cops and unsuspecting citizens at high rates of speed with seemingly little regard for human life. At this point, it was an extremely high-stakes game of cat and mouse.

Mac had gotten a glimpse of the bike about a month ago when his friend Deputy Kevin Charm had called out a pursuit on the southern end of the town. Within seconds after arriving to assist Charm, the bike accelerated into triple digits on Onondaga Road in the 35 MPH zone and was in the ether.

It was just a matter of time before the wrongdoer killed himself, an unassuming citizen, or a cop, and everyone from the police to the dispatchers knew it.

This time, as fate would have it, Mac was at Fairmount Fair and engaged in the pursuit as the bike turned into the Wegman's Grocery Store parking lot with Scooby on his tail. There were also one Village of Solvay unit, two Sheriff's cars, and a State Police cruiser all immediately on him. With all the units coming from different directions, it looked like the hellion was finally out-maneuvered and boxed in.

The police cars all converged on the bike and tightened the circle as he juked this way and that in the parking lot, and it looked like they would have him as he was running out of room to navigate and was being slowly pinned up against a guardrail, which protected a stream through the center of the mall parking lot. Mac was just about bumper to bumper with the cars on both sides of him, with the motorcycle reduced to riding inches, instead of feet, when the miscreant accelerated at the last second and found freedom, scraping off the fenders of his pursuers.

Mac knew he could've knocked him off his bike, but thought better of it. He couldn't risk one more accident, and the risk of seriously injuring the biker was foremost in his mind. Mac wanted to end it, but at what cost?

The cop cars started to unscramble from the parking lot, but everybody knew it was a lost cause. The bike immediately got on the Route 5 Bypass and they could hear by the acceleration that he was well over 100 MPH as he got out of Dodge.

All the cops regrouped in the parking lot and got out of their cars to commiserate the latest unsuccessful apprehension of the suspect when the MRD dispatcher advised Scooby that Fire Control was dispatching an ambulance to the other end of the Town of Geddes, at State Fair Boulevard and Walters Road for a single motorcycle accident with injuries. Everyone looked at each other and not a word was spoken as the cops got back into their cruisers and headed in that direction.

Upon arrival, the WAVES crew were loading the battered body of a young twenties' white male into the back of the ambulance. He was screaming in agony as his right leg was apparently amputated below his knee. The cops took up positions on both sides of the rig and proceeded to golf clap as the technicians worked on the poor soul.

Mac looked at Scooby, who responded by saying, "Karma's a bitch..."

And with that, the shift came to a close. On A-Watch, you never really knew what you were in for.

I am a part of everything that I have read.

- Theodore Roosevelt

CHAPTER

TWENTY-TWO

The next Tuesday, Mac and Twist were both off on their pass days with no overtime to be had. It was decided that they would go on a double date of sorts. It turned out that Twist had become interested in NMI's little sister, as she too had started working at TJ Big Boy's as a waitress. Upon finding this out, Wide-Body had made constant cracks in their presence about being future in-laws, incessantly saying, "Hey Moe! Pass the mashed potatoes!"

That night they all went out to Morgan's Restaurant in

Westvale and had dinner. The restaurant clientele was an older crowd, but the ambience and food were better than average fare. The sisters didn't find it strange to be dating friends that were cops, and that kind of helped the process for Twist. Within weeks, they were a steady item.

Mac's brother Michael was due to graduate in the next couple of months and he needed a place to live when he came back home. They agreed that he would live on Skyline Drive, taking over Mac's responsibilities of caring for their grandmother, and that left Mac and Twist to arrange to get a two-bedroom apartment in the Village of Camillus.

Mac continued his workouts at the dojo and had just completed his purple belt test in front of Master Hidy Ochiai himself, at his main training facility in Vestal, New York. The workouts were grueling, and Mac's gi would be soaked after training in the dojo located in the basement at Nottingham Plaza. Even though the routines were arduous, going two to three times a week, they gave Mac a sense of balance and inner peace that couldn't be duplicated. He was excited to start training for his brown belt as those practitioners were the gateway to the all coveted black belt in Washin-Ryu.

As an added bonus to his workouts there was an obscure Chinese take-out place right next to the dojo. Never mind the fact that Washin-Ryu was Japanese in origin and this may have violated some ancient faux pas in the time continuum of martial arts.

As a reward for his endeavors in the oriental arts, Mac would get an order of sweet and sour chicken to go and eat it when he got home. This was an extravagant meal compared to what he normally ate in his grandmother's basement. Mac didn't like intruding on his grandmother in the upstairs of the house, and rarely if ever used the kitchen. There was a full-sized refrigerator by the bar area in the basement where Mac kept milk and juice. He didn't have very much time to eat, and got into a habit of buying a Friehoffer birthday sheet cake and keeping it in the fridge. It was a less expensive, quick, and convenient source of sustenance that Mac would sometimes have for all three meals of the day.

On his third past day he spent it with his children and NMI. The days flew by too quickly and before he knew it, his three pass days were over, and it was time to go back to work for six days in a row. The routine was crushing, but there was light at the end of the tunnel as he was getting close to graduating from OCC. Then he could get off of A-Watch and resume a normal (or semi-normal) rotational shift of two weeks of A-Watches / two weeks of B-Watches / and then two weeks of C-Watches…and repeat.

For now, he was back on midnights driving around on the endless routine of business and park checks. Again, it was a beautiful summer night, which happened to be on a Friday night late in July. Mac knew these nights were fleeting and appreciated them greatly. Sooner rather than later, the air would chill and eight month's worth of wet, rain, sleet, and snow were just around the corner.

On this particular A-Watch shift, Mac was conducting his

patrol through the town's business districts, working alone, just before 2:00 AM when he pulled into the parking lot of Elm Hill Plaza. The parking lot was fairly full this time of night because the Back-Door Tavern was getting ready to close, and patrons were also enjoying the evening in the parking area as they made their way to their cars.

Mac didn't usually spend much time in the lot because he didn't want people to think that he was just there poaching for DWI's. He did pull through the lot on the weekends to make sure there weren't any fights in the parking lot, which happened from time to time. Mac and his coworkers didn't patronize the bar for any particular reason except that most people in town knew who they were, and they didn't want people staring at them if they decided to go out and have a drink after work. Thus, the reason why they hung out at Molly Malone's in Solvay.

Tonight, as Mac made his way through the lot in his marked patrol vehicle, most customers were wrapped up in their own revelry and barely noticed him as he crept across the asphalt area. Mac's vehicle windows were down, and he could hear competing car radios playing mostly some form of rock music. The radios weren't all that loud; most patrons knew that if they were, they would get unwanted attention from the patrolling units, since residential apartments were adjacent to the plaza. 'Midnight Rider' from the Allman Brothers seemed to be the over-riding melody on this early morning disbandment from the drinking hole.

As Mac was just about to leave the plaza, he spied

something unusual coming from across the back of the lot. It was a lone figure with a dark baseball cap with the front bill pulled down tight, so you couldn't see most of his facial features. This wasn't the unusual part. The subject was wearing a long black duster coat, like cowboys wore in old westerns. If this was October through May, the coat itself would have been unique but not totally out of place, but it being summertime and at this time of night hovering around seventy-seven degrees, it all made the coat a red flag to Mac. A sign that something wasn't right.

Mac hit the brakes on the police unit and started slowly turning it around to intercept the subject as he made his way across the plaza towards the front door of the Back-Door Tavern. As Mac was doing this, he reached for the police radio microphone to call out his location for a suspicious person., but before he could key up the mic, the subject noticed Mac coming back around, and startled with a jolt. The subject changed his direction one hundred and eighty degrees and took off running towards the back of the lot, with his coat flapping behind him in his wake, and what looked like a shotgun underneath his coat down by his legs.

Mac couldn't change directions fast enough in the parking lot due to the pedestrians all around going to their cars, and by the time Mac navigated the people and the parked cars, the subject was inside the driver's seat of an old Dodge Diplomat police car, throwing it into gear and peeling out of the plaza through the nearest exit.

"Shit!" Mac yelled as he had to double back around and head towards the exit that he was just at a moment ago.

"Unit #3103A to Dispatch copy a pursuit."

"Unit #3103A your location and direction of travel?" Felicity Flynn answered right away.

"Unit #3103A just exiting Elm Hill Plaza heading east on Milton Ave. Suspect vehicle is a dark gray Dodge Diplomat occupied by one unknown race male armed with a long gun. No plate information at this time."

"All West Zone units hold the air! Unit #3103A is in pursuit of a dark gray Dodge Diplomat, unknown registration on Milton Ave. eastbound from Elm Hill Plaza. Units be advised, the lone unknown suspect is armed with a long gun. Unit #3103A your status?" Felicity asked.

"Unit #3101A the suspect vehicle turned north onto Hinsdale Road and then took a right onto the Route 5 Bypass, heading eastbound," Mac advised.

"All Channel Four units be advised the suspect vehicle is proceeding eastbound on the Route 5 Bypass."

Multiple units from surrounding town and villages, sheriff and state units keyed up their mics and advised the MRD Center that they were responding to the call. The situation went from zero to one hundred miles per hour in seconds. In his periphery, Mac could hear Roxy McCall (NYSP) and Gerald Hair (NYSP) acknowledging the call with their vehicle's engine screaming to life in the background. He also could hear Kevin Charm (OCSD) struggling with his mic as he answered up from the Onondaga Indian Reservation (The Res).

The suspect had just enough gap on Mac that he couldn't close it to no more than thirty yards. He had his foot through the floor and the vehicle was pegged at one-hundred and twenty-five miles an hour. Thank God, Mac thought, no one was up on the highway at this time of night.

With everyone wanting to acknowledge the call, which Mac appreciated greatly, knowing that he wasn't alone, Felicity had to take back control of the channel so that Mac could advise which direction the pursuit was heading.

"All units hold the air! Unit #3103A your direction of travel?"

"Unit #3103A...coming up on Route 690 Eastbound. Felicity advise the city," Mac requested.

The City of Syracuse Police Department was on a different radio frequency and patrolling units would have no idea that Mac was hurtling at them behind an armed suspect bent on getting away.

"Advising them now, Mac. I've also advised Channel Three," Felicity responded in kind.

The northern and eastern units of the MRD dispatch system were on Channel Three, and unless they were scanning Channel Four, they also would have no clue that Mac and the bad guy were coming to them in a hurry.

"Thank you! Can we take this to Channel One?"

Channel One was used for In-Progress crimes and for car-to-car transmissions that could tie up the regular channels from dispatching calls for service. Channel One usually had a dispatcher standing by called the TA that would coordinate the controlled chaos.

"Affirm Mac the TA is standing by. All units on Unit #3103A's pursuit go to Channel One. All units on the pursuit go to Channel One."

The Police Academy instructors were of course right...the most fun a cop could have with their clothes on was driving a police vehicle with the lights and siren on...however, it was also pretty terrifying. Since there were no supervisors on A-Watch, it was up to Mac to balance the threat of the pursuit with the danger of the bad man getting away and still being a menace to the public.

Mac formulated in his mind that the suspect was either going to forcibly rob the Back-Door Tavern or he was going to shoot a rival inside or outside the bar; either way, he most certainly was a danger to the public to justify a high-speed pursuit. This of course was ever evolving, dependent upon traffic conditions, time of day, weather conditions, and if the suspect was known to the police or not. Supervisors would normally monitor all these deciding factors, because once a cop was invested in the pursuit, it became harder for them to be dispassionate, and with just letting the suspect get away, due to environmental or other conditions, was harder to do.

As Mac was adjusting his police radio to Channel One, he saw a Town of Geddes Police Department vehicle getting on the on-ramp to Route 690 at the Fairgrounds, followed by two Village of Solvay Police Department cars. He could see Scooby's determined face in the lead car for a transitory second as the red and white overhead rotating lights from Mac's police unit reflected off his face.

Within seconds they were in the city, and Mac could see SPD police vehicles converging from behind as he passed them at dangerous speeds.

"Unit #3103A to the TA...is Air-One up?" Mac asked, trying to get the sheriff's department helicopter involved.

"Negative Unit #3103A...it's down for maintenance," the TA responded.

"Received," Mac acknowledged on the radio, but said "Shit!" yet again to himself.

"Unit #3103A, your direction of travel?" The TA inquired.

Mac knew why the TA was inquiring. Besides all the city off-ramps, there was also a split off to Route 81 Southbound. If that occurred the MRD Center would have to start notifying the southern county of Cortland.

"Unit #3103A still eastbound on Route 690."

When Mac reached the eastside of Syracuse, it started to rain. This resulted in a mumbled "Fuck!" as Mac upped his profanity verbiage in the pursuit.

"Unit #3103A be advised the suspect vehicle is exiting at Kirkville Road in Minoa."

By this time the rain had picked up as they were slowing down to get off the winding off-ramp and Mac could see at least twenty police cars in his rearview mirror, each with their overhead emergency lights on. It reminded Mac of the movie *Blues Brothers* starring John Belushi and Dan Aykroyd.

The suspect vehicle then proceeded on Kirkville Road East at an extremely high rate of speed again, and this time not on a highway, but on a surface street. The lighting conditions were poor, since there weren't street lights along the roadway, the rain wasn't slowing and the odds of something very bad happening with a pedestrian or a citizen driving down the road increased the threat level to the public as well as the pursuers. Mac didn't like it, but it was the right thing to do...

"Unit #3103A to the TA."

"Go ahead Unit #3103A"

"Unit #3103A...I'm calling off the pursuit."

"All southwest and northeast units...Unit #3103A has cancelled the pursuit. All units report back to your respective channels. Channel One is clear. 0213 hours."

Letting anyone go that was that dangerous and reckless did not sit well with Mac. He brooded all the way back to the Town of Camillus. He knew he made the right decision. The odds of a civilian getting hurt or killed on the surface streets was immense, and also the safety of his brother and sister officers assisting in the pursuit was in the back of his mind. That's the thing with responsibility, it weighs heavy on the one that wears the crown.

Several weeks later, Mac heard through the grapevine who the suspect was in the pursuit. He was a white male who had a criminal record and lived out in Minoa where they had called off the pursuit. It appeared he was indeed going to rob the Back-Door Tavern, however there wasn't enough circumstantial evidence to obtain a warrant of arrest, nor a search warrant for his vehicle or residence.

Approximately a year later, Mac heard from a deputy at the Onondaga County Sheriff's Department that the suspect had been involved in a fatal one-car crash off the roadway in Minoa. All the evidence pointed out that the suspect had been drinking and had struck a tree in the early morning with his wife in the vehicle. The deputy went on to say that the wife died in the crash and indications at the scene depicted the wife being dragged into the driver's seat after the crash by the suspect, to portray her as the driver...nothing could be proven, and he was never arrested.

It behooves every man to remember that the work of the critic is of altogether secondary importance, and that, in the end, progress is accomplished by the man that does things.

- **Theodore Roosevelt**

CHAPTER

TWENTY-THREE

M ac was entering into his third year with the department, and most cops would be offered a specialized In-Service training school to attend when a slot opened up in applicable schools. To attend these schools was based on seniority, and usually a cop would only be able to attend one every several years depending on funding and needs of the department. Most cops opted for Evidence Technician School or Traffic Enforcement (Radar) School, but

Mac had his heart set on the two-week Drug Enforcement Administration (DEA) School.

This aspiration was most likely due to being enamored by *Miami Vice* when he was younger. Although, for practical purposes, working drugs as a patrolman in a rural town police department didn't seem too likely. Twist and Wide-Body had made the sensible choices by attending the other practical schools when they were offered. The DEA school didn't get presented that often and Mac was headstrong on attending. He saw the offering one day before his shift and sent a memorandum to Lt. Max Johnson for the opportunity to attend. The LT oversaw training and was hesitant at first, but soon relented. Mac was enrolled in the training, which coincidentally would be held at the Town of Camillus Police Department. This would be no-cost training for CPD and the department wouldn't charged any extra money for lodging, fuel, per diem, etc., thus the main reason for the LT relenting.

It also coincided with summer break at the college. Mac had taken summer classes in the past, but decided that this In-Service course was more important than trying to speed up his formal education.

Perhaps not a coincidence at all, was that the DEA Task Force was located on the third floor of CPD across the hall from the police locker rooms. The task force was comprised of DEA agents, New York State Police—Special Investigations Unit (SIU), Onondaga County Sheriff's Department—Special Investigations Unit (SIU) and the City of Syracuse Police

Department—Special Investigations Division (SID). Although this was a clandestine office, off-the-books, so to speak, many cops knew it was there. Mac would see the undercovers in the hallways, going to their Concealed Identity (CI) vehicles, or sitting in the reception area hanging out with the secretary for CPD, Betty Masters.

One of the cops assigned to the DEA Task Force was an African American detective from the Syracuse Police Department named Wally Howard. He was young, good-looking and unassuming, and had a broad smile on his face every time Mac saw him. Wally on his downtime would come downstairs and sit in the reception area and carry on lighthearted conversations with Betty while playing with his drumsticks on top of a desk or against a chair.

For a city cop working undercover for the DEA, Wally was not pretentious at all. He always had that engaging smile and constantly acknowledged your presence with something nice to say in passing. Mac was in awe of his company in Betty's office every time he saw him. This also added to his desire and affirmation to attend the DEA school and to forgo the other offerings that the cops usually chose.

The DEA school couldn't come fast enough, and the weeks dragged until the school finally started. The school itself would run Monday through Friday 8:00 AM until 4:00 PM in the bottom floor of the Town of Camillus Municipal Building. Like most of the unused spaces in the building, the room that held the training resembled an elementary classroom, which indeed it was. Complete with a chalkboard, low countertops, a pencil sharpener, and pull-down beige shades on the windows. The major change was that the miniature desks had been replaced with long free-standing fold-out tables and adult-sized metal chairs.

The class size was approximately thirty (30) cops, comprised from all the police departments in Central New York. The Central New York Region was made up of seventeen (17) counties through the middle of the state, from the Canadian border through Syracuse down to the Pennsylvania border. Mac didn't know any of the other attendees, but this didn't dampen his excitement for the training.

The DEA instructors were seasoned agents and looked the part of narcotic investigators with long hair, earrings, facial hair, and tattoos. For teaching purposes, they wore DEA dark collared polo shirts and tan 511 cargo pants. Each agent, before presenting the material in their block of instruction, would give a brief biography of their education, background, and work experience thus far with the agency.

Instruction for the two weeks consisted of; specialized narcotics and dangerous drug law enforcement, asset forfeiture, intelligence training programs, clandestine laboratory training, pharmaceutical diversion training, and development of confidential informants. The curriculum was an extensive scaled-down version of the DEA agent training in Quantico, Virginia. It was also tailored to the specific part of the country in which it was being taught, as there are large variations geographically from the illegal narcotics used, to the distribution methods involved.

Mac sat in rapt attention as all this information was being imparted to the cops. It was a crack in a doorway to another world that was all around them, but invisible just the same if you didn't know where to look or what you were looking at. Mac especially paid very close attention on how to develop a confidential informant and in what way to implement this into a solid recruitment.

The two weeks flew by, and Mac was filled with just enough information about narcotics work to get him into trouble if he wasn't careful about how he went about applying the tutorial he received. He thought he might have a way of implementing some of the coursework he undertook and went about finding Detective Sergeant Billy Cole in his office upon his next regular shift assignment on C-Watch.

"Hey Sarge! I'm glad I caught you in," Mac said as he eased his way into the tiny investigations office.

"How's it going, Mac? What can I do you for?" Det. Sgt. Cole replied.

Cole was wearing a red plaid button-up long-sleeved shirt, jeans, and had his running sneakers propped up on the corner of his desk as he leaned back in his chair reading police reports. The radio was on featuring Led Zeppelin's 'Ramble On' playing gently in the background.

"You know I just got done with the DEA school, and I wanted to run something by you."

"Go ahead...shoot," Cole replied.

"I think I can come up with an informant for some drug work inside the town. My father has a cook working for him that's on parole for possession. I thought I would approach him and see if he would be willing to work off some of his parole time for information leading to arrests on dealers."

Cole gave him a long look and then flashed him a small smile. "Mac, I didn't think it would take you long to figure this out. It sounds like a good start. There are some nuances to getting an informant up and running. I'll have to take a look at his sheet and see if he's worth working with. If his convictions aren't that bad and he's willing to give it a try, we can sit down with him and his parole officer to try and work out something equitable for everybody. What's his name?"

"Andrew Jenkins. He's one of the cooks at MacKenna's Pub in the village," Mac answered.

"I can't say I've heard of him, Mac."

"He's not from around here. He just had his parole changed to Onondaga County. I think originally, he's from the Buffalo area."

"You know Mac, as much as he might want to cooperate, he may not know the players around here, so don't get your hopes up."

"You know, I didn't thing that far ahead. If it's all right with you, I can feel him out unofficially and see where it goes from there. He knows who I am and what I do, and we've had some innocuous conversations about stuff in the past. I think he might want to work with me to get out from under the parole thing."

"All right Mac, that's fine with me. This will be strictly off the books on your own time until we see a way to move forward, though."

Now Mac had his own smile. "I know. I'm glad you're giving me a chance. Thanks, Sarge!"

With that, Mac went upstairs to change into his uniform and start the evening shift. His mind was already spinning with different scenarios on how he was going to approach Andy and win him over to the informant world.

The shift went on as another uneventful tour, and Mac mulled over the circumstances on how to conduct the unofficial approach to Andy the next day. He decided to head down to the pub for lunch the following afternoon. The kids were in school and he would be seeing them this weekend. NMI was working doubles at the restaurant and the bank as of late and this gave Mac some extra time to put this new course of police work into play.

Mac pulled into his father's pub the next day at noon in the Camaro as he listened to Lyle Lovett finish up 'Which Way Does That Old Pony Run.' Mac's brother Michael had turned him onto the artist. Mac agreed with Michael and thought that Lyle Lovett was a great songwriter, and often spent time thinking about the lyrics to his songs. This one seemed to resonate with him more than most.

While still thinking about the lyrics, he exited the sports car he'd parked in the back lot of the building and made his way through the back door to the pub. Through the years, Mac's father had softened his stance on Mac becoming a cop and eventually was quite eager to tell acquaintances that Mac was a Camillus Police Officer. Any transgressions in the past were left unsaid, and an uneasy but peaceful truce had been forged amongst the father and the son. Mac still bore some weight on trying to make his father proud of him, and maybe this pushed him along to try and thrust himself harder and further in his chosen profession.

"Hiya, Speed!" James MacKenna said from behind the bar as Mac walked up the back hallway. James occasionally called Mac 'Speed' due to Mac's fast pace and sometimes impetuous speech.

"Hi Dad! What's good for lunch today?"

"You never just come down for lunch. What's up?"

"I've got a small break in my schedule. I don't have any overtime right at the moment, the kids are in school, and NMI is working, so I thought I'd stop by and grab some lunch."

"We're indebted to have your presence amongst us. The fish sandwich and fries are really good today if you want to try them,"

"That'd be great, Dad. Thanks! Who's cooking today?"

"Andy's back there today. Are you eating it here, or having it to go?"

"Here will be fine. Thanks."

"Okay, one order of fish and chips coming up," and with that James went into the kitchen while writing the order down on a green colored guest check.

Mac didn't want to tell his father of his real reason for coming down for lunch. As Mac learned in the DEA School, a relationship between a cop and a CI was very protective. If word leaked out, the CI could be placed in great harm by those on the wrong side of the law. And he wasn't sure if his father would approve of that relationship with one of his employees. Mac thought, not for the last time, that maybe it was better to ask for forgiveness than for permission.

Mac's dad was right—the fish was really good. It was served golden-brown in a red mesh basket with white wax paper and fries all around it. Mac had a Diet Coke and ate at the bar. The patrons were fewer than usual, and most of them sat at four by four tables on the other side of the bar.

After the lunch crowd started to dwindle, the day bartender came on and James came out from behind the bar.

"I've got your lunch, Speed. I'm off to the Elks Club to meet up with Charlie, Fritz and Buddy."

"Thanks, Dad, you didn't have to do that."

"Like I said, it was an honor for you to grace us with your presence. I'll see you later!"

"Thanks again, Dad. Say 'Hi' to Mom for me!"

"Will do," he said, and with that his father walked out the

266

front door, got into his maroon Chevy Suburban and drove down Main Street.

Mac finished his lunch, got off his barstool, picked up his empty red food basket and brought it into the kitchen to dispose of it. The barmaid was attending to other patrons and didn't notice Mac cleaning up his space and retreating to the back of the pub.

"Andy, that lunch was great!" Mac said as he walked between the double doors and threw away the wax paper putting the red basket into the kitchen sink.

"Hey, Mac!" Andy said by way of greeting as he was cleaning up from the lunch rush. Andy was wearing a white chef's shirt with black and white striped chef's pants and black sneakers. He was about the same age as Mac, a little shorter and darker, with longish black hair covered by a Yankees ball cap.

"You got a minute, Andy?"

"Sure Mac. Mind if I keep cleaning? I got to start doing prep for dinner soon as I'm done here."

"No worries. I remember you telling me that you were on parole. Do you mind me asking how much time you have left on it?"

"Yeah, that stupid drug charge. I've got two years left. I can't wait to get out from under it. Why do you ask?"

"Well, I was thinking that I might be able to help you shave some time off of it if you could help me with some drug work around town. That is, if you think it's a good idea, and of course, if you knew anyone dealing around here. I know you haven't been here that long."

Andy stopped working for a moment and looked at Mac with a blank expression on his face. Mac couldn't read what he might be thinking and just gave him some time to digest what was said.

"Sure, I know who's dealing around here. At least a couple of the dealers. How much time are you going to be taking off my sentence?"

"Well, that's up to how much work you put in and how successful we are. I'd have to set up a meeting with your parole officer, my detective sergeant, and ourselves to come to a firm understanding on what was expected from both sides, but I think it's doable if you really want to work some of it off."

"Well you know, Mac, I moved out this way because my girl wanted to move back home with our infant son. I'd do just about anything to get off parole. Let's set it up and see where it goes!"

Mac agreed. Two days later, the meeting was adjourned with Andy on board. The parole officer stipulated that if Andy got a good conviction on a dealer, he could get the judge to knock off half of his time. Andy was more than excited to get going. By that weekend, Mac was in plain clothes sitting in the back of an old red Town and Country Carpet cargo van listening to Andy on a wire that Det. Sgt. Cole had placed on him under his shirt. They kept a visual on him and the potential targets he met with at Camillus Mall.

Over the next several months, Andy was good to his word and had two separate dealers down for selling eight-balls (1/8 ounce) of powdered cocaine. He was also able to learn that their supplier was an ex West Genny lacrosse player who was currently attending Syracuse University on a scholarship. Coincidentally, it turned out to be NMI's first real boyfriend before Mac.

What secrets lie in a small community until someone starts looking with the proper tools. Andy was able to get the rest of his parole expunged due to his diligent narcotics work, and Mac continued to work angles with the other dealers to try and get to the ex-lax player who was supplying a lot of people with poison in the Town of Camillus. No one ever suspected Andy's involvement, and Mac's first foray into drug work and informants was a homerun. He was soon to learn, however, that not everyone he worked with was enthusiastic about his good fortune.

It is only through labor and painful effort, by grim energy and resolute courage, that we move on to better things.

- Theodore Roosevelt

CHAPTER
TWENTY-FOUR

With summer again in full swing, Mac was enjoying time with his children playing outside at Shove Park. They would get Happy Meals from McDonalds and eat them on the picnic tables and then go explore the stream and the trails through the woods beyond. Nature was fascinating, but the swing sets and the jungle gyms were the main focus for the children. Mac was always smiling watching them play without a care in the world for all of them.

Mac had enrolled the kids in Catholic Youth Organization

(C.Y.O.) basketball in the fall at Holy Family Church, and took them every Saturday morning. Joseph was still playing baseball in the spring and Mac enrolled the girls in ballet and dance in a dance studio in Camillus. Fall would soon be approaching, and Mac intended to sign up the kids for Pop Warner Football in Westvale. He found out that Joseph could play Mighty Mites and that both girls could cheer for his team. The children's mother was content to have him enroll the kids in extracurricular activities as long as Mac was paying for it, and of course, transporting them back and forth to practices and games.

Mac had played each of these sports as a kid, and thought the team building exercises, spirit, and comradery were invaluable. Yes, his mother even talked Mac and his brother Michael into taking tap dance lessons as kids, saying that dance would improve their coordination for sports. Turns out their mother was good friends with the neighborhood dance teacher, and she needed boys to play certain /male roles in her dance revue, so there might have been an alternative motive.

After four years at Camillus PD, Mac was comfortable with most aspects of the job. But he was starting to get a bit burnt out from working every overtime detail that came up, as well as trying to finish his associate degree from OCC. He wasn't as concerned about losing his job as he once had been. He had certainly proved that he was somewhat worthy to the PD after all. Life had transformed somehow, and he wasn't struggling as much about the apprehension of providing for his children.

He was now seeing a brighter future, with NMI as a big part of it.

Prior to joining the Camillus Police Department, Mac had worked minimum wage jobs and didn't have any vacation time to speak of. Whatever little time he did have he just would work another job to make more money. The security job paid better than the others, but Mac still never took any time off, seeing that it was his responsibility to make sure everything in the company ran smoothly. So, having an allotment of vacation, personal, and compensation days was a novel concept that Mac started using in earnest.

He and NMI had started taking day trips with the kids to Niagara Falls, Sea Breeze Amusement Park in Rochester, NY, Sylvan Beach, NY located on Oneida Lake, and Enchanted Forest Amusement Park in the Adirondacks just above Utica, NY. Eventually NMI planned out an Amtrak train trip to Walt Disney World in Orlando, FL with the children in tow. It was exhausting traveling by rail (especially without a sleeper cabin) but it was cost-effective enough where Mac could afford to do it, staying off-site in a cheap motel just outside the main gate.

When the children were with their mother Mac and NMI started taking time off to take brief trips by themselves as well. Traveling to Alexandria Bay, NY in the Thousand (1000) Islands Region was one of their first trips. The village is known locally as "A-Bay" and is populated by just about one-thousand residents but swells considerably during the spring and summer months. Tourism generates a large chunk of the revenue for the hamlet, as it sits on the northern border of New

York State, just across from the Canadian Border with the mighty Saint Lawrence River running between the two countries. The Saint Lawrence Seaway is a series of locks, canals and channels in Canada and the United States that permit large freighters from the Atlantic Ocean to transport goods through the Great Lakes of North America.

Throughout the Thousand Islands Region there are more than a thousand little islands (thus the name) that cover the expanse through the Saint Lawrence Seaway, from the eastern shore of Lake Ontario in Oswego, to Massena on the United States side, and Kingston to Cornwall on the Canadian side. A-Bay is billed as "The Heart of the Thousand Islands" for geographically being in the middle of that span.

Mac and NMI explored Boldt Castle on Heart Island, traveling by boat with Uncle Sam Boat Tours. The castle was built around the turn of the twentieth century by George Boldt for his beloved wife Louise. Mr. Boldt was a wealthy hotelier who most famously built the Waldorf Astoria in New York City. Tragically, the castle was never completed due to the unexpected death of Louise in 1904, and all work was stopped just before completion with George never returning to the island.

The castle eventually fell into disrepair due to the elements. It was eventually sold and used as a tourist attraction as to what grand splendor had held so much promise out of an affluent family's love affair. Eventually the poor condition of Boldt Castle became too much, and the island property was handed over to the Thousand Islands Bridge Authority (TIBA) in the late seventies for restoration and preservation.

"It's beautiful here!" NMI said, as they walked on the green grassy island by the stone Arch near the boathouse.

The sky was a cloudless blue and a gentle wind came off the river as the two walked around and admired the castle in the dazzling sunshine. The river itself shimmered like diamonds on the water's crest around the ring of the isle. It was quite the site on this summer's day.

"I know. Can you imagine if they had finished this? It would have been amazing!" Mac answered.

Police work seemed so far away. Mac was content to enjoy this time with a woman he loved so much, and to put it all aside and just enjoy this space in time. NMI reached for his hand as they strolled through the castle on their own, admiring the stone architecture and carvings. They had been together for a while now and Mac was trying to work out the next step in his head about their relationship. Being married the first time had turned out to be a catastrophe. He was forever ashamed for being divorced, and the bad sting it had left on him, but he did truly love NMI. And at that moment Mac started to formulate future plans so that they could be together.

One warm July evening on NMI's birthday, Mac did indeed propose while taking a dinner cruise on Onondaga Lake. Mac had brought his brother Michael along as a ruse, so NMI wouldn't expect the gesture. They celebrated with all their friends later on that night at Molly Malone's.

In due course they ended up taking trips by themselves to the New England area after that. Visiting Boston, Cape Cod, and Nantucket Island, which were all amazing places, but A-Bay would always hold a special place in Mac's heart, due in part to the great show of George Boldt's expression of love of for his wife Louise.

The man who loves other countries as much as his own stands on a level with the man who loves other women as much as he loves his own wife.

- **Theodore Roosevelt**

CHAPTER
TWENTY-FIVE

Mac was back at work on A-Watch and refreshed from taking some time off with his children and his fiancé over the spring and summer months. Summer still had some time left and the air was still hot and humid at night as he patrolled the town on this dark starless night. Tonight, Mac was patrolling with a new part-time police officer who had started working part-time at the Village of Jordan Police Department the previous year.

Hogan Draper was his name, he was several years older

than Mac, on the tall side, slight of build and resembled a young Ichabod Crane. He seemed nice enough at first blush. Hogan had been filling in, on and off, on the midnight shift to supplement time off by the full-time cops for their summer vacations.

Since Mac was senior, and Hogan was brand new to Camillus PD and fairly new at police work all together, he was sliding by most of Hogan's calls to make sure he didn't need any help, or to answer any questions he may have during the course of the shift. Sgt. Jake Smith had asked Mac to look out for Hogan seeing that there were no supervisors on A-Watch, and Mac was doing his best not to let the sergeant down.

During the past several weeks he had introduced Hogan on-shift to Deputy Kevin Charm from the sheriff's department, Officer Kevin "Scooby" Geertzen from Geddes PD, troopers Roxy McCall and Gerald Hair, and EMTs Donna Johnson and Vaughn McCabe from WAVES. Hogan seemed to get along with everyone, but Mac's little voice was telling him that everything may not be as it seemed. Mac tried to brush it off as Camillus PD was a small department and they really didn't get that many new cops coming aboard, and that this was just an anomaly.

On this night Hogan was patrolling the western part of the town and was assigned as Unit #3102A. Mac had the eastern side and was working as Unit #3101A. The radio air traffic was kind of slow on Channel Four and Mac was conducting property checks on the businesses on West Genesee St. in Fairmount.

"Unit #3102A to dispatch...copy a vehicle and traffic stop

on New York registration Boy Frank Charles 2138...BFC-2138...it should show on a blue four door Honda...occupied by one," Hogan called out over the police radio.

"Unit #3102A copy...your location?" Felicity Flynn acknowledged from the MRD Center.

"Unit #3102A...Route 5 just before Ike Dixon Drive," Hogan responded.

Hogan sounded fine on the radio although he should have given his location to Felicity in his first transmission. Just a rookie mistake which Mac made his fair share of when he was first learning. Hogan liked doing V&T stops which Mac knew the chief steered new cops away from, but everyone's different on how they take direction. He didn't appear to be in distress, so Mac continued on with his property checks.

A few minutes later, "Unit #3102A to dispatch...can you have Unit #3101A start this way with an Alco-sensor?" Hogan asked.

Before Felicity could key up her mic Mac answered, "Unit #3101A en route from Fairmount Four Corners."

Felicity acknowledged Mac's response, "Unit #3101A...0007 hours."

Mac started making his way west knowing that Hogan had a possible impaired driver. DWI's weren't all that uncommon in Camillus on the midnight shift. Mac had made a number of NYS VTL 1192 arrest working primarily A-Watch since starting school full-time. He most often though would take the affected driver's home and have their cars towed for the $75 towing fee placed upon them by the tow companies. Most of Mac's encounters with people driving slightly over the legal limit were that of town residents who admitted right away that they may have over imbibed without knowing it. Mac didn't mind taking them home and police officers did have a lot of discretion on how to handle simple stops involving these subjects. However, if the subject was combative, unruly, way over-served and was clearly not going to learn a lesson from some compassion from the police, Mac would gladly take their freedom and lock them up. If the drivers were involved in accidents, that automatically sealed their fate with a DWI charge.

Mac arrived approximately five minutes later shielding his eyes from the overhead emergency lights as he parked his car on the Route 5 shoulder behind Hogan's marked car. Traffic was non-existent as Mac exited his marked car and made his way to the driver's window of Unit #3102A.

"Hi Mac! She's totally boxed. You got the Alco-sensor for me? Hogan asked.

"I got it out of the glove box and put it in my pocket. How'd she do with the field sobriety tests?"

"I haven't given them to her yet, but I know she's drunk."

"Well, we still have to give them to her first and then the Alco-Sensor test if she fails. How many drinks did she say she had?"

"She said she had two. You believe that...the proverbial

two!"

"Did she say where she was coming from?" Mac asked.

"Yeah, she's a nurse at Community. She said she worked twelve hours and then stopped at Kelley's on Onondaga Hill."

Mac cringed inside a little. Cops worked hand-in-hand with doctors and nurses, and usually they would get a little bit of courtesy if warranted, but this wasn't his stop and that was up to Hogan.

"Okay, let's get her out and you can administer the test. I'll stand back and watch," Mac responded.

"Okay Mac, I got this!" Hogan said as he got out of his patrol vehicle and made his way to the blue Honda. Once there, opening the driver's door and asking the driver to step out and walk with him between her car and the patrol car, protecting them from any potential vehicle traffic.

Mac stood just to the rear of the passenger headlights from Unit #3102. He was mostly in the shadows with only the red and white emergency lights lighting up his ghostly figure intermittently, as he stood near the white fog line on the side of the road and observed the process.

Hogan asked the middle-aged nurse to recite the alphabet (without singing it) beginning with the letter "J". He then asked her to walk on the fog line ten steps up, turn, and take eight steps back, heel to toe. Hogan then had her stand on one foot with the other foot six inches off the ground and count to ten, with her arms remaining by her side. He then finally had her close her eyes and on direction take a hand indicated and touch the tip of her nose with the index finger of that hand.

Mac watched as the nurse progressed through the tests, and according to Mac's perception, pass each one. She was a little unsteady on the raised foot six inches off the ground, but that could've been because they were standing on a slight hill, or that she was tired from a long day at work. It certainly did not look alcohol induced. Adding to Mac's assumptions, her uniform was not disheveled, her speech was clear, and her eyes weren't glassy.

After Hogan got done, he had the nurse lean up against her vehicle and he came back to where Mac was standing by the patrol car. "You see. She's off. I knew she was drunk!"

"Hogan, I think she's a little tired. From what I saw I wouldn't say that she flunked the field sobriety tests," Mac said.

"She was hesitant on the ABC's and she was wobbly on the other stuff. Can you give her the Alco-Sensor now?"

"Um...yeah. But I wouldn't get my hopes up. She doesn't look intoxicated to me."

Mac moved forward and introduced himself to the nurse. He described the Alco-Sensor as being a pre-screening device for DWI and asked her to take it. The nurse agreed and when Mac asked her to, she placed her lips around the clear disposable tube on top of the machine (which was slightly bigger than a pack of cigarettes) and had her continue to blow out air out of her lungs, as she made a whistling sound out the other end of the tube, until he told her to stop.

Mac then took it away from her mouth as he pushed the READ button on the device. The LED numeral lights at first didn't read anything but .00 % Blood Alcohol Content (BAC). Eventually, very slowly, the numbers started to creep up. When they stopped at .04 % BAC Mac first showed Hogan and then the nurse.

Mac told the nurse "Please wait here. We'll be right back." And he turned and walked to the rear of Hogan's patrol vehicle with Hogan in tow.

"Sorry, Hogan. I tried to tell you she wasn't intoxicated," Mac said once they were out of earshot of the nurse. At the time, a 0.1 % BAC or above was the classification of legally intoxicated in New York State.

"I'm sure she's on the way up Mac. I'm going to arrest her for common law DWI and you can run the Breathalyzer Test when we get back to the station and it will confirm my arrest," Hogan said.

Mac was conflicted. He wasn't a supervisor and technically couldn't tell Hogan not to undergo an arrest. He was trying to mentor Hogan and follow up with Sergeants Smith's guidance to look over him, but Hogan wasn't having any of it. Mac suspected that Hogan was trying to justify a full-time position for himself with Camillus PD, but he was going about it entirely the wrong way. Mac also slightly suspected that maybe Hogan had an inferiority complex and took delight in lording over the public. Either way Mac didn't feel right about the whole thing.

Before Mac could respond, Hogan went back to the nurse, placed her in handcuffs and then put her in the rear of his patrol vehicle. Mac was just slightly nodding his head back and forth in a disapproving way when Hogan looked at him. Hogan called for a hook for the nurse's vehicle and transported her back to the station to start the paperwork, while Mac waited for the tow truck to show up. Mac being a Breathalyzer Test Operator (BTO) he would be required to run the Breathalyzer test within two hours of the arrest, and Hogan was betting the more time that he waited that the test would be above .10 % BAC.

Jimmy Yeager from Pete Kitt's Towing showed up about thirty minutes later. Mac turned the nurse's vehicle over to him and started back to the station. When he got there Hogan had already filled out the arrest form and was in the process of fingerprinting her in the same room where the Breathalyzer was. Mac told him that he was ready anytime Hogan was, and he went on the other side of the partition to put his clipboard down and waited to be summoned.

Approximately ten minutes later Hogan had finished processing the nurse and stated that they were ready for the Breathalyzer. Mac resurfaced and set up the Breathalyzer as required by New York State, making sure everything was satisfactory. He then had the nurse come over to the machine which looked more like a science experiment than a state-of-the-art law enforcement alcohol detection tool and administered the test to her.

When she had finished expunging the gases from her lungs Mac dialed the proper knobs until they revealed the results. BAC was again confirmed at .04 % BAC. Hogan observed the findings over Mac's shoulder and then led the nurse back to the holding bench where suspects were detained.

Hogan came back as Mac was shutting down the Breathalyzer. He lowered his voice and said, "Dial a drunk?"

What Hogan said to Mac was incredulous. 'Dial-a-Drunk' was a fantastical phrase that was rumored to be what troopers did to make so many DWI arrest. The theory behind it was that the BTO would just simply turn up the knobs to achieve the higher reading than what was actually attained by the driver, resulting in a DWI charge, where in fact there wasn't one. This was in fact patently not true about the New York State Police. The phrase was used in jest by cops and only amongst themselves.

Mac thought he must've misheard Hogan and asked, "What did you say?"

Again, Hogan replied with, "Dial a drunk? You know, redo the results so that she's over the limit."

Mac was stunned. He'd been a cop now for about four years and no one had ever asked him to do something so wide of the mark. In essence of the law, Hogan was asking him to commit perjury and violate his oath to defend and protect the constitution of the United States, let alone violate someone's constitutional rights as a citizen who hadn't done anything wrong. Mac could barely speak. The only word he could muster to say was pierced with anger, "No."

Mac composed himself, told Hogan to unarrest the nurse, call Pete Kitt's and get her vehicle released, and not least of all, if not the most important, apologize to her. Mac was beside himself. He'd never been so blindsided by anyone who was supposed to be as principled in carrying out the law as he was. He wanted to call Twist, Kevin Charm or Orsen Alvey, but they were all off shift and it was much too late to wake them up. Mac left the station and drove around aimlessly for the rest of the night. He was trying to figure out on how to deal with Hogan's blatant disregard for the law. It was a position he never foresaw for himself. Mac honestly thought that everyone that wore the badge was forthright, honest, and unwavering in the protection of those who couldn't protect themselves.

When Mac came back to the station Hogan was waiting for him in the parking lot.

"Mac, I was wrong. Can we just keep this between us? I should have listened to you. I don't want to get in trouble. You've got to help me out." Mac was too tired to have that conversation right then. All he could say to Hogan was, "I'll let you know." And with that Mac climbed up the stairs to the locker room and changed into his civilian clothes. In hindsight, Mac should've reported him to Sergeant Smith or Lieutenant Johnson that very morning.

Mac had to double back and be in at 3:30 PM for an overtime shift at the mall. He had barely gotten enough sleep during the day and was still trying to process what Hogan had done the night before, when Lt. Johnson met him on the first landing to the stairs, just outside the patrol office.

"Mac, I need to see you in my office," Lt. Johnson said as he went into the administrative door walking back to his workplace.

Mac figured that the nurse complained, and that Hogan was being fired. He couldn't have been more wrong.

"Mac come in and close the door."

Mac took the sole seat across from the seated lieutenant.

"Mac I've received a complaint from Hogan Draper that he has a serious personality conflict with you, and that he has asked not to be put on the same shift as you in the future."

For the second time in just about twelve hours Mac was dumbfounded. He literally sat there with his mouth open. Mac's mind couldn't catch up with what was going on in the lieutenant's office. Finally, he was able to form somewhat of a cohesive sentence, "Lieutenant... Hogan made a bad arrest last night and I fixed it as best I could."

"That's not the story I'm getting from Hogan. He says you're caustic to people on the midnight shift, that your officer safety precautions are lacking, and that everything came to a head last night when you gave him bad advice on a DWI arrest."

Mac could feel his blood starting to go beyond the boiling point. He went from confused to ballistic in a nanosecond.

"Max that's bullshit and you know it. I've been here a long

time and I've always tried to do the right thing. This kid just tried to set up a nurse from Community on a DWI charge and I wouldn't let him. For Christ's sake, he asked me to perjure myself!" Mac exploded.

"Officer, you will address me by my rank, and you will never raise your voice to me!" Johnson shouted back. "Now get out of my office. I'm done with you. Any other complaints and I'm putting you on the beach!"

Mac composed himself as best he could. He could feel tears forming at the corner of his eyes he was so angry. He stood up and filed out of the office as quick as he could. Mac got to his locker upstairs and slammed the metal door open as hard as he could. He'd never felt so betrayed, and so unjustifiably judged.

This wouldn't be the last run in with Lieutenant Johnson over something that was so obviously misplaced blame. The bias that Johnson had towards Mac's dad was abundantly clear now, but it was the last time he would ever give a misguided cop the benefit of a doubt. Mac would never again work with Hogan, but he had the pleasure of giving him a lifelong incurable nick name known by all other cops in Onondaga County as "Dial-A-Drunk" Draper.

The most important single ingredient in the formula of success is knowing how to get along with people.

- Theodore Roosevelt

CHAPTER

TWENTY-SIX

Mac regrouped enough to foster another idea to help him be a better cop. There were always burglary complaints coming in through the road patrol that were assigned to Detective Sergeant Billy Cole to sort through and decide if they were viable enough for follow-up investigation. Cole couldn't keep up with the number of burglary reports that far outweighed the hours he had available each day, along with his other duties as with following up on all felony complaints, crimes against persons, as well as trying to stay apprised of the narcotics tips that came in.

Mac saw Cole in the parking lot as he was coming in to fill

a C-Watch shift position during the week.

"Hey Sarge! Got a moment?" Mac asked as he was getting freshly dry-cleaned uniforms out the back seat of the Camaro.

"Sure Mac. What's on your mind?"

"I've been taking burglary reports while filling in on C-Watch and was wondering if you'd mind if I followed them up during the day on my own time. I wouldn't put in a slip for overtime unless I made a decent amount of headway with them. Do you think that would work out for you?"

Cole gave it a little thought, rubbing his cheek as he worked through it in his head. "I'm pretty sure I can get that by the chief. I'm not going to ask Johnson. I've heard the rumors of how he's been dogging you. Draper is a boot licking piece of shit and he should've been fired. Everyone knows it and Johnson has been keeping the chief in the dark over it. Sure, I'll run it by the chief and let you know. Keep your chin up!"

And with that Cole got into his take-home company ride and scooted out of the parking lot.

A few days later Mac got an inter-departmental memo in his work mailbox from Cole. It formally gave Mac the go ahead to start doing follow-ups of his burglaries on his own time. Mac couldn't help but smile.

Later that week Mac came in on his day off and sorted through the open burglary cases he had taken in the last several weeks. He chose the ones with no physical evidence. No fingerprints, leads, or witnesses. Sgt. Cole could easily solve the others where there were viable leads, Mac wanted to work on the ones that fell through the cracks and therefore would most likely not be solved without his follow-up work.

Mac decided to start with a day-time burglary that occurred less than a week ago at the Meyers' residence on Maxwell Street in the village. Mac had been on thirds and taken the report shortly after the shift started. The residence was a white single-family Cape Cod dwelling built just after World War II in a neatly nestled neighborhood in the village of Camillus. The family who lived there were a married couple with two teenage children. Both parents worked during the day and the children stayed with relatives in another neighborhood in the village while they weren't in school.

On the original neighborhood canvass, the surrounding neighbors had not been home and therefore Mac had not learned anything worthwhile to add to the investigative report. The proceeds of the burglary were small items like jewelry and emergency cash that the parents kept secreted in their bedroom. The house was not ransacked, and nothing had been damaged in the break-in. Entry appeared to have been by an open downstairs bathroom window and egress was most likely out the back door to the attached garage. All in all, it was a pretty straight forward burglary for the Town of Camillus.

Mac had learned in the police academy that most residential burglars were opportunist that avoided confrontation with the public. They were most likely in their teens or early twenties and had a familiarity of the neighborhood or more specifically of the target house. Consequently, Mac knew he had to revisit the neighborhood and go knock on doors again. It was the most basic principle to solving these types of crimes and it just involved leg work and time.

Although Det. Sgt. Cole didn't set the parameters for how Mac should work the case, he decided that he would follow Cole's example. Mac had come to work in a dark blue short-sleeve polo shirt, tan khakis, and brown dress shoes. He wore his badge on his right side just in front of his holstered duty weapon, which was secured to his dress belt, with his loose silver handcuffs dangling off the belt just behind the gun.

Like most cops, Mac had visions of working investigations as a detective. Unfortunately, Camillus PD only had Det. Sgt. Cole in that position. It was rumored that the department may create another position, but more than likely that would be filled by seniority. Mac had four years on the job at this point and really wanted the position, however there were many cops in front of him that wanted the same thing.

At this time though it appeared that Mac was the only patrolman being proactive about conducting investigations at Camillus PD. Mac had his on-going drug investigations and was now delving into solving crimes against property. It really was where his heart was, but he also knew he had to wait his turn. In the meantime, he could gain invaluable experience by trying it out on his own. Hopefully if nothing else the residents of the town would reap any benefits Mac made during his foray into these areas.

Mac poked his head in with Betty Masters as she sat at her desk and chatted for a few minutes. He wanted someone to know that he was working the follow-up detail just in case something came up. Betty listened to the MRD police radio while sitting in the office and every now and then used the base unit (KVD-648) for contacting officers out on the road to forward messages that came in through the phone to the department.

Grabbing keys to an old unmarked gray Dodge Diplomat, Mac made his way out to the parking lot and put his file on the burglary and his clipboard of forms into the front passenger seat of the police car. He started it up, rolled down the windows and listened to the police chatter on the radio, as he made his way out of the parking lot, onto Male Ave. and then took a right onto West Genesee Street for the five-minute ride down to the Village of Camillus.

Bassey was outside the Fairmount Fire Department washing his chief's truck as Mac rounded the corner and continued westbound on this warm sunny day. They both waved at each other as Mac's mind went to figuring out how the suspect(s) had navigated the burglary on that day and where they might've gone after they committed it. Mac was intrigued on how to get inside someone's head to help solve the crime, and spent the time traveling down the road to explore other possibilities of the burglary.

Mac arrived on Maxwell Road in his concealed identity police vehicle, and not for the first time took a look around. It was an older peaceful neighborhood with mostly honest, blue-collar families who worked during the day. The forty or so homes were close together and most parcels looked to be quarter acre plots of land. Houses were equally spread apart from one another and were mostly one car garaged and under one-thousand square feet of livable space beneath the roofs.

As Mac sat in his car taking in the scenery, he observed an elderly lady in his rearview mirror just coming out of her house on First Street carrying a little dog in her arms. When she got to her front yard, she gently put the brown and black ball of fur on all four feet in the grass.

Mac hadn't found anybody home on his first neighborhood canvass and decided she was a viable first point of contact. He exited the unwrapped police car carrying his patrol box clipboard and slowly made his way across First Street to where the woman was monitoring her pet.

"Good morning, I'm Officer Patrick MacKenna from the Camillus Police Department," Mac said as his feet touched the proprietor's driveway.

The woman was a little startled as was her dog, who started to yap in defense of her human. "Good morning. I'm sorry I didn't see you pull up."

"Sorry about that. I'm parked in that gray car over by Glen Meyers place. The family had a burglary last week, on Thursday, during the day. I'm asking neighbors if they saw anything or anyone unusual in the area last week."

"Well, I'm not sure, let me see. Last Thursday? Hmm…" The lady seemed to consider her recollection before verbalizing it for Mac. Mac was content to wait and reached down and gave the dog a little scratch under the chin. The dog seemed relaxed now that her owner was conversing with Mac in a gentle tone.

"I'll tell you what. I'm retired and I'm home a lot, but I didn't see anyone break into any homes. Although, now that I think about it, I play Bridge on Thursday's at noon and when I came home around 2:00 PM I saw Stephen O'Reilly standing on the corner of First and Maxwell, across from my house. Now that you mention it, Stephen did seem strange. Once he saw me, he didn't wave. He just turned around and started walking down Maxwell past the Meyers place."

"Does he live on Maxwell?" Mac inquired.

"No, no, he lives with his mother on North Street. I hardly ever see him down here. Usually when I see him it's at the corner of Main Street and North Street outside the pizza shop."

"Are you sure it was him?"

"Yeah, I'm pretty sure. I taught his mother Maureen, science at the middle school. I see her every now and again in the village and up at Camillus Mall. She's introduced me to him since he was a baby."

"About how old would you say he is now?" Mac asked.

"Oh, I'd say about fourteen. He's a good kid, but some of the kids he hangs around with at the pizza shop are older and may not be as nice as he is."

"You've been quite helpful…I'm sorry, I never asked for your name."

"Becky Mattli. I've lived in the village my whole life and we usually don't have any problems down here. Is it something I should be worried about?"

"No, Ms. Mattli. I suspect it was just kids. Stephen may have seen something that may help, but I wouldn't be worried. However, if you do see anything or anyone out of place please call the police department and let us know. Plus, your canine companion would keep most people up to no good away," Mac said with a flash of a smile and another pat for the pooch.

Mac got the rest of Ms. Mattli's pertinent information for the report and said goodbye. He went back to the station and ran Stephen's name through the database and came up empty. Mac looked up the family's address in the street guide and saw they lived at 43 North Street. Mac packed up his report pad, clipboard and headed out again to the unmarked car in the parking lot to once again make the five-minute ride back to the village.

Mac was more familiar with this part of the village. His father had owned 55 Main Street for a long time and leased it out as the Black Horse Tavern for years, before moving the original Mac Kenna's Pub, where Mac had worked for his father, from around the corner on Elm Street to the Main Street location, where it currently sat. Main Street in the Village of Camillus is actually West Genesee Street, but the name changes for about four or five blocks while it runs through the business district of the village. There are the usual small businesses you would find in any small hamlet, hairdressers, barbers, flower shops, restaurants and inns, a saddlery shop, and a small local grocery store, as well as a bank, churches, and a post office.

Mac Kenna's Pub was just about across the street from Main Street and North Street, and just a little east and on the opposite side of the street from the pizza shop. As Mac made the turn from Main Street onto North Street, he could see four or five teenage kids hanging out by the pizza shop. He thought the best thing to do was contact Stephen's parents and feel out if he had any involvement in the burglary down the street before talking to the kids on the corner.

Mac parked on the side of the street, as most of the houses on North Street didn't have driveways. The homes were similar in construction and size as the ones on Maxwell street although, the biggest difference was that North Street was a long, busier side street set on an incline going away from the village center.

As he got out of his vehicle a middle-aged woman with red hair was just pulling up to the same address. Mac waited to see if she indeed was going to 43 North Street, and she was. As he started going up the cement steps with a wrought iron rail to the house after her, he stated, "Excuse me, Mrs. O'Reilly?"

"Yes?" She said as she turned around with a brown paper sack of groceries in her arms.

Mac explained to Maureen he was investigating a burglary in the village and that her son Stephen may have been in the area and maybe he could assist in his investigation. Maureen took this in and while shifting the weight of the sack in her arms, blew a red ringlet out of one of her eyes and said, "You'd better come in officer. This may take a while," as she led the way up the rest of the stairs and unlocked the front door to her home.

Maureen told Mac they could talk in the kitchen as she put her groceries away. She went on to explain that she was a single mom and Stephen was her only son. Maureen said her husband moved out about two years ago and Stephen had lost direction without having a father figure around.

"He's a really good kid. He rarely asks for anything. Stephen knows I work hard, and we really don't have a lot of money, but he never complains. Lately he's been hanging out with some older boys at the end of the street before I get home. Matter of fact, he's there right now. I passed him and gave him a wave just before I saw you.

Anyway, one of the kids is named Vernon. Vernon Simonds. He's been in trouble before. I'm not keen on Stephen hanging around with him and I've told him so, but when I'm not around I know they're probably still hanging out."

"How old is Vernon?" Mac asked.

"I'm pretty sure he's sixteen. His family lives around the corner on Elderkin."

"Maureen, is there any chance you could go and get Stephen so I can talk to him? If he's a good kid like you say, I think that we can probably work this out right here. I won't have to bring him to the station, and with your permission, I'll ask him some questions to try and figure this out right now."

"Oh, he is a good kid. You'll see. Just give me a moment and I'll walk down and bring him back up," and with that she put the last item in the cupboard and walked back out the front door.

Mac was left alone in the kitchen and took in the environment. It was a tidy space that smelled of clove and other spices. There were no dishes in the sink and no clutter on the counters. The modest wooden kitchen table was set with four placemats with a metal napkin holder in the middle. Unopened mail was set neatly on the counter by the house phone.

Approximately five minutes later Maureen walked in with Stephen. Stephen was dressed like a skateboarder, longish brown hair, slender build, flannel shirt, ripped jeans and black Ked sneakers. "I've told him why you're here officer," Maureen said as she came in and sat down at the head of the table. "Please sit," she said to Mac and then she turned and looked at Stephen and eyed him into one of the other seats at the table.

Mac took a seat as Stephen was pulling back the chair to get into his. "Hi, Stephen. I'm Officer Patrick MacKenna from the Camillus Police Department. I've spoken to your mom about you helping me with a burglary investigation I'm working on. She told me you're a good kid and that you'd be happy to help me with it."

Stephen had a fidgety worried look on his face. His blue

eyes would dart back and forth between Mac and his mother as Mac spoke. "Um, yeah. If I can. I'll help."

"Okay, great! Last Thursday during the day we had a burglary over on Maxwell Street. Some people saw you in the area at the time and I'm hoping that you can give me some information."

Stephen looked down and away but didn't say anything. After a while, Maureen glanced at Mac and he knew by her look that her mothers' intuition was telling her that her son knew something. "Stephen, I told Officer MacKenna that you would help in any way possible. You should tell him what you know. It'll only get worse if you don't cooperate now."

Stephen looked up with a tear in his eye and said, "I'm sorry mom. I really didn't do anything that bad. I mean I know it was wrong, but I didn't go in the house. I just stood outside and watched as Vern went in. He said that the kid who lived there owed him money. When he came back out with jewelry, I knew he lied to me. I'm sorry mom."

Maureen looked at Stephen with a visible disappointment on her face and a tear of her own in her eye.

"Stephen you did the right thing by telling me this. Was there anybody else involved? What did Vernon do with the jewelry and the money?" Mac asked.

"He kept the jewelry and most of the money. He gave me ten dollars. I didn't know what to do with it. It's still in my sock drawer rolled up in one of my socks. Nobody else was involved.

Vern put the rings and necklaces under his mattress. I'm not sure what he's going to do with them."

"When was the last time you saw the jewelry and the money?"

"Today. We went over to his house to drink some soda and he showed me where he hid them. His parents don't know. They'd kill him if they did. His father beats the shit out of him. Sorry mom. His father hits him a lot."

"Okay. If you give me a written statement I can try and get the money and the jewelry back. Technically, you were a look-out, an accessory to the burglary, but with you being forthcoming with cooperation I can write it up so you can stay out of trouble. This time. If you do anything else in the future, I can't help you and you most certainly will get arrested."

"Dang, I'm sorry and there won't be a next time, but I don't want to get Vern in trouble," Stephen said.

"Well Stephen, Vernon is already in trouble. This way I can mitigate it a little by getting the victims property back and giving them a little peace of mind that we know who did it. That's more important at this time," Mac said.

Stephen looked at his mother, who nodded the affirmative, and he said, "Okay. Let me get the money from my room first."

Stephen left the kitchen and Maureen looked at Mac and mouthed the words, "Thank you!"

Stephen returned with the ten-dollar bill and gave it to Mac. He then gave Mac an affidavit as to what he first told him about the burglary and the whereabouts of the missing currency and jewelry. Mac left Stephen and his mother on their front steps as he went back to the station to apply for a warrant on Vernon Simonds's bedroom for the stolen property.

Mac was typing up the warrant and researching Vernon Simonds at the counter in the Patrol Office when Twist and Wide-Body came in to start their shift on C-Watch.

"Hey Moe! Are you a defective now?" Wide-Body cracked as he walked by.

Mac ignored him as he concentrated on his work, but he could tell over the past month or so, while he was working with Detective Sergeant Cole on the narcotic investigations and now this, that they were becoming jealous to a certain degree. Mac understood there was a pecking order at the PD but didn't comprehend their attitudes toward him. Anybody could do what he was doing, they just chose not to. Twist had always been a good friend, but academy mates were always thicker than thieves, and Mac thought that Wide-Body was the one leading the sentiment against Mac at the PD about conducting collateral investigations.

Mac obtained the search warrant from a local town magistrate. He then went to the Simond's residence located at 23 Elderkin Ave. and served the warrant on Mr. and Mrs. Simond, who were cooperative. Vernon was home, and after Mac located all the jewelry and most of the money under his mattress, he confessed to committing the burglary and was taken into custody, processed, and released back to his parents after Mac arraigned him in front of the same judge who signed the search warrant.

The Meyers' were excited that Mac recovered their property and solved the crime. Detective Sergeant Billy Cole was enthralled that on Mac's first foray into their little venture he had brought the burglary to a successful conclusion. Subsequently, Mac had a sense of accomplishment that he could do a capable investigation, but was left with some pause that his co-workers weren't as pleased for him as he thought they would be. Regrettably, Mac was unknowingly heading on a collision course with them that would once again put him squarely in Lieutenant Max Johnson's crosshairs.

It is hard to fail, but it is worse never to have tried to succeed

- Theodore Roosevelt

CHAPTER

TWENTY-SEVEN

Mac continued to work the odd burglaries that he came across in his own time and solved some other ones too. The tension with the other cops dissipated as they kept up their routine of going out to Molly Malone's once a week after C-Watch, but Mac was spending more time with NMI and after four years it seemed like things were changing.

Twist had just bought a house and moved out of the apartment with Mac. He also put in a lateral transfer request to go to the sheriff's department. New part-timers were being hired in lieu of the anticipation that they would become full-time upon retirements or transfers. Connor Coke was getting restless in his routine at the PD and was expressing his need to be an entrepreneur in one way or another. The close family group that Mac had started his law enforcement career was shifting. Evolution is expected in one's life, but when it comes it is still unsettling just the same.

The New York State Fair is the unofficial end to summer in Central New York. People come from all over the state, as well as all over the country to attend its annual gathering. The Fair is a ten-day event on 375 acres in the Town of Geddes that showcases agriculture, technology, education and entertainment. It has a dirt racetrack for the racing of cars and horses, two outside concert venues for nationally known acts, buildings that contain cows, horses, sheep, pigs, and rabbits to just to name a few. A midway that has all sorts of carnival rides and games, and vendor booths and concession stands' that pop up all over the expanse of the property for all kinds of food and drink.

Twist had organized a trip to the Fair on a rare Sunday afternoon when Mac didn't have his children. It was intended to cheer up Wide-Body who was going through a messy divorce from his wife. Twist thought a venture to the annual event might take Wide-Body's mind off his impending marital dissolution. Even though Wide-Body didn't have kids the divorce was hitting him hard. Mac knew through experience that once the lawyers got started it would create a toxic environment for all involved.

Wide-Body rarely came out drinking with the other cops to Molly Malone's and Mac only saw him have some beers at the yearly police picnic that was held jointly with Geddes PD. It was more of a family setting where there was more food than alcoholic drinks served, and the competing PD's would participate in a softball game as the main event.

Even so, Mac usually saw Wide-Body go from happy to brooding as the day went on. Most cops could handle their drinking and it wasn't an issue, but some cops, just like ordinary people, couldn't handle their booze. Mac suspected that's why Wide-Body didn't hang out with the rest of them on the regular.

Twist also invited Orsen Avery from the state and they all agreed to meet at noon that Sunday. Twist would drive the trio to the next town over for the Fair in his new Chevy Blazer. It was a stellar day with highs predicted to be in the upper seventies with no chance of rain as Mac pulled into the parking lot of the PD. Twist, Orsen and Wide-Body were already there waiting outside Twist's truck.

"It's about time Moe. We're burning daylight. Let's go!" Twist said as Mac climbed out of his Camaro.

"All right Jorge. Give me a second. It was a long shift last night and I barely got any sleep," Mac retorted, as he walked across the paved parking area. He still felt like he was sleep walking as he got into the SUV.

"Morning Carl! Morning Orsen!" Mac said turning towards them as they sat in the rear seat.

"Hey Mac!" Orsen said.

"Technically it's afternoon Patrick," Wide-Body responded.

"Yeah, I know, but I'm still trying to wake up. What's on the agenda today?"

"I thought we'd catch the Beach Boys at the grandstand at four. It should be a pretty good show," Twist said.

"Sounds good to me Twist. Do you think we can get something to eat when we get there? I haven't had a thing to eat and I'm starving," Mac said.

"I could go for food also," Wide-Body added.

"Me too!" Orsen chimed in.

"Of course, That's the best part of the Fair! The food! Then of course we can have a few pops after that," Twist said, referring to beers.

And with that they were off for the ten-minute ride to the fairgrounds. Mac pulled his Red Sox hat down over his sun-glassed eyes as he rested on the ride over. They talked about rumors about who may be promoted at the PD, who may get the other pending detective position, about how the new part-timers were doing, about Twist's progress getting into the sheriff's department, and finally Orsen spoke up about a new state contract that would pay the troopers a healthy wage. Cops could gossip like old ladies and anyone else listening in wouldn't know the difference between the two.

Once inside the main parking area Twist made his way to the inner security perimeter where he showed his badge. He told security that they we're going back to the trooper's barracks. Orsen had advised that there was always extra police parking below the seating for the grandstand for cops only, and Twist repeated the process of showing his badge to the female trooper who was guarding the area when they arrived. She waved them in, and everyone told her thank you as they exited the vehicle and made their way for the long walk across the infield to the midway for some sustenance.

Upon walking underneath, the tunnel from the infield the foursome arrived at the bottom part of the midway to the fairgrounds. There a dunk-tank sat where a clown in face paint parked himself on a wooden bench behind the cage and above the water. Using a microphone and a loudspeaker, the clown insulted fairgoers as they walked by. Hoping to elicit a visceral response from the victim to retaliate for the affront, by buying three baseballs for two dollars and throwing them at a pie plate target in the hopes of submerging the offensive prankster. They watched as the clown insulted just about everyone who was unfortunate enough to cross in front of his gaze. Sometimes the rudeness worked, and balls were purchased, and attempts were made to silence the comedian, but more often than not, the clown remained high and dry and the challenger walked away more ashamed than when he started his retaliation.

The cops continued on and saw endless games of chance as they walked to the top of the midway. There was the ring-toss the bottle game, lob the ping-pong ball into the goldfish bowls game, stand the bottle upright with a pole and rubber circle attached to a string, fire an automatic B-B gun to try and shoot out a red star on a playing card, pop balloons with darts, and shoot a basketball into a hoop, to name a some of the games. They were scattered all along the Midway between the carnival rides.

The rides themselves were the usual for a field day event. The Bumper Cars, Fun Slide where you rode down a giant yellow chute in a brown burlap sack, the red colored Tilt-A-Wheel, the Himalayan, the Enterprise, the Flying Swings, and of course the Ferris wheel.

The best part of the Fair though, besides the food, was the people watching. Folks from all walks of life circled the acreage. They saw cowboys, bikers, farmers, yuppies, gang bangers, and what some would refer to as trailer trash. It was quite the diversity all in one spot.

They ended the walk up the Midway and stopped outside the poultry building at a small free-standing structure painted gray and white, named Page One, to get some greasy cheeseburgers and some drinks. As fate would have it, this was the same stand that Mac's father owned, and Mac worked at for five years when he was growing up.

"Hey Moe! How come you're not having a beer?" Twist asked Mac.

"I can't eat and drink alcohol. It upsets my stomach. I'll just have a diet soda," Mac responded, taking a big bite of the cheeseburger.

"Your loss," Wide-Body said as he took a big swig of his frosty cold draft beer.

"Plus, I'm not much of a day drinker and I'm not too particular to beer. They don't serve mixed drinks here either, so I guess I'll just take it easy on my alcoholic intake today if that's all right with you boys," Mac said to the inquiring faces.

"You better agree to have a couple of beers later at the concert then," Orsen replied, taking a sip of his own beer.

"Of course, I don't want to rain on your parade Alvey."

They finished their food and walked around the rest of the fairgrounds until it was time to go to the Grandstand at 4:00 PM and see the Beach Boys. They ordered several rounds of beer at the concession stand inside the of the Grandstand. Mac as promised, had his two cups of suds. There was nothing wrong with beer, matter of fact Mac would have a beer if he was a bit overserved and just wanted to nurse a drink in his hand while still socializing, he just preferred Captain and diet soda.

The concert was pretty good, with the Beach Boys ending with 'Surfin' USA.' The guys continued walking around the rest of the fair after the concert and the others had a couple of more beers on their stroll around the venue. Once the sun went down, they were getting ready to make their way back to Twist's SUV. The fair stayed open until midnight, but they had no plans to stay that late.

"Hey! Are we going back to TJ's when we get back?" Orsen

asked.

"Why?" Wide-Body inquired.

"Well, all the girls are working tonight, and I thought we'd go surprise them."

Orsen had also just started dating a waitress from T.J. Big Boys, which added to Mac and Twist dating sisters from there already.

"You guys are a bunch of homos!" Wide-Body exclaimed. Although it sounded like he said it in fun, everyone could tell he was put out. Even though he didn't drink that much, the guys could tell he was starting to turn the corner on his good mood.

"Yeah. We should get going," Twist said, and they walked back to the trooper's barracks and retrieved their car.

Once in the car and up on the highway heading back home, 'Pump up the Jam' by Technotronic came on the radio, and Twist being Twist, he started to playfully rock the SUV back and forth to the beat. He wasn't being reckless, just a little playful, and it was kind of funny seeing Wide-Body and Orsen almost collide into each other in the back seat. Orsen was laughing so hard Mac thought he was going to piss himself. Mac and Twist started chuckling as Wide-Body shouted, "Knock the shit off!"

He was serious, and everyone knew it, and the good times ended. Twist turned down the radio and drove like a nun to T.J. Big Boys. Twist parked right outside the front door and Orsen hustled out of the back seat and ran inside. As Twist and Mac stood outside their open doors Wide-Body glared at them as he exited the back seat and said, "You guys are bunch of assholes! I'm walking home. Fuck off!"

And with that he started walking out of the parking lot. Mac looked at Twist who seemed bewildered on what to do. Mac decided to jog after Wide-Body and have him come back to the restaurant.

"Hey Carl, Twist was just fooling around. He didn't mean anything by it..." Mac said, as he reached him and placed his hand on the back of his shoulder.

Without warning, provocation or anything said, Wide-Body spun around and threw three haymakers, alternating between blows, right-left-right at Mac's head. Mac saw just a blur of fury coming at him. He was on his heels attempting to back out of the way and just caught glancing blows off of each cheek as he retreated. Out of pure instinct, Mac threw one direct right hand into the middle of Wide-Body's face. It was his karate training kicking in and Mac responded to the overt aggression without even realizing that he had.

Mac stood there in shock as Wide-Body crumbled to the ground on his knees holding his nose which was leaking copious amounts of blood onto the black asphalt.

"You broke my nose! You fucking asshole! You broke my fucking nose!" Wide-Body howled.

Mac was frozen. He didn't know what to do or say. He turned around and looked at Twist who stood there stunned just fifteen feet away. Twist finally came back to reality and came over to Wide-Body. He cautiously put his hand on Wide-Body's back and said, "Shit Carl! You got to get to an ER. Let's get you in my truck."

While Twist was trying to stand Wide-Body up, Mac went into the restaurant and got some clean dish rags and handed them to Twist as he walked Wide-Body back to his car. Mac opened the front passenger door as Wide-Body took the rags from Twist. Wide-Body held them to his face as Twist lowered him down into the seat. Wide-Body was only unintelligibly muttering now to himself about his broken nose.

Twist closed the passenger door and mouthed the words, "Holy shit," to Mac, got himself into the driver's seat, backed the SUV out of the parking lot and headed to Community General Hospital. Mac silently watched them drive off and shook his head as he tried to make sense out of what just happened. It was so surreal he couldn't put it together.

Wide-Body would've killed him if he didn't bob and weave out of the way. He felt bad about instinctively throwing the punch, but under the circumstances he wasn't sure what else would have stopped Wide-Body from coming after him.

As he went inside T.J. Big Boy's to tell NMI what had just happened, he had a foreboding feeling. His little voice was getting louder, telling him that it somehow was going to get turned around on him at the PD. He had no idea how bad it was going to be.

In any moment of decision, the best thing you can do is the right thing, the next best thing is the wrong thing, and the worst thing you can do is nothing.

- Theodore Roosevelt

CHAPTER
TWENTY-EIGHT

That next afternoon after their Fair excursion Mac reported to the station for overtime work at Fairmount Fair. Betty Masters saw Mac walking by the office on the way up the hallway and stairs and quietly called him into her office.

"What's up Betty?"

"I'm pretty sure you know this already, but the lieutenant is looking for you," she said in a hushed tone.

"Well, I expected something, but not this soon. What

happened? Mac asked quietly.

"Carl Sorbie called in sick today. He was supposed to work B-Watch. Carl told the Chief that you attacked him for no reason. I know that can't be true, but that's what he said. I'm pretty sure he told Johnson the same thing."

"That's not what happened Betty. Wide-Body was drinking all day at the fair and you know how he gets. He got mad at Twist on the way back and tried to walk off on his own when we got to TJ's. I tried to reason with him and get him to come back and HE attacked me. He threw several punches at my head and without thinking, I reacted and threw one punch to defend myself, as I backed out of the way and I bloodied his nose. That was it. Twist was right there. He saw the whole thing."

"That sounds more like the real story Mac. But be careful with Johnson. You know how he feels about you. I don't think it will go as smoothly as you think," Betty said in a concerned tone.

"I'll be all right Betty. I do appreciate your concern, though. Is the LT in his office?"

"Yes. The door has been closed all afternoon. I think he's been on the phone most of the day."

"Thanks again Betty. I better go see him now and get this over with." And with that, Mac walked back and knocked on Lieutenant Johnson's door.

Mac had a split second to think about the fact that Twist hadn't called him today to talk about what happened last night. Mac's small voice was telling him that something was quite wrong about it.

"Come in," was the answer behind the door. Mac walked in and said, "You wanted to see me, lieutenant?"

"Yes, as a matter of fact I did. Would you care to share what happened last night?

"Well, yeah, I mean, of course LT." Mac said. He stood in the middle of the room holding his dry-cleaned uniforms as he wasn't told to take a seat. "Jorge, Carl, Orsen Avery from the state, and I went to the fair yesterday afternoon. We saw a concert, got some food and a little to drink and headed back to town about dusk. Carl got mad at Jorge on the ride back and tried to walk home from TJ Big Boy's. I tried to convince Carl to come inside TJ's when he got upset and threw some punches at me. I reacted by instinct and reached up once with my closed hand as I tried to get out of the way of his fists and struck him in the middle of his face. I didn't mean to hit him. I was just trying to get away from him. Jorge ended up taking him to Community to get looked at. I still feel bad about it, but I didn't instigate it with Carl. He's going through some bad things with his divorce, but I never thought he'd come after me like that."

Lieutenant Johnson just sat there looking at Mac for what seemed liked five minutes.

"Well, the REAL story I got from Carl was that you got drunk at the fair and attacked him unprovoked, beating him so badly that he has a severely broken nose which needs reconstructive surgery to fix."

Again, Mac had been in this situation with the lieutenant before, but still couldn't understand why he was believing what Wide-Body had told him. It took Mac a few moments to compose himself and not shout out his defense.

"Lieutenant, Jorge was ten feet away and saw the whole thing," Mac said evenly.

"I've already spoken with Twist. He said he didn't see anything."

Mac was again caught off-guard. He been good friends with Twist for almost five years. They lived together for a year. They were dating sisters! How could anyone do something like that? It was incomprehensible. Mac had nothing else to say. He was too hurt to defend himself anymore, he just looked down at the floor.

"This is your last chance here, Patrick. I don't need someone who can't get along with everyone else. You appear to be the odd man out and next time you will be. You're dismissed," Johnson said, ending the conversation as it was.

Mac walked out of the office and couldn't meet Betty's expecting eyes. He went up into the locker room, changed as quickly as he could, and drove to Fairmount Fair in his personal car to begin his shift at the mall. He ended up working alone that night. It turned out that Wide-Body was supposed to be his partner and obviously he didn't get a replacement. Mac strolled around the mall lost in thought, trying to sort things out in his head on what direction to take.

He was entering into his last semester at Onondaga

Community College in the fall which was rapidly approaching, and he was more focused on graduating than thinking about Lieutenant Mendoza's offer at a transfer to the Syracuse Police Department, but now...

He formulated a plan to talk with his brother the next day. Michael was in town going through the background paperwork and interviews to become a road patrol deputy for the Onondaga County Sheriff's Department. It was a departure from using his economics degree from Boston University, but he'd caught the police bug from all his late-night ride-a-longs with Mac. Michael agreed to teach Mac how to lift weights properly, as he had lived with the strength and conditioning coach from BU, and they met up at Pine Grove Fitness Center and Country Club on Milton Ave. Mac had just put an offer on a small old farmhouse across the street, which was accepted, and he figured this would be the most convenient place for them to work out.

After they got done working out, Mac and Michael walked out of the gym and across the golf course to the thirteenth green, where they could see the house that Mac had just purchased. It was only nine-hundred square feet, but it had an acre and a half of fenced in yard which Mac wanted for the children to play in. The house was white, which matched the picket fence that ran across the backyard.

"Well, what do you think?" Mac asked, as they stood across the street on the golf course.

"About the house or you transferring to the city?

"Both."

"The house is cute. I think the kids will love it. Them living with their mother in Solvay in a house behind a house, with no yard, this will be perfect. As far as leaving Camillus PD. It seems like the whole place is in flux. From what you tell me about that Dial-A-Drunk guy, the issue with Wide-Body, the lieutenant not believing anything you say, and Twist not having your back, I'd think you must be crazy about not going.

You said you never really wanted to work for Camillus in the first place. It was where they offered you a job first Patrick, but you always wanted to do investigations and be a city cop. I don't know why this is so hard for you to make a decision."

"You're right Michael, but there are still a lot of good guys and girls here. They trained me and looked out for me. It seems like that I'd be letting Johnson chase me out of a place that I've learned to call home," Mac said staring at the house across the street.

"As long as he has a burn for dad, he's going to torture you and ultimately get you fired, and then you couldn't transfer anywhere else," Michael said as he backed away from the green when he noticed an approaching foursome coming up to the tee.

"I know. It's the right decision. I guess I'm just afraid of the unknown. I'd have to start all over from the bottom up and that place is huge. I know some cops from my academy class there, but that's it. They have five-hundred and twenty sworn personnel, not counting support staff. That's the biggest PD in seventeen counties through the middle of the state. Only NYPD, Buffalo and Rochester are bigger, as far as city cops go."

"Hey, I don't really know anybody from the sheriff's department. I know Kevin Charm through you and that's it. It's a whole new beginning for me too. Nothing ventured, nothing gained. I think you know what to do," Michael added.

"Fair enough. Thanks for listening. Let's go back. I'll put it into play tomorrow and see how it turns out."

The brothers walked back across the golf course to their cars and after giving each other a big hug, went their separate ways.

The next day Mac called SPD personnel and put his transfer in. He still hadn't seen or heard from Twist. Mac wanted to know why Twist didn't tell the truth, but in the end, it was too late for him to do anything with that information.

Not too long after that Twist transferred to the sheriff's department and Wide-Body decided that being a cop wasn't for him. He moved out of state and was never seen again by Mac.

If there is not the war, you don't get the great general; if there is not a great occasion, you don't get a great statesman; if Lincoln had lived in a time of peace, no one would have known his name.

- Theodore Roosevelt

CHAPTER

TWENTY-NINE

College had started back up and Mac was on a steady diet of A-Watch tours while he got his day classes in order for the semester. Summer was still in swing, but it was getting a bit colder at night which meant that fall wasn't that far off. Mac had immediately heard back from SPD and he was jumping through the hoops to try and secure his transfer to the city. Interviews, medical examinations, and polygraphs were conflicting with his class schedule, but that couldn't be helped.

It was all part of the process and the classes were suffering to no lack of his desire to graduate.

Michael was also on track with the sheriff's department going through the same type of hiring process. He had secured a beverage manager's job in the meantime at the Marriott just outside the city and was adjusting to living with their grandmother and taking care of her.

Mac had just started another A-Watch by himself, calling into service and having Felicity Flynn from MRD dispatch acknowledge his availability. He started driving his circuitous route around the perimeter of the town with little to no radio traffic to listen to. Mac was again getting melancholy about leaving Camillus PD. Even though he didn't like not being constantly busy, he had become accustomed to his solo rides around the town and the rural aspect to his jaunts.

The fear of the unknown is a crazy thing. It's almost paralyzing in nature, even though a change would drastically improve one's situation, the mind still belies what good can come of it, nurturing a false sense of reverie that really shouldn't be there. Mac knew this was true, but still had trouble processing it in his head, with the cogs and wheels constantly turning and gearing in his brain.

The slow night on the radio continued until about four o'clock in the morning with Mac alternating between business checks and checking rural routes around the town.

"Unit #3103A and any other units in the area of the Town of Camillus...burglary just occurred...202 Jones St. in

Fairmount...complainant, Walker Bish stated that the family just awoke to an unknown white male in his twenties, standing in their family room...last seen wearing a dark T-shirt and blue jeans...suspect exited out the front door, last seen running west on Jones Street towards Myron Road," Tiffany Flynn dispatched from the MRD control room.

"Unit #3103A received. En route," Mac acknowledged.

"Unit #4505A en route from Onondaga Hill," Deputy Kevin Charm answered up on the radio.

"Unit #4506A en route from the South Station," Deputy Howie Marcus replied.

"Unit #2D41 add us also please, Route 5 and the Bypass" Roxy McCall voiced her and Gerald Hair's response.

Mac wasn't that far away as he was doing a drive-by checking on his parents' house in Fairmont Hills, the sheriff's units and the state unit were most likely at least five minutes away. He arrived in under a minute, calling arrived over the air as he turned from West Genesee Street onto Myrtis Road. Mac turned off his headlights as he slowly started crawling through the neighborhood, with his windows down, and scanning and listening as he went.

It was a dark night void of the moon or any stars. This time of night there was nobody out on the streets and Mac had to squint into the darkness to see through the shadows between the unlit houses.

Mac soon saw Scooby from Geddes PD trawling through one of the side streets with his lights off also, along with two cars from Solvay PD. Mac knew they would probably slide over without calling out and he greatly appreciated their help.

"Units #3103A, #4505A, #4506A, #2D41, another caller from Sherry Drive stated that she just witnessed a white male going through vehicles on her street...she states that she no longer has a visual on the subject," Felicity advised.

"Received. Advise the responding cars I have Geddes and Solvay units on scene." Mac didn't want Kevin, Howie or his state partners driving too fast responding, thinking that he was alone in a precarious situation.

Both units acknowledged before Felicity had a chance to relay the information to them. Shortly after that both units called arrived in the area.

After fifteen minutes of the seven police vehicles all darked-out circling past each other in the nine adjoining blocks, Mac called out with the original complainant, while Kevin spoke with the woman that called in the vehicle larcenies from Sherry Drive.

As Mac pulled up in front of 202 Jones Street, a middle-aged man wearing pajama bottoms and a white T-shirt came out of the front door of the all lit up house.

"Did you catch him?" the man asked.

"Sorry. Not yet. Is everybody okay? What did he get from your house?" Mac asked.

"Yeah we're fine. He scared the bejeezus out of us. I

thought one of my kids had gotten up when I heard the noise. I went into the family room and saw him standing there as I turned on the light. At that point he looked as frightened as I was. He took off lickity split through the front door."

"What did he look like?"

"A stocky kid with brown wavy hair, I think he had tattoos on his forearms as well."

"How do you think he got in?" Mac asked.

"I think he came in through the garage door to the house. I didn't check it before we went to bed tonight. To be honest, we never have problems like that here and the house is nearly never locked up unless we're on vacation or something."

"Is anything missing?"

"I'm not quite sure. I'll have to look officer," the man said.

"All right. If it's okay with you, I'll keep looking for him and come back later to take your police report when you know more about what might have been stolen. We've had another caller stating that most likely the same suspect was going through neighbors' cars the next block over as well."

"No, that's fine, go ahead officer."

As the man walked back to his house Mac could see his wife and three small children huddled around her legs, all in their nightwear, standing in the threshold of the front door. By the look on their faces, Mac knew they weren't going back to bed anytime soon.

He got in his cruiser and went over to Sherry Drive and caught up with Kevin Charm as he was just getting back into his patrol vehicle.

"What do you have, Kevin?"

"It wasn't her car. She heard a noise with her bedroom window open, looked out and saw a guy going through her neighbor's car across the street from their driveway. When she was on the phone reporting it, she saw him go to the adjoining neighbor's vehicle and do the same thing. The vague description of the suspect is about the same as the burg suspect. I went over and checked the vehicle she pointed out and they were indeed gone through. Stuff from the glove compartment strewn throughout the inside of the cars. The ashtrays taken out and loose change on the vehicle's floors."

"Did you get her bio info?"

"What do you take me for Mac? A rook?" Kevin said, smiling as he tore a piece of notebook paper from his tablet and handed it to Mac.

"Thanks Kevin! I'll be all set if you want to clear. I'm just going to take a few more laps around the neighborhood and see if I can come up with something. Maybe there was two of them. Seems kind of odd that after you're almost caught in a burglary you go around the corner and do vehicle larcenies," Mac said.

"Maybe he was looking for spare keys to get the fuck out of dodge. Who knows? By the way I didn't wake up the neighbors to get their info. Do you want me to do it now?"

"No Kevin, I have to go back and get all the information

from my original complainant a little while later, after they inventory their house. By that time the sun will be coming up and I'll get their info then and see what's missing from their vehicles."

"All right, bud, I'm going to clear and head back to the South Station. I've got some paperwork to get caught up on before the end of the shift," Kevin said.

"Sounds good bro. Stay safe!"

And as Kevin drove off and was clearing on a Code-10 (ASSIST) with Felicity over the air, Troopers McCall and Hair pulled up car to car along Mac's drivers' side.

"Thanks guys!" Mac said as they pulled up.

Jerry was driving, and Roxy was riding shotgun. "Thanks for what Mac? We didn't do anything," Jerry said.

"Well you showed up and helped look. I appreciated you answering up and coming just the same," Mac said.

"Sorry we couldn't find the bastard. Sounds like he was on a one-man crime spree," Roxy said as she opened up a purple Gatorade bottle and took a swig.

"Well he's long gone now. I'm going to do one last sweep and take the reports. It's after five aren't you guys out of service?"

"Yeah, I've got to get Roxy back to the barracks and call it a night if you're going to be okay without us," Jerry said.

"I'm good, guys. Thanks just the same. I'll see you both back again tonight. Go home and get some rest."

"Thanks Mac. Keep it positive!" Roxy said as they slowly pulled away and cleared with Felicity as well on a Code-10.

Howie, Scooby, and the Solvay cars had also stopped circling the blocks, and Mac assumed they had returned to their respective jurisdictions as well.

After everyone was gone Mac had a chance to think about the assorted crimes that occurred in the neighborhood tonight. It was strange. This was a quiet neighborhood and it seemed weird that a bad guy would be so persistent.

Mac remembered seeing a number of vehicles parked on the street when he originally arrived on scene. There was no overnight parking ban in the town during the spring and summer months, so residence could park their vehicles on the street instead of their driveways if they wished. He knew it was a long shot, but he thought he would start running license plate numbers on the street to see if one of them didn't belong.

He disliked bothering the dispatcher working the Data Channel this late into the shift, but he couldn't think of anything better to do. Plus, he hated the fact they'd got beaten by this guy.

After the sixth vehicle registration he'd run through the dispatcher on Channel Two that all came back to Camillus residents, Mac was second guessing his strategy when he got a hit on number seven.

"Unit #3103A...copy 10-32 (Caution Indicator) on the

registered owner," the Data dispatcher advised across the airwaves.

Mac felt instantly energized. This finally could be something.

"Unit #3103A go ahead." Mac answered.

"Unit #3103A...the vehicle is registered to Miguel Olivier D.O.B. 05/13/1968...residing at 666 West Onondaga Street #13 Syracuse, New York...on a 1980 Ford 4 DSD color brown showing valid...Mr. Olivier shows a suspended New York State driver's license for failure to answer a summons in the Village of Solvay.

"Mr. Olivier also shows an active traffic warrant out of the Village of Solvay...caution indicators for resists arrest and armed...he also shows to be on parole until 06/01/1995."

Mac couldn't believe he found the vehicle. This had to be the guy. Why else would it be parked in this neighborhood in Camillus?

"Received," Mac advised the Data dispatcher.

"Unit #3103A would you like me to have Channel Four start you another unit," the concerned dispatcher asked Mac.

"Negative. I'm not currently out with the owner," Mac picked up the mic and answered back. It was nice that the unknown dispatcher was concerned for Mac's safety, but all he had for now was a suspicious unoccupied legally parked vehicle on the side of the road. If Olivier was smart, he had abandoned the vehicle and beat feet out of the area. Mac was still hesitant to give up completely. He had a decent suspect for the crimes in the neighborhood, but he wanted to catch him red-handed at the scene.

The vehicle was parked in front of 11 Gifford Drive. Mac quickly formulated a plan in his head. It would be getting daylight in about an hour and he figured if Olivier was still around, he would get his car before the neighbors woke up and spotted the suspicious car in front of their homes.

Mac drove his police vehicle back onto West Genesee Street and parked it behind a Car Wash that was adjacent to Myrtis Road. He then got out of his vehicle and hurried through the backyards of Gifford until he was behind number 11. He thought that he was too exposed and too far away from the suspect vehicle if Olivier came back for it, so as an afterthought he crept into the front yard and climbed a full-grown maple tree, hiding in full uniform among the leaves on the lower branches.

There he sat spying between the foliage as the first signs of sunrise illuminated around him into the neighborhood. Again, not for the first time, Mac felt quite foolish with his current predicament. This was not taught in the academy. He literally chuckled to himself over his dilemma, thinking that the other cops would have a field day with his present improvising. As a harbinger of things that may come, his little voice was articulating concerns of its own, about Mac not telling anyone else about him doing this, nor requesting a back-up unit. In his defense to his little voice, Mac knew this was an extreme longshot and that shift change was coming up for the rest of the departments, and he didn't want to put anyone else out on his hairbrained idea.

Forty-five minutes later as the sun continued its' rise into the new day, Mac was just about to call it off and go take the reports from the victims, when a man carrying a tan suitcase, dressed in a uniform for Grossman's Lumber bearing a neon orange work shirt complete with an embroidered name tag of 'Tom', blue jeans and brown Timberland work boots, was nonchalantly walking down the middle of Gifford Drive. He looked like an executive for the big lumber store located less than two miles away in the town, at the corner of Milton Ave. and Hinsdale Road. Mac was getting more confused the closer he got to the suspect car. Could he have it wrong after all. It was late, and his brain was getting kind of soggy, it was the midnight shift and the human body was not preprogrammed to operate efficiently during these hours.

Mac waited until the man was just ten feet from the vehicle. He slid silently out of the backside of the tree and ran unnoticed to the man as he attempted to put his door key into the driver's side vehicle lock to open the car. Mac said, "Camillus Police! Can I see your identification please?"

The startled man just stood there open mouthed looking at Mac. Mac couldn't tell if it was because Mac just materialized out of nowhere, or because it was Olivier. Mac then did make a rookie mistake; instead of cuffing him right then and there behind his back and sorting it out later, Mac asked the subject to put the suitcase down, turn around and place his hands on the vehicle so Mac could pat him down for weapons.

As Mac was patting him down, this gave the subject time to think and the shock was wearing off, as Mac felt a large amount of loose change in one of the pockets and knew this was most likely the proceeds from one of the vehicle larcenies. Mac also knew by touching the subject's back through his shirt he could feel tight, taught, muscle of someone who worked out every day in state prison. The gig up, Olivier pushed back off the car, knocking Mac back. and it was off to the races.

Mac reached for his portable radio off his belt and called for immediate assistance as he ran down Gifford Street after Olivier. Mac knew it was shift change for all the police agencies and there weren't any cops on the road close by, but he wanted MRD to know where he was and what he had. Mac swiveled the portable radio back into place and in earnest kept up the foot pursuit as Olivier ran into the backyards to get away. He was built like a tank and once the initial flow of adrenaline wore off Mac was able to run up along beside him, yelling that he was under arrest and to stop running, as he tried to push him to the ground. Olivier outweighed Mac by about fifty pounds of pure muscle and this tactic was not working.

Olivier briefly sped up and jumped over several fences when Mac had to take his portable radio off his gun belt again to advise Felicity where he was. He could hear responding units coming with their sirens on in the background but didn't know who was responding and where they were coming from.

Olivier had gone around a corner during this brief period

and Mac lost him. He knew he couldn't have gotten very far. It wasn't like he was even close to being a track star. Mac looked underneath a porch where he had last seen him and then behind some trash cans of an adjoining house with no luck. He then spied a shed in the backyard of a third house and thought that must be it.

Mac opened the shed and found Olivier cornered. Grabbing Olivier by the arms Mac tried unsuccessfully to throw him out of the interior of the shed. Olivier then reached back and was attempting to get an axe off of a rack hanging on the wall behind him.

"Shit!" Mac exclaimed, as he withdrew his ASP baton off his belt and jerked his right hand backwards to extend the metal tubing which made an audible metallic sound. Olivier seeing this fought even harder trying to get any weapon he could out of the shed to repel Mac.

Mac started hitting Olivier as best he could in the confined space with forty-five degree strikes on Olivier's elbows and knees trying to take him down and away from the improvised weapons. All this did was distract Olivier from obtaining the implements. It did not seem to faze him in any other way. After striking him for more than a minute with countless strikes Mac couldn't feel his right hand anymore. He dropped the ASP and grabbed Olivier by the front of his shirt with both hands and finally flung him out of the shed.

Olivier was bleeding profusely from his head. Several of

Mac's strikes from the ASP must've inadvertently struck him in the head and now they were both covered by the effusive body fluid that was freely flowing over both of them. Olivier had turned around from the supine to the prone position and was attempting to push himself off the ground to get up. Mac was sitting on his back which had no effect in keeping him down.

Mac started throwing punches into the back of Olivier's head over and over again until he finally went limp. Mac got his slippery hands on his handcuffs from his back-cuff case on his gun belt and wrenched one hand back cuffing it, then the other.

With that Mac rolled off Olivier as he heard the approaching sirens coming to a halt somewhere around him.

Mac was fading fast. The last of the will he had during the fight was subsiding faster than he thought possible. The front of his baby blue short-sleeved uniform shirt was covered in blood, and he felt the warm stickiness up both arms past his elbows. He supposed it felt like molasses, although he couldn't be sure, because he hadn't been immersed in any substance like that before. He simultaneously thought to himself as he laid there that it was a strange thing to be thinking about. Mac, however, had been around fresh blood before, and the unmistakable coppery smell was all around him. As he looked up from his supine position on the freshly cut grass in whatever backyard he was lying in, he thought he must have some of it in his eyes as well.

He saw figures standing over him, but it was difficult to focus on them through the emerging light of daybreak on this warm September morning. Mac felt bone-tired and thought to himself—maybe he said it out loud to those above him—"Just give me a minute to rest, and I'll be all right. Just one more minute..."

And with that, he closed his eyes as the faceless bodies above murmured to one another in an unintelligible conversation that he apparently wasn't meant to be a part of ...

I wish to preach, not `the doctrine of ignoble ease,
but the doctrine of the strenuous life.

- Theodore Roosevelt

CHAPTER

THIRTY

In the light of day, with all the commotion from the responding units coming full tilt with lights and sirens to Mr. Olivier's follies, the neighbors took stock of their valuables. It turned out that Mr. Olivier had committed at least three burglaries and six vehicle larcenies that morning, with pretty much nothing much to show for it. He had stolen the Grossman's work shirt out of someone's garage, which the neighbor didn't want back now that it was soaked in blood and irrevocably ruined. The briefcase was stolen from another home and contained highly specialized electronic tools, which weren't useful to anyone else but someone in that niche profession. There were also miscellaneous items that Mr. Olivier put into the briefcase from the various vehicle larcenies he committed, such as, more loose change, sunglasses, cigarettes, lighters, a small flashlight, and a pair of driving gloves. A career crook mastermind he was not.

Sergeant Jake Smith had B-Watch units from CPD take the original burglary report from Mr. Bish, as well as the other burglary and vehicle larceny complaints from the aggrieved neighbors. Mr. Olivier's vehicle was impounded by Sergeant Dianne Powell, as it was used in a crime. It was quite a mop up day for the day shift, but they artfully got it all taken care of before noon that day.

Connor Coke was working dayshift as well and coordinated with WAVES Ambulance to have Mr. Olivier medically checked out before he could be arraigned and transported to the Book (Referring to the Booking Desk of the PSB Jail). EMTs Donna Johnson and Vaughn McCabe were on duty for WAVES just finishing up their overnight tour. After cleaning off the head wound and putting a butterfly bandage over the small cut to the side of the head, Mr. Olivier was medically released. He had refused to go to the hospital for any further treatment. It would be up to the jail nurse on whether she would accept him into the PSB Jail in that condition or not.

Subsequently, Connor arraigned Mr. Olivier in front of the town justice and then transported him to the Public Safety

Building and lodged him on the parole sticker, and; Burglary in the Second Degree (three counts), Grand Larceny in the Fourth Degree, Petit Larceny (six counts), and Resisting Arrest.

With all that going on, Mac drove himself up to Community General Hospital and had his right hand looked at. While he was there waiting to be treated, Chief Ronan Whitlock came to check on him.

"How are you feeling, Patrick? Chief Whitlock asked, as he parted the flimsy curtains to one of the treatment rooms in the ER.

"Fine, Chief. You didn't need to come. It's really nothing," Mac said, startled at his emerging presence.

"Glad to hear it. You did pretty well last night. Although, you really should have called for backup from one of the other agencies," Whitlock said, as he made himself comfortable on a chair by the gurney that Mac was sitting on.

"I know, Chief. I wasn't really sure if he was still in the area. Then when he did appear, I wasn't certain it was him. But I know better now," Mac said, grimacing as he tried to manipulate his hand.

"You said it, Patrick. Now you know. I'm just glad you didn't get hurt much worse. It could've easily gone that way. I also wanted to talk to you about your transfer to the city. Officer Marty Henry from the Syracuse Police Department was in my office yesterday inquiring about you."

"Yes, Chief. I should have touched base with you and let you know that I was attempting to transfer. The process is moving a lot faster than I thought it would. I apologize for not giving you a heads-up."

"That's fine, Patrick. I hate to lose you. You've come a long way. I'm proud of your determination last night, and I'm sure a lot of our residents are quite pleased with your performance as well. You'll do well in the city. It seems to fit your aspirations well. You do know that you will be the first member of CPD to transfer to SPD, don't you?"

"No sir, I didn't know."

"Well, you are. Most guys and gals go to the sheriff's department. I gave Officer Henry a glowing recommendation, and I'm sure it won't be long until they take you. You think last night was bad, that's an everyday occurrence in the city. Just so you know what you're getting into," Chief Whitlock said.

"I sort of know Chief, but thanks just the same. I really do appreciate the good review you gave me. You have me for a while more it seems. I'm sure we'll talk before I get a start date. Thank you again!"

"My pleasure, Patrick. Get well and we'll see you back to work when your cleared by the Docs," Chief Whitlock said as he hoisted himself off the chair and parted the curtains on his way out.

The aftermath of Mac's tree roost adventure left him with a severely sprained right hand and left him out of work from CPD for a week. The fact that he had broken it on the job four years earlier didn't help with the healing process. He knew better than to punch someone in the back of the head, especially after striking them with the ASP baton repeatedly until his hand went numb, but at the time it seemed somewhat sensible, not letting Mr. Olivier continue with his great escape.

Shortly after returning to his regular schedule at the Camillus Police Department, Mac received word from Officer Marty Henry that his start date with the Syracuse Police Department was going to be October 19, 1990. He was excited to have his transfer accepted and to have the opportunity for urban police work, but as he expressed to Michael before, there was a certain sadness with leaving CPD.

Mac had been mentored by some really first-rate cops, and he knew by experience, that after he left CPD, those relationships would be left behind as well. Chief Whitlock had helped him through his divorce, which he didn't have to do at all. That meant more to Mac than Whitlock would ever know.

Sergeant Jake Smith, Sergeant Dianne Powell, Sergeant Russ Parker, and Detective Sergeant Billy Cole were superb in their supervision and taking care of all the cops. It had to be like herding cats at times, overseeing brand new police officers that all come on at the same time, but they made it look easy.

Connor Coke was the only peer left at CPD he was leaving behind. Mac knew Connor wasn't long behind him in leaving himself, but it was still bittersweet. Mac envisioned Connor moving to Hollywood and dating starlets, but that chapter had not yet been written.

Hogan Draper "Dial-A-Drunk" had sicked out Mac's last week at CPD. According to the other cops, Draper was afraid that Mac would settle up with him for lying to Lieutenant Johnson about his ill-fated attempt on arresting the nurse, before leaving to go to the city. The other cops didn't care for him, so it's just as likely they started the rumor to watch him squirm for a while.

Mac could've cared less either way. He was glad he was leaving Lieutenant Johnson and Draper in his rearview mirror. That part of his experience with the Camillus Police Department he was looking to forget and move on.

Conversely, he would also always miss Betty Masters. She surely earned her keep at the PD, playing den mother to all the boys and girls. Mac knew her steadfast guidance would never be replaced, and he was sad again.

Twist was still dating NMI's sister and making his way at the Onondaga County Sheriff's Department. Michael had received the fantastic news that he also would be starting the academy for them in the coming weeks.

Mac's mom, Searlait, was now doubly concerned that her only boys were both cops, and upped her daily prayers to reflect her worry for her kids. Mac's dad, James, seemed to be mellowing with age somewhat, but still hadn't slowed down his drinking. Mac had always had rules for drinking since he witnessed his father's meltdown which resulted in Mac's broken nose. These included not drinking or being intoxicated at all around his children, not drinking until the sun set, and not drinking alone, amongst other sensible rules. He'd also given up drinking for Lent for the first time earlier that year, and vowed to make it a yearly tradition, so that he didn't get caught up in that trap.

Mac's children were getting older and Mac was still trying to spend all the time he could with them. He spent time watching their practices, games, recitals, school events, mass, and religion classes, taking them to the park, the movies, and out to dinner. Mac still especially missed checking on them at night and watching them sleep. He was hoping that his transfer to the city would afford him more time to do the same.

NMI had been supportive of his transfer and was excited to see what lay before him. She had started taking a paralegal program held at Lemoyne College and was anticipating changes for herself as well.

For Mac's schooling, he had one Oceanography Lab Class left at Onondaga Community College, that he couldn't complete with the impending onboarding at SPD. That's all that stood between him and his associate degree, but Mac couldn't control the sequence of events to make graduation this year. It would have to be put on the backburner, which didn't sit well with him, for all the work he put in and the sleep he missed, to get that close and not finish it right away.

All in all, Mac had been on a pretty good ride since becoming a cop. He started off on shaky ground with back to back vehicle accidents but had rebounded and found some moderate success in taking on different kinds of self-initiated investigations. He was looking forward to a challenge with more responsibility and excitement being a city cop, and his little voice was telling him that it all was going to be okay...or he thought that's what it was saying.

It is not the critic who counts; not the man who points out how the strong man stumbles, or where the doer of deeds could have done them better. The credit belongs to the man who is actually in the arena, whose face is marred by dust and sweat and blood, who strives valiantly; who errs and comes short again and again; because there is not effort without error and shortcomings; but who does actually strive to do the deed; who knows the great enthusiasm, the great devotion, who spends himself in a worthy cause, who at the best knows in the end the triumph of high achievement and who at the worst, if he fails, at least he fails while daring greatly. So that his place shall never be with those cold and timid souls who know neither victory nor defeat.

- Theodore Roosevelt

EPILOUGE

"**M**acKenna...Unit #442C?"

"Here sir," Mac answered the Third Platoon captain.

Captain Winters went down the rest of the Roll Call list giving car assignments as he went.

The Roll Call Room was on the first floor of the Public Safety Building (PSB) in room #102. The PSB was located at 511 South State Street and was home to the City of Syracuse Police Department. The City of Syracuse Fire Department had its' administrative offices located on the 5th floor, of the five-story building, but the rest of it belonged to the cops.

The PSB was built in 1963 and not much had

changed, on the exterior or the interior of the building, as the autumn of 1990 was coming into full glory. The Roll Call Room had about twenty old metal folding chairs in front of the lectern, as you first came into the room. Most of the chairs were full for this late roll call. Early roll call was an hour earlier to provide shift coverage equally, so all the cops weren't off the street at the same time. This was the same for all the platoons.

First Platoon was the midnight shift (early 2200-0600 hours / late 2300-0700 hours), Second Platoon was the day shift (early 0600-1400 hours / late 0700-1500 hours), Third Platoon was the evening shift (early 1400-2200 hours / late 1500-2300 hours), and Fourth Platoon was the swing shift (2000-0400 hours). Third Platoon was the busiest shift and where most of the new cops were assigned. Some unlucky few would go to First Platoon or Fourth Platoon.

Sergeants and the sole lieutenant would stand against the walls during roll call. The size of one roll call was just about equal to all the cops that worked for the Town of Camillus Police Department, and to say the least, Mac was a little overwhelmed...and it was about to get worse.

After roll call was over, and all the cops had received their unit numbers for the evening, Officer Safety bulletins were read, along with Wanted for Questioning Bulletins, and Wanted and/or Stolen Vehicle bulletins were passed out, the North Zone sergeant called out, "MacKenna!"

"Yeah Sarge?" Mac answered, as he made his way out of his seat with his posse box full of forms and bulletins.

"You're the transfer from Camillus, right?"

"Yes, Sarge."

"Nice! Welcome to Third Platoon...here's a Street Guide...and oh, by the way...you've got a rider. Good Luck!

And with that, the sergeant made his way out of the Roll Call Room. This was Mac's third night, he had ridden with two separate cops in two different territories and he didn't know where his Unit #442C territory was in the city, let alone any streets in the city besides the main thoroughfare.

Mac looked up from the Street Guide the sergeant had handed him and saw an eighteen-year-old college intern looking expectantly into his face. "I guess you're the rider," Mac said.

"Yes sir, I am," the freckled face kid said.

"Well, here's a Street Guide. You're going to have to read it to me since I'm brand new and it's my first shift on my own," Mac said.

The kid brightened up, "This is going to be exciting. It's my first time too!"

"It's going to be something, kid..." Mac said as he walked out of the Roll Call Room, not having a clue of where to go or who to ask.

ABOUT THE AUTHOR

Dennis Patrick Murphy, M.S.C.J. is a Navy veteran, former United States Air Force Reserve-OSI agent, and an adjunct professor who attained a graduate degree in criminal justice and has held the following titles in law enforcement and the military; Police Officer, E.R.T Operator, Detective, Task Force Agent, Police Sergeant, Detective Sergeant, Police Lieutenant, Detective Lieutenant, Supervising Criminal Investigator, Senior Federal Investigator, Intelligence Specialist, Operational Representative, and Special Agent, but his favorite title is being called 'Dad' by his four children.

https://www.thethinbluelineseries.com/